The
SISTERS
of
CORINTH

The SISTERS *of* CORINTH

ANGELA HUNT

BETHANYHOUSE
a division of Baker Publishing Group
Minneapolis, Minnesota

Published by Bethany House Publishers
Minneapolis, Minnesota
BethanyHouse.com

Bethany House Publishers is a division of
Baker Publishing Group, Grand Rapids, Michigan

Printed in the United States of America

Library of Congress Cataloging-in-Publication Data
Names: Hunt, Angela Elwell, author.
Title: The Sisters of Corinth / Angela Hunt.
Description: Minneapolis, Minnesota : Bethany House, a division of Baker
    Publishing Group, 2024. | Series: The Emissaries ; book 2
Identifiers: LCCN 2023051315 | ISBN 9780764241574 (paperback) | ISBN
    9780764243226 (casebound) | ISBN 9781493446636 (ebook)
Subjects: LCGFT: Christian fiction. | Romance fiction. | Novels.
Classification: LCC PS3558.U46747 S57 2024 | DDC 813/.54—dc23/eng/20231102
LC record available at https://lccn.loc.gov/2023051315

Scripture quotations are from the Tree of Life Version. © 2015 by the Messianic Jewish Family Bible Society. Used by permission of the Messianic Jewish Family Bible Society.

This is a work of historical reconstruction; the appearances of certain historical figures are therefore inevitable. All other characters, however, are products of the author's imagination, and any resemblance to actual persons, living or dead, is coincidental.

Cover by Peter Gloege, LOOK Design Studio
Cover images from Adobe Stock, Shutterstock, and iStock

Author is represented by Browne & Miller Literary Associates.

Baker Publishing Group publications use paper produced from sustainable forestry practices and postconsumer waste whenever possible.

24 25 26 27 28 29 30   7 6 5 4 3 2 1

Introduction

In Paul's letters to the churches he founded, we can see his love and concern in the way he praises, encourages, and admonishes the Gentile converts. But although the Scriptures paint an overall picture of the age in which these people lived, the modern reader may find it difficult to fully appreciate the pressures facing the fledgling believers.

THE EMISSARIES series features the stories of men and women who came to faith through Paul's missionary efforts in cities of the Roman Empire. Our own society—which grows ever more saturated with anti-biblical worldviews—is not so different from that of ancient Corinth. May we be challenged by the first-century believers' vision, courage, and commitment to Messiah Yeshua.

Since reading involves "hearing" words in our heads, you might find it helpful to know the pronunciation of several words and names used in this story. The early church was the *ecclesia* (pronounced ek-la-SEE-ah), and *Achaia* (Ah-KI-ah) was the province in which Corinth was located.

Ancient Corinth hosted the Isthmian games, forerunner of the modern Olympics. The games featured several events, but the most anticipated was the relay race. Competitors, each carrying a torch, positioned themselves at the starting line, while other groups of runners waited at fixed points in the distance.

When the signal was given, the first group ran, holding their lighted torches aloft. As a runner reached his teammate at the next position, he would hand over his torch. And so the race continued until the final team member crossed the finish line.

With that relay in mind, the Greeks coined the phrase *"Let those who have the light pass it on."*

May we do the same.

One

MARIANA

AD 60

When Salama stepped into my bedchamber, her face twisted with distress, I dropped the scroll I had been reading. "D-Domina," my handmaid stuttered. "I know you want to read without interruption, but your mother commanded me to fetch you."

Irritation wrestled with curiosity as I picked up the scroll and furled it. "Do you know why?"

"Unexpected guests have arrived."

"Friends of my mother's?"

"I do not recognize them, Domina. But the woman mentioned you by name."

My curiosity flickered. Few of my mother's friends had time for me, and none of them would seek me out.

"Our visitors are women?"

Salama shook her head. "A man and a woman. Their tunics are faded, they have the tanned skin of fieldworkers, and they do not look like they live in Corinth."

My irritation vanished. I knew only a few people from outside Corinth, and all of them were dear to me.

I stood, shook the wrinkles out of my tunic, and checked my reflection in the looking brass. I had not dressed for visitors but did not want to disrespect this couple by appearing unkempt in their presence. "Should you rearrange my hair?"

"You look beautiful, Domina. And these guests do not seem overly concerned with appearances." A blush darkened Salama's cheek. "I apologize; I do not mean to insult your—"

"Do not worry. I have many friends who are not overly concerned with appearances." I smiled to put my handmaid at ease and moved toward the door. "Are they outside?"

"Yes, Domina."

I left my chamber and strode toward the garden. Once I stepped through the doorway, I heard the mingled tones of a man and woman in conversation with my mother. My pulse quickened when I recognized their voices, and a peek around the rose arbor confirmed my hunch: "Aquilla and Priscilla! How wonderful to see you!"

"Mariana!" They stood, opening their arms, and I hugged each of them, holding Priscilla for an extra-long moment. "When we said farewell," I whispered in her ear, "I did not think I would ever see you again."

"Adonai had other plans." Priscilla stepped back and pinned me in a quick scrutiny. "You have grown into an attractive young lady! How old are you now? Fourteen?"

"Fifteen," I answered, not knowing whether I should be pleased by her interest or embarrassed by my unmarried status.

Priscilla smiled and gestured to an empty space on a garden bench. "Please join us. We were telling your mother about Paulos."

A flush of pleasure warmed my cheeks. Paulos had changed my life, mine *and* Mother's, by introducing us to Yeshua of Nazareth. But we had not seen the fiery emissary in months.

I sat next to Mother. "Is Paulos well? Is he still being held in Caesarea?"

Priscilla looked to her husband, who tugged on his silvered beard before speaking. "He has been sent to Rome. He has been there several months, but we have received letters, so we know he is well. Luke is with him, also Epaphras and a few others. They see to his needs while he is confined."

"He is still in prison?"

Aquilla nodded. "But he is grateful for a good situation. He is kept in an apartment, under guard, but he is free to write."

"And his health?" Mother asked. "He develops a severe cough in these months of cold weather."

"Luke takes good care of him," Aquilla assured her. "And we are on our way to visit them."

A crease wrinkled Mother's brow. "Are you concerned about going back to Rome? It has not been so long since the Jews were expelled."

Aquilla snorted softly. "Claudius is dead, and thus far Nero appears to be tolerant of those who hold different religious beliefs. Still, Paulos has warned us not to attract attention when we begin our work. We will no longer preach in synagogues. Instead, we will hold meetings in our home."

"So we will be shopping for a large domicile," Priscilla said, dimpling as she squeezed her husband's arm. "We do not care if the building has fallen into ruin, so long as it can hold dozens of people. Our budget is limited, but we believe the Lord will lead us to the right house."

"One with a walled garden," Aquilla added. "To avoid prying eyes. As long as we do not disturb the peace, we should not attract undesirable attention."

Mother glanced toward the house, then lowered her voice. "Mariana and I know all about not attracting attention. Narkis and his daughter . . . they do not worship Adonai. We have had to be *discreet* about our faith."

Priscilla's narrow face furrowed with concern. "I am so sorry," she whispered. "Does your husband—does he feel threatened by your beliefs?"

"No." Mother managed a tremulous smile. "As you said, Mariana and I take care not to disturb the peace of the household. Narkis is a good man, and he knows we worship Adonai. He does *not* know we no longer worship the Roman gods. He would not tolerate such dissension."

She leaned forward, clearly intent on changing the subject. "Tell us about this new emperor. I have asked Narkis about him, but I do not think he knows as much as he would have me believe. Is Nero a good man? Can he be trusted to let us worship in peace, or will he expel believers as Claudius did the Jews?"

Aquilla cleared his throat. "According to what I have heard, Nero has done many good things. He put an end to secret trials and gave the Senate more independence. He has given slaves permission to bring legal complaints against unjust masters. He has even pardoned men who plotted against him. But . . ."

Mother lifted a brow. "What else have you heard?"

Aquilla blew out a breath. "Whatever good Nero may have done in public pales in the light of what he is reported to have done in private. He believes himself to be a skilled actor, musician, and charioteer, but he is not, so he forces people to offer false praise. He has taken a lover, committing adultery against his wife. But the worst thing he has done is murder his mother."

A chill spidered up my spine. "His mother," Aquilla continued, his voice low and gruff, "spoke against the emperor's new mistress, and he refused to tolerate her interference. They say he arranged for her to sail across the Bay of Naples after a feast, but then sabotaged the boat. When the vessel broke apart during the journey, his mother managed to swim to shore."

"A brave woman!" I said, grinning.

Aquilla gave me a rueful smile. "Unfortunately, that is not the end of the story. When Nero heard his mother had escaped, he sent one of his officers to her home. When she realized death had come for her, she confronted the soldier, pressed the tip of his sword against her belly, and commanded the guard to pierce her in that spot because the fruit of her womb had engineered her demise."

My stomach dropped. Though I had not held any regard for the emperor's mother before hearing Aquilla's report, I could not help admiring her. If only I could meet death with such courage. If only I could face my stepfather with such bravery.

Mother reached out and took our guests' hands, but a deep line remained between her brows. "In going to Rome, you may be walking into a pit of vipers, so I will pray for you. Every morning and night, I will lift your names to the Father and ask Him to bless you and Paulos."

The conversation had taken a turn toward adult matters, yet I loved Paulos and wanted him to remain alive and well. "Please tell Paulos we miss him," I added, my cheeks burning.

"We will tell him," Priscilla said, smiling at me, "and knowing how you love to read, Mariana, we have brought you a copy of one of his letters." She nodded at Aquilla, who pulled a rolled set of papyri from a leather bag. "It is a copy of his letter to the believers in Rome. Have you read it?"

I smiled in pleased surprise. "No, but I would love to."

Aquilla placed the pages in my hand. "I am sure you have already read his letters to the believers here."

"Many times," Mother said, a note of resignation in her voice. "I am not proud that Paulos had to scold us, but since it is important that people learn from our mistakes, we have hired copyists to reproduce his letters for the ecclesia throughout Achaia. We ask all new converts to read them."

"Paulos loves and misses you." Priscilla's dark eyes filled with tears. "When we were with him in Ephesus, he could not speak of you Corinthians without weeping. Despite the trouble you went through, he has not stopped praying for all of you."

"I hope the troubles are well behind us." Mother straightened her spine. "And where are my manners? Have you eaten? I will have the servants bring food and honey water, and you must agree to stay with us tonight. You are welcome to rest in our home, knowing you are among friends."

Priscilla gave Mother a smile of pure relief. "Thank you, dear Hester. You may never know how much we appreciate your hospitality. The journey to Rome will take many days, and I daresay none of our accommodations will be as pleasant as this house."

"Most evenings"—Aquilla grinned—"we spread our blankets and sleep beneath the stars. I have learned to appreciate dead leaves; they can be fashioned into a remarkably soft mattress."

Mother caught the attention of a house slave stationed near the doorway. "Prepare one of the bedrooms for our guests, then bring food to the *triclinium*." She glanced at Aquilla. "Do you have animals outside? A conveyance of some sort?"

"Only a donkey," he said. "Loaded with provisions."

"I will make certain your beast is properly tended," Mother said, ringing for the *ianitor*. The doorkeeper appeared almost instantly. "Albus, direct the stable hands to unload and care for the donkey outside. He will need food, water, and a place in our stable for the night." Albus bowed and hurried away as Mother turned to our guests. "I will give you time to relax, then I will join you for some refreshments."

We stood, but the light tap of sandals on the tile distracted us. I turned and saw Prima, my stepsister, peering around the arbor. "Oh!" She lifted a questioning brow, then looked at Mother. "Friends of yours?"

"And mine." I forced a smile. "Prima, let me introduce Aquilla and Priscilla, formerly of Ephesus, now on their way to Rome. They will be our guests tonight."

"Lovely." Prima showed her teeth in an expression that bore little resemblance to a smile. "Has Father approved?"

"He will," Mother said, stiffening slightly. "He is a hospitable man."

"Then we will welcome you for one night." Prima nodded. "I hope you rest well."

"I am sure we will," Aquilla said, bowing. "And tomorrow, after we greet some of the other brethren, we will be on our way."

"Of course . . . though I am certain Hester and Mariana would love to spend hours praying with you." She waved in a dismissive gesture, spun on her sandal, and left us.

Priscilla broke the silence. "Your stepdaughter, I presume?"

As Mother struggled to regain her composure, I attempted to smooth the disruption to what had been a perfectly peaceful afternoon. "Prima believes we are fools for believing in Adonai. I have tried to share the Gospel with her, as has Mother, but she does not want to hear."

Aquilla folded his hands. "A great many people do not want to hear the glorious Gospel," he said, his voice grave. "But she is young, and God is patient. Give her time, Mariana, and pray for her. The Spirit must open her heart so she will receive the truth . . . in His perfect time."

I was not sure Prima would ever be willing to abandon the Roman gods, but Mother was gesturing toward the house. "I am certain your room is ready," Mother said, nodding at Priscilla. "Come, I will show you the way, and within the hour I will meet you in the triclinium. I look forward to hearing more about your time in Ephesus."

"I will join you as well," I said, but my thoughts had turned to Prima's abrupt appearance. Had she come outside for a breath of fresh air, or had she come to the garden to spy?

Two

PRIMA

I ducked around a corner, quietly delighted by the discomfited expression on my stepsister's face. My appearance had embarrassed her *and* Hester, a result more satisfying than I could have imagined.

I could not understand why my stepmother insisted on welcoming common laborers into our home, especially a pair who had not visited a public bath in only the gods knew how long. The man reeked of sweat and beast, and the woman's hair was in complete disarray, sprouting from her head like Medusa's snakes. Yet despite their lowly and foreign appearance, Hester had invited them to stay overnight!

Shuddering, I walked back through the house. I would bar my chamber door at sunset. Not because I expected the man to enter my *cubicula* with inappropriate intentions, but because I would die if either the man or woman sullied my bedchamber with their grime and sweat.

I returned to my chamber and found Gilda, my handmaid, folding garments that had come from the fullers. My white tunics were now spotless, every trace of dinginess removed.

They had worked a miracle with my blue tunic—I could find no trace of the wine I spilled when I last wore it.

I dropped onto my bed and stared at the elaborately painted ceiling. "I wish Father would come home. Hester has invited vagabonds to sleep under our roof."

Gilda nodded. "I thought I heard voices in the garden."

"They are poor as mice, from the look of them, and ignorant as well. I believe they have visited us before—about the time Hester and Mariana started listening to that rabbi. Mariana was so young and foolish then. She drank in every word the Jews uttered."

Gilda pressed her lips together and folded another gown. I wanted to warn her that her lips would flatten and she would look even older than she was, but why should a slave care about her appearance?

When Gilda refused to respond, I rose on my elbows to better see her. "By all the gods, slave, I could smell that pair when I walked through the atrium. Surely you have some comment about them."

Gilda shook her head. "I am sorry, Domina, but I was folding your tunics. I did not see them."

The woman kept her gaze focused on the contents of my trunk, causing me to wonder if she harbored some secret sympathy for the poor . . . but surely she could not. In our home she wore a good wool tunic and ate whatever was left over from my dinner trays. Compared to others, was hers not a life of luxury?

But I did not know this slave well, as she had been a member of our household for only a few weeks. "You never told me," I said, sitting up, "where you were before Father bought you."

A smile curved her lips. "You have never asked that question, Domina."

"I am asking now. Before you came to Corinth, where were you? Where were you born?"

She inhaled a deep breath. "I was born in Britannia. Before I came here, I served in Rome."

She uttered the words in a grave voice, as if I should be impressed that she was born in a land inhabited by uncivilized barbarians. Yet though I cared nothing about Britannia, I cared a great deal about Rome.

"Did you learn to speak Greek in Rome?"

She shrugged. "And some Latin."

I studied her. She was thin, as most slaves were, and could have been anywhere from twenty to thirty-five. Her face was pale, and her lashes blond and barely visible, which gave her the frightened look of a rabbit. A twisted knot of fiery hair sat atop her head like a rebel's crown.

"Do all people in Britannia have pale skin, blue eyes, and copper-colored hair?"

She shrugged again. "Many do, but not most."

I nodded, finally understanding how she had come to be my handmaid. At the slave market, standing among so many dark-haired, brown-eyed women, my father must have thought Gilda looked like a daughter of Aphrodite.

"Unbind your hair, slave."

The woman blinked, then dropped the tunic she was folding and silently pulled out her hairpins. An unruly river tumbled over her back, waves of bronze lit by copper flashes. I was amazed at its fullness, and despite her age, I could not see a single silver thread.

I rose and combed my fingers through the tangles. I lifted

it with both hands and felt its weight. "It might do," I murmured.

She turned her head. "Domina?"

"Put it up again."

She twisted and pinned her hair while I picked up the looking brass and studied my reflection. The face staring back at me was neither pale nor unique, but it was not unattractive, particularly when cosmetics had been properly applied.

Hester and Mariana could have their strange new god, but Father and I would remain true to the deities of Rome. They had made us part of an empire that brought its citizens power, slaves, and unimaginable luxuries.

Father and I enjoyed being Romans because Rome had proved itself invincible. The gods of Rome had taken a tiny settlement on the River Tiber from obscurity to leadership of the known world. How could the God of the Jews possibly compete?

Even though we lived in Corinth, many miles from the imperial city, Father was fond of dreaming about the capital. "One day," he frequently assured me, "you and I will journey to Rome and stand on the steps of the Forum. We will visit the Senate and gaze upon the Pyramid of Cestius with our own eyes."

I adored the idea of visiting Rome. Who would not, since everything powerful and good came from that city? Yet I also enjoyed life in Corinth where, thank the gods, I would never have to compete with the daughters of senators and patricians who resided in Rome.

In my sixteen years, Father had firmly impressed one principle upon my heart: life was a competition. For a female, the competition centered on marriage, and my marriage should have been arranged two years before.

But soon, Father promised, I would marry a powerful and wealthy man. My father's well-known declaration that I would marry the best prospect in Achaia was the only reason tongues had not begun to wag about my advanced age.

Yet time was slipping away like water through my clenched fingers.

Three

MARIANA

The next morning, I dressed quickly and went directly to the triclinium, where Aquilla and Priscilla were already reclining near trays of fruit and bread. Mother must have had the kitchen slaves rise early because a standing tray of warm nut cakes had filled the air with the aromas of cinnamon and cardamom.

The couple looked much better than they had the day before. Both had damp hair, the result of visiting the luxurious marble bath, and I could not see even a trace of dirt beneath their fingernails.

"Good day to you," I said, sinking onto the end of Priscilla's dining couch. "I trust you slept well."

She swallowed a bite and smiled. "Indeed, we did. We are most grateful to you and your mother—and your father, too, of course."

I glanced around. "Have you seen him this morning?"

Aquilla pointed toward the vestibule. "He stopped to wish us a good journey, then went on his way. He mentioned something about urgent business at the governor's palace."

I frowned. "But we have no governor."

"You soon will," Priscilla said. "We heard the news a few days ago. The Roman Senate has appointed a new governor for Achaia, who will soon be coming to Corinth. Your father must be making preparations for his arrival."

Aquilla lifted a brow. "Narkis is still the chief magistrate, is he not?"

I dipped my chin in a nod. "I believe so. But I do not often concern myself with government or politics."

"You are young," Priscilla said. "When you are married, you will learn that such things are important, especially when they affect your family."

I picked up a nut cake as my mother came into the room. She gave each of our guests a light embrace, then reclined on another couch and folded her hands.

"I wish you could stay longer, but I understand why you wish to reach Rome as soon as possible." She gestured to the trays of food. "Please, take all this with you. I will have one of the servers wrap the bread and fruit. You will need sustenance on your long journey."

The hint of a smile shone in Aquilla's beard. "Thank you," he said, "for anticipating our needs."

"What will you do when you reach Rome?" Mother's bracelets tinkled as she rested her elbow on an armrest. "I am sure you will visit Paulos as soon as possible."

Aquilla nodded. "We will. And with your permission, we will assure him of your love and prayers."

"Of course." Mother smiled. "What will you do after you have seen him?"

Priscilla lifted her right hand, displaying her palm. "I am glad my fingers still have calluses. Aquilla and I will make tents while we are in Rome, just as we did here and in Ephesus. When we are not cutting or sewing goatskin, we will tell people about Yeshua. And once we have found a place, we will begin to hold meetings in our home."

"I promise to pray for you," Mother said, her eyes sobering. "Although our current emperor seems willing to allow people to continue worshiping as they always have, Rome has never been a safe place for those who resist the emperor's edicts . . . and who can predict what he may decree tomorrow?"

"We will also pray for you." Priscilla's eyes darkened as she lowered her voice. "I am sure it is not easy to live in a divided household. Clearly, your husband and stepdaughter are at odds with your convictions."

"And do not forget," Aquilla said. "Pray for your sister. Since Yeshua told us to love our enemies, surely you can love your stepsister."

"Narkis and Prima are good to us," Mother protested, her cheeks coloring. "They do not prohibit us from worshiping Adonai, and Mariana and I do not belittle their Roman gods. When I kneel at the household *lararium*, I pray to Adonai, not Jupiter."

As Mother spoke, I winced at a stab of guilt. To keep peace in our household, she and I went through the motions of worshiping Roman gods, but I felt no peace about our charade. What must the slaves think when they saw us kneeling before an image of Jupiter? They could not hear the prayers in our heads, so how could they tell we were not worshiping the demons represented by false gods?

Priscilla and Aquilla would *never* kneel before a Roman shrine. Neither would Paulos. I had read enough of the Jewish sacred writings to know about the time when Israel abandoned Adonai and sacrificed to demons, non-gods, new gods and old ones, forgetting the God who brought them out of slavery in Egypt.

Paulos had taught me that the Roman gods—new and old, known by Greek and Roman and Egyptian names—were not gods at all, but *shedim*, or demons, who delighted in leading people away from Adonai.

"We will pray for you," Priscilla repeated. "We will ask Adonai to use you and give you wisdom."

"And courage," Aquilla said, looking at me. "The courage to do His will."

Priscilla and Aquilla stood, so Mother and I did as well.

"Thank you for Paulos's letter," I said. "I will begin to read it today."

"We will load your donkey and send it out," Mother said. "May the shalom of Messiah Yeshua comfort you until we meet again."

We embraced each other, then Mother sent me to the stable, where slaves were loading Aquilla's donkey with water jars. A pair of cats zipped through the straw, apparently chasing a mouse, and a moment later a kitchen slave came out with two baskets of bread and cakes, which other slaves lashed to the donkey's pack.

I followed the stable hand who led the donkey to the front of the house, where Mother waited with our guests. Aquilla took the donkey's lead rope and thanked Mother again as Priscilla gave me a warm hug.

"I hope this is not the last time I see you," I whispered.

"Adonai knows," she answered. She kissed my cheek. "Be strong and courageous," she murmured. "Adonai will be with you."

I stepped back as she took her place next to her husband, then, with a final wave, they moved down the street.

"May the Spirit of Yeshua be with you," Mother called, her hand at her throat.

Anxiety and envy swirled within me as I watched them go. They were walking into a potentially dangerous situation—after all, Paulos was in prison because he had preached the Gospel—but oh, what joy they must feel, knowing they would be used by the Spirit of God.

"Sometimes, my pet," Mother whispered, "I feel I am not doing enough to serve Adonai."

I glanced up at her, wondering if she shared my guilt for kneeling before a pagan altar.

"Then again," she continued, "I am doing the best I can where Adonai has planted me. Surely that is enough." She squeezed my shoulder. "And now we have work to do. Let us get busy."

Mother refused to meet my gaze as we returned to the house. I wanted to learn the source of her disquiet, but she wiped her eyes and said she had things to do, so I should go to my chamber and read.

I went to my room, but I couldn't forget the quaver in Mother's voice and the glimmer of tears on her cheek. Feeling as though a hand had closed around my heart, I asked Salama to join me in prayer.

"But mistress, I do not know your God."

"You can learn about Him."

Kneeling by the bed, I closed my eyes and spoke to Adonai: "Father and Creator of all, please hear my prayer. Bless

Paulos, keep him well, and preserve his life. Go with Aquilla and Priscilla and keep them safe on the road. Guard them from thieves and protect them from evil. When they reach Rome, help them find the perfect house and let them be able to do their work in peace. Send them clients for their tent-making and send the people who need to know about you and your Son, Yeshua. Remind me to pray for them and assure Mother that all will be well because you will give us the courage to do whatever must be done. Surely you know that I lack courage, and have far too many fears . . ."

I fell silent, aware that I had begun to babble. I did not know Adonai nearly so well as Paulos and his friends, but I was eager to learn and become more confident in my faith.

"Domina?"

Salama's soft voice startled me. "Yes?"

"Why are you so afraid for your friends? Many people travel to Rome without incident, so I do not understand why you find this situation so distressing."

Salama, who had recently been given to me, did not know me well, and I did not think she knew anyone outside my family who worshiped Adonai. I shook my head, not sure I would be able to explain why fear had been part of my life since the day my father died.

"I do not know why I am often afraid," I said, turning to see her better. "Yeshua said we should not fear because Adonai will take care of us. But it is easy to be distracted by situations we cannot control . . . and since I am only a girl, I cannot control anything."

Salama threw an arm around my shoulder, giving me a relaxed smile with a good deal of confidence behind it. "I am not afraid in this house," she said, directly meeting my gaze—an unusual action for a slave. "Do you know why?"

I shook my head.

"I see goodness in you," she said, her eyes shining. "We have only been together a few days, but I know you will not be cruel to me. Perhaps it is the same with your God—if you know He is good, you can trust Him to be kind."

"He *is* good." I repeated the words slowly, hearing them as if for the first time. "Paulos spoke often about Adonai's love and kindness."

"I will look forward to learning about Him." Salama lowered her arm and adjusted her smile. "You must forgive me if I am too forward. But since we are the same age—"

"We can be friends," I said, finishing her unspoken thought. I took her hands, and together we rose from our kneeling position. "I would like that. Because until this moment, save for my mother, I have not found a friend in this house."

❖

I looked up and groaned when I heard my stepfather's booming voice in the vestibule. Narkis was home, and he would want to eat dinner as soon as possible. Within the hour I would have to set aside Paulos's letter and eat with the household.

Paulos's epistle to the believers in Rome fascinated me, in part because I had never read a letter to Jewish believers. Paulos's letters to the Corinthian ecclesia clearly pertained to issues we had experienced, but his letter to the Romans referenced Scriptures and situations I knew almost nothing about. What was the Law, and why had the Jews been so intent on keeping it? Who was Abraham, and out of all the people alive in those ancient days, why had Adonai chosen *him* to bless the world?

The chiming of a bell warned that dinner was being served, so I tied the curled papyri together and hurried to the triclinium. Mother, Narkis, and Prima had already reclined on their couches. Mother caught my gaze and lifted a finger in a subtle warning: my stepfather had something important on his mind.

"I apologize," I said, moving a gray cat from the center of my dining couch. I lowered the feline to the floor and took my place. "I was reading."

Prima plucked a bunch of grapes from a platter on a nearby stand. "As usual. Reading is all you do."

"Your tardiness," Narkis said, lifting his goblet, "is forgiven because tonight we have much to celebrate. May the gods be praised! Today the news was finally confirmed. Our new governor, the emperor's most recent appointee, will arrive in Corinth before the end of the month. As chief magistrate, I will greet him, and afterward I will expect you to introduce yourselves with the greatest humility and charm." His eyes flicked at each of us and settled on my mother. "I cannot stress how important this opportunity is for our family. Servius Memmius Lupus is a powerful senator, and we must do everything we can to ensure that his term in Achaia is a pleasant and profitable experience."

Mother bowed her head. "Do not fear, husband. We will do everything we can to please you."

"Thank you, my dear."

Mother reached for a honeyed fig. "Memmius Lupus, you said? I have heard the name."

Narkis nodded. "He is from a long line of distinguished senators. In his letter to the council, Memmius mentioned that the governorship of Achaia is a highly sought-after post, so he is honored to have been chosen to serve us."

"I am thrilled for you, Father, but what about the other council members?" Prima arched a brow. "Will they curry the senator's favor as well?"

"No doubt," Narkis answered, the corner of his mouth twisting, "but a senator only has two sides, and I intend to stand at one of them. Despite problems from that upstart Titius Justus, I made myself indispensable to Gallio, our previous governor. I am certain Memmius has already heard that I can be a valuable and loyal friend."

I glanced at my mother, who appeared to be concentrating on her food. She had never cared much for politics, and probably cared even less since forswearing the old gods and deciding to follow Yeshua. But she was also determined to be a good wife, so she would do everything she could to please her husband.

"Hester." Narkis leaned toward her. "For the next week, I would like the cook to prepare something extravagant each night. I want to sample several dishes that might appeal to Memmius. When he arrives, we will hold a banquet and feature the most delicious."

A faint line appeared between Mother's brows. "Did you have anything specific in mind?"

Narkis tapped his stubbled chin. "The sow's udder stuffed with kidneys is quite memorable, as is the roasted boar. But I leave the choice to you."

Mother lifted her cup. "I have recently learned of a new twist in serving a wild boar. The animal is roasted, but before being served, the cook cuts a narrow opening into the beast's side and inserts a live bird. When the server makes the initial cut behind the head, the bird flies out and astonishes everyone in attendance."

For a moment I thought Narkis's eyes would fall out of their sockets, then he slapped his thigh and roared in approval. "That is precisely what I want—something unexpected for the man who has surely seen everything. Yes, let us try that. And if you hear of any other unique presentations, give the cook explicit instructions. I do not want this Roman to think he has been sent to a cultural wasteland."

Prima tossed a grape stalk over her shoulder. "What is so special about this Roman?" she asked. "We have hosted other senators."

"Ah." Narkis smiled and lifted his chin. "*This* Roman has a son of marriageable age. And for you, my dear daughter, I can think of no better husband than the eldest son of a senator."

Prima's eyes widened with pleasure, and I turned away lest she see the knowing smile that had to be playing on my lips. I knew—everyone in the household knew—that Prima had grown weary of being the oldest virgin in any gathering. If Narkis had his way, he would arrange Prima's marriage to the senator's son, and father and daughter would finally be content. He would be happy to be linked to a prominent Roman family, and she would be relieved because everyone would know that her father had refused to give his greatest treasure to anyone but a truly extraordinary man.

"Do not doubt me, my dear Prima." Narkis lifted his goblet. "I will arrange a marriage to the senator's son if it is the last thing I do. My only regret"—his gaze shifted to me—"is that while the senator does have *two* sons, only the eldest is coming to Corinth."

When I returned to my chamber, I caught Salama standing by my bed, the loose pages of Paulos's letter in her hands. When I cleared my throat, she dropped them as though they had burned her fingers.

"I am sorry, Domina." She cringed as if expecting a blow. "Forgive me. I am far too curious, I know. I should not be looking at your things—"

"I thought you were not afraid of me." I bent my head to catch her gaze. "I will not strike you, Salama."

She nodded slowly. "I apologize. It is an old habit."

"A handmaid ought to be familiar with her mistress's possessions." I picked up a page and offered it to her. "I do not mind if you read this letter. It is from Paulos, the man who told me about Adonai and His Son, Yeshua. This is a copy of his letter to the ecclesia in Rome."

Salama shook her head. "I cannot read Greek. I learned to read Latin in my former position, but not Greek."

I snorted softly. "I'm surprised you can read at all."

"My master insisted." Salama's eyes softened with memory. "All children in his household were taught to read and write because literate slaves were worth more."

I bit my lower lip and considered the girl I had begun to consider a friend. I had accepted her into my chamber without question but had not thought to ask about her past. "Where . . ." I hesitated, not wanting to wake any painful memories. "Where did you live before this?"

"Rome." She blinked wetness from her eyes and gestured

to the papyrus in my hand. "You were about to say something about the letter."

"Oh . . . yes." I studied the page in my hand. "I can read Greek, but Paulos's meaning is not always easy to understand." I sat on the bed and found the page I had been reading. "There is much here I cannot grasp. Paulos is writing to Jews in Rome, but I had never met a Jew before I met him. I do not fully understand their traditions and their Law."

"So why are you reading a book meant for other people?"

"Because his letter is not directed to Jews *alone*. In his opening, Paulos says he is writing to 'all those in Rome, loved by God, called to be *kedoshim*.'"

When her brows slanted in a question, I laughed.

"The word is Hebrew, meaning *holy* or *set apart*. He is writing to anyone who has decided to leave the old gods and follow Yeshua."

Salama cast a nervous glance over her shoulder, so I rose and closed the door. When I was certain we would not be overheard, I climbed back onto the bed and gestured for her to sit across from me.

How could I explain everything that had happened in the last few years? Salama barely knew me and had never heard of Paulos, so how could she conceive of a God I still struggled to understand?

I drew a deep breath. "Mother and I worshiped the gods of Rome like everyone else—until one afternoon," I began. "We were in the marketplace at midday, and many of the merchants had gone to the well for water. Paulos stood in the town center, and he was speaking in a loud voice. Mother knew he was a Jewish rabbi—a religious teacher—by his dress. We had never heard anyone talk like he did, so we stopped to listen."

Salama frowned. "Why would a religious teacher speak at the marketplace? I would expect to find such a man at a temple."

"He was working in a tentmaker's booth with Aquilla and Priscilla, the couple who left this morning. I cannot explain why Mother and I stopped to listen, but we were not disappointed. Paulos spoke of familiar things while describing them in a new way. We went again on the next market day, and the next, and after a few weeks we were convinced that Adonai, the God of the Jews, had to be the one true God and Creator of the world."

"How could *that* make sense?" Salama frowned. "Why Him and not Jupiter or one of the Egyptian gods?"

"The gods of other nations are *human*," I pointed out. "They argue, they fight, they are jealous of one another. Shouldn't a god be less petty and selfish than mortals?"

Salama bit her lip. "I have never thought of the gods as petty, but perhaps you are right."

"Exactly. Paulos explained that Adonai is not like us. He is constant, always loving what He loves and always hating what He hates. He hates evil, but He loves people. He yearns to know us because He created us."

Salama's brows drew together. "If He loves people and hates evil, how does He feel about evil people?"

I smiled, appreciating the logic behind her question. "Paulos said none of us is holy or perfect, but if we turn from evil, Adonai will forgive the wrongs we have committed. But a price must be paid for the evil we have done, so Adonai sent His Son to pay that price."

Salama shook her head. "I do not understand. How can anyone worship an invisible God? We can *see* the gods of the Romans and Greeks. And in Egypt, where I was born, the priests offer food to images of Isis and Horus and Osiris, and clothe and care for them—"

"But what do those gods do for the people?" I asked. "Paulos said everything we see in the world—the mountains and sky, forests and trees, everything beautiful and good—must come from a creator, and that Creator was Adonai. He created this world from nothing, but people have given the praise and glory due Him to lesser immortals that have no creative power at all. Most people are deceived and act like their false gods, lying and stealing and murdering because they want to please themselves, not the true Creator. So Adonai sent His Son to earth. He was called Yeshua, He lived in Israel, and during the time of Tiberias Caesar, the Romans crucified Him."

"Why?" Concern flickered in the depths of Salama's wide eyes. "Why would they kill the son of a god?"

"They killed Yeshua because the religious authorities feared His popularity with the people. They also feared antagonizing Rome. But three days after His crucifixion, Yeshua came out of the tomb and promised that those who follow Him will never die."

Salama flinched. "How can anyone be dead for three days and live again? It has never happened."

"But it has! And Paulos has actually spoken to people who were dead until Yeshua brought them back to life."

Salama shook her head. "I am your slave, so I must do what you say. If you want me to worship this God and His Son, I will do as you command."

I took her hand. "I would never force you to worship Adonai, and following Yeshua is more than chanting prayers and burning incense. Those who follow Him must believe in their hearts that God has raised Him from the dead. When we have true faith, we surrender—we become *His* slaves out of gratitude and love for Him. I would not ask you to do that unless you can believe in Him with all your heart."

Salama gave me a penetrating look. "You are a slave? To this Yeshua?"

I nodded.

"But how does He tell you what to do?"

I stared past her into my own thoughts. Did I know Yeshua's voice? Would I recognize it if I heard it?

"He tells me—" I hesitated, fishing for an answer— "through the holy writings." I lowered my hand to the papyri. "He tells me through rabbis and other holy teachers who know Him better than I do. And sometimes"—I touched my chest—"He tells me in a silent, strong voice that speaks to my heart."

Salama studied me, then swallowed. "I do not understand your God," she said, "but I am grateful to serve you. If your God arranged it so I would be your birthday present, I will forever be grateful to Him." She lowered her voice. "I have often thanked my gods I was not given to your sister."

I caught my breath, instinctively alarmed by her honest words. Many women would have beaten a slave for expressing disloyalty to another member of the household, but how could I blame Salama for feeling as I did? Even after following Yeshua, I continued to wonder why Adonai placed me with a stepfather and stepsister who neither loved nor appreciated me.

"Prima is not so bad," I said, "but she does not know Yeshua, so she cares more for herself than for others. I have been praying for her . . . and trying to love her." I sighed, knowing I had scarcely begun to teach Salama about Adonai. "It is not easy living in this household," I continued, keeping my voice low. "Every morning when we stand at the lararium and Narkis sacrifices to his gods, I know I should not be standing with him. But he is the *paterfamilias* of this house, and I cannot defy him without risking my life. My mother feels the same way."

"But surely he cares for you. He has been your paterfamilias for how long?"

"Five years. Do not misunderstand, I am grateful he married my mother after my father died and we lost everything. He seemed to truly admire Mother, so I promised her I would do my best to respect him and bring honor to his household. Yet while I hold him in high esteem, I do not believe he considers me anything but an obligation. Prima does not love me, of that I am certain. But Mother does. And so does Yeshua. That should be enough. It *is* enough."

I lowered my head to meet her gaze. "I cannot stress how important it is that you do not speak of my belief in Yeshua to anyone. Narkis knows we worship Adonai, but he knows nothing about Yeshua or that we have ceased to worship the Roman gods."

Salama pressed her fingertips to her lips, a sign of silence.

"And I would know more about you," I said. "You were born in Egypt and came here from Rome. Have you lived in other places?"

Salama's gaze flitted to the ceiling as she blinked rapidly, then she shook her head. "My mother was a slave from Gaul, owned by an official in the Roman army. She gave birth to me when he was stationed in Egypt."

I nodded slowly. "And your father?"

Salama lifted one shoulder in a shrug. "I do not know. My mother's master sold us to a Roman, who took us to Rome. Mother worked for his wife while I learned reading, writing, and the special skills of ladies' maids. Once I began to bleed, I was taken to the market and sold to a trader, who brought me to Corinth."

"I am sorry," I whispered. "You must miss your mother."

Salama drew a deep breath. "A slave's feelings are of no consequence," she whispered, averting her eyes. "But if it matters, since my arrival my dealings with you have been pleasant."

"Truly?" I lay back on my pillows and smiled, amazed that a slave's statement could bring me so much pleasure. "Then as long as we are friends, I am blessed indeed."

Four

PRIMA

After dinner I found Father scowling behind his desk in the *tablinum*. A ledger of accounts lay open on his desk, while behind him the ancient family treasure chest sat locked and chained to the floor. My father was proud of his wealth, but far prouder of his position.

"Father?"

His scowl eased as he looked up. "Prima! Do you need something?"

"I have no needs, but I fear you do." I sat on a nearby stool and propped my elbow on the edge of his desk. "I know you are greatly stressed not only by your daily responsibilities but also by the preparations that must be addressed before the governor's arrival. That is why I am offering to help you."

"You want to help?" One corner of his mouth rose. "You are a girl, and this is an important event."

"I am no longer a girl, so assign me some of the responsibilities for your banquet and let me show you what I can do. I can oversee the cooks. I can create the guest list, engage the musicians, rent extra slaves. With Aphrodite's help, I can handle anything this occasion requires."

Father looked at me, speculation sparking in his eyes. "Why would a girl—a woman—who has never volunteered for anything want to handle the governor's banquet?"

"Perhaps I would like to show the governor that I am capable." I rested my chin in my hand and smiled up at him. "I want what you want, Father. We are about to welcome an important new governor, and you have much on your mind, so let me help you. Over the years I have attended dozens of these banquets, yet I have never embarrassed you, have I?"

Father shifted in his chair. "No, Prima, you have not. But I have already asked Hester to oversee the menu."

"So let Hester tend to the dinner and allow me to arrange everything else. I will not disappoint you."

Father tented his hands and stared at me over his fingertips. I knew he was calculating the risk, but was my risk not as great as his?

He had to realize there had never been a more important time to demonstrate my gifts and abilities. The new governor had a son who needed a wife. Perhaps the young man had not found a suitable woman in Rome. Perhaps he had grown tired of meeting senators' daughters. A banquet was the perfect way to display my charm, sophistication, and suitability for the role of a patrician's wife.

Father finally lowered his hands. "You are right, and you are old enough to take on such a responsibility. I daresay your impulse is well-timed, and I will be happy to introduce you to the governor's son." He leaned forward and lowered his voice. "I have heard that Memmius would like his son to marry a girl from Corinth. A union with a local family would give the young man a good reason to remain in the city while Memmius travels to and from Rome. While the governor is away, his son would oversee the capital."

"Why would Memmius need an overseer?" I lifted a brow. "You have always been able to stay abreast of important matters."

"Indeed I have. But Memmius does not yet know how capable I can be."

I nodded. "Thank you, Father. Your trust in me will be rewarded."

I was about to leave him, but stopped when a shadow crossed the threshold.

"Narkis," Hester said, stepping into the room, "should I begin to compile the guest list for your banquet? I assume you want to invite the city council members and their wives, plus the leading merchants—"

"No need, my dear." Father smiled at me. "Our beautiful Prima has already volunteered to oversee all the details except the menu, which I will leave in your capable hands."

Confusion flickered over Hester's face, then she gave me a tentative smile. "Are you certain, Prima? I am accustomed to handling such things."

"Running a large household is demanding enough," Father said. "So let Prima do this for us. If Fortuna smiles on us, Prima's efforts will impress the governor. I believe she will even impress his son."

I lowered my head, basking in his ambition while my heart simmered with satisfaction. Let Hester handle the cooks and kitchen slaves. Let Mariana hide away in her bedchamber with her papyri and scrolls.

For sixteen long years I had watched my father manipulate and impress others with his insights and skills. Soon I would show all of Corinth that I had learned my lessons well.

After breaking my fast the next morning, I met Father and the rest of our household at the *lararium*, the recessed niche built into the north wall of our enclosed garden. A slave played the double pipes while another lit a cone of incense, filling the air with a sharp scent I would always associate with our household gods.

Above us, a scattering of clouds hid the blue of the sky while a brisk breeze chilled our bare arms. Our one hundred and twenty-seven household slaves huddled under the roofed peristyle, enjoying one another's body heat and a respite from the cold wind of Ianuarius.

I stood at Father's right hand, my assigned spot, while Hester and Mariana stood at his left. Like a snake, Hester's favorite cat played around her ankles, gliding and rolling to the music of the pipes.

When the last slave had shuffled into place, Father lifted the edge of his pleated toga and draped it over his head, showing respect to the gods. Then he recited the morning prayer, his palms uplifted, reading from a scroll held by his amanuensis. He read slowly and carefully because a single stutter or slip would require him to begin the entire ceremony again. One did not offer an imperfect prayer to immortal gods.

"O Vesta," he began, addressing the goddess of hearth and home, "hear my words. We ask you to warm our home, warm our hearts with your flame, and keep us in your hearth fire. Watch over our family and keep us safe. Help us honor you and prepare for our work on this day. May our labors be prosperous.

"O Janus," he continued, "god of beginnings, I pray for a start of new prosperity through this act of worship, so we may please you and the divinities. As paterfamilias, I seek your vision and protection at this important time."

He gestured to a waiting kitchen slave, who stepped forward with a bowl of raw pork. Father set the meat upon the altar in the niche, then lifted his hands again. "O great Jupiter, god of Rome, I welcome you to our home. I ask you to look with favor upon our family at this time. I ask for your blessing and in return, I give thanks and roasted meat to satisfy your hunger. I give to you so you may give to us."

At that instant, another slave—one who had probably been abruptly rousted from wherever he slept in the house—swayed on his feet, earning a reproachful glance from my father. The man next to the sleepy slave elbowed the youth, who stiffened and lowered his head.

"O mighty Jupiter," Father went on, "this family faces a monumental task. You have blessed us with peace and prosperity. You gave me a successful relationship with my wife. You have provided me with a high position and good health. I have many friends and a large household, and with much gratitude, I thank you. Look upon us with favor and bless us with wisdom and foresight as we prepare for the arrival of the new governor, Servius Memmius Lupus. May he bless us, and may you bless him, so we and our fellow Corinthians may prosper. Through your bountiful grace, I ask that he will look upon us with favor and increase our wealth and standing. In return, I will give many sacrifices to you and support the priests at your temples."

As Father lowered his hands, a female slave stepped forward. She carefully poured a small amount of wine into a dish, then placed the dish into the niche.

Father extended his arms again, palms upward, as if he expected blessings to drop at any moment. "Through prayers and sacrifice, I give you an offering of fine wine in recognition of your kind blessings to me. I open my heart and trust in you, Jupiter. With gratitude, I thank you and feel your presence before me."

With his major petitions made, my father lowered his hands and dipped his head toward the statues of the Penates, the spirits of our storeroom. "We are trusting you, Penates, to provide us with the food and supplies we need for health, sustenance, and the important banquet that lies ahead of us."

He lifted his gaze to the crimson death masks of his parents and grandparents, which hung on the wall above the altar. "Lares," he said, "spirits of my ancestors, we know you are watching. May we honor you in our activities today and in the coming weeks."

Father bowed his head for a moment and then turned away from the altar, setting off on his right foot—to step off on the left would have been a sinister omen.

As he left the lararium, I studied Hester and Mariana. They stood quietly like the slaves, though Hester had not closed her eyes during the prayers, and Mariana appeared bored with the morning sacrifices. If he had seen their faces, Father would not have approved.

I smiled. Father knew, of course, that Hester and Mariana

had begun to worship the Jewish God, but as long as they did not disrespect the gods of Rome, he did not seem to mind.

Still . . . one day, I might need to tell him of their obvious disinterest.

Five

MARIANA

While Salama sat in a corner spinning, I lay on my couch, the pages of Paulos's letter to the Roman ecclesia scattered around me. I sat up when Mother entered the room with an odd look on her face.

My pulse quickened. "Is all well?"

Mother clasped her hands together and sat at the end of the couch. "I am probably being silly."

"Why would you think so?"

She glanced at Salama, who had not looked up from her spinning, and sighed. "Prima has asked Narkis if she can handle the arrangements for the governor's banquet. I should probably be grateful for not having to worry about anything except the food, but if this governor holds our fate in his hands, perhaps Narkis should not place so much confidence in Prima's abilities."

The slope of Mother's shoulders betrayed her genuine apprehension, so I resisted the temptation to wave her concerns away. "If Prima wants to handle things, let her do her best. Do not worry—Narkis will not allow her to fail."

Mother gave me a pained smile. "But if she does not complete the preparations, I will be responsible for setting things right, probably at the last moment." She shuddered, then sighed and kissed the top of my head. "What sort of mother bothers her daughter with her worries? I should not be here. Let us speak of other things." She gestured to the papyri on my couch. "What wisdom does Paulos impart to the believers in Rome?"

"He addresses many issues . . . and some of his writing is truly beautiful." I turned to a section I had just read. "'I will call those who were not My people, 'my people,' and her who was not loved, 'Beloved.' And it shall be that in the place where it was said to them, 'You are not My people,' there they shall be called sons of the living God.'"

Mother's brow furrowed. "I think he is quoting from the Jews' holy writings. Paulos often does that."

"Adonai was talking about us, right? The Gentiles?"

"Perhaps. We are not Adonai's chosen people; the Jews are. But Yeshua came to save anyone who believed in Him. So those—Jew or Gentile—who follow and obey Yeshua are now His people and beloved of Adonai."

Mother's face lit with an inner radiance as she pondered the words, and in that instant I wanted Narkis, Prima, Salama, and the entire household to understand and believe Paulos's message. They were all lost, dutifully worshiping false gods, living as they pleased while completely ignorant of the God who had sacrificed His Son so they could have eternal life.

I looked up and saw that Mother's brow had again creased with anxiety. "If you think it would help," I said, touching her arm, "I could suggest that Prima allow you to oversee her efforts for the banquet. Having oversight might put your mind at ease in case she forgets an important detail."

Mother shook her head. "Prima would be offended at such a suggestion. No, Narkis rules this house, so if he wants Prima in charge, that is the way it will be. Perhaps he wants her to gain experience . . . or perhaps he intends to exhibit her suitability as a wife. I do not know his intentions, but I will bow to his will. Because that is what a wife should do."

My breath caught in my lungs. "It is not right that a daughter should overrule the concerns of a wife."

"But it is fitting that a wife honors her husband," Mother answered. "So I will."

"If you need me to help with anything—"

"I might," Mother said, "but for now, I will oversee the food and summon the designer from the fuller's guild. If we are to welcome the new governor at a festive banquet, we will all need new garments."

❖

Three days later, Mother summoned me to her bedchamber. I found her holding a length of lovely fabric while the jeweler waited with a tray of polished gemstones. Across the room, the designer from the fuller's guild sorted through her materials.

"I have sent for your sister," Mother said, running her hand over the fluid fabric. "Prima will come in a moment, I am sure."

"While we wait," the dress designer said, "shall I begin with you and your daughter? We can design your tunics now, and the other girl's later."

Mother snorted a laugh. "Prima will want first choice. So rather than have a heated argument when she arrives, we will wait." She set the fabric on the bed. "Would you like some honey water? I could have one of the slaves bring figs and nut breads—"

Prima sauntered into the room, followed by Gilda, her handmaid. Prima's eyes widened when she saw those who were waiting. "You did not say the jeweler would be here as well!"

"I wanted to surprise you," Mother said. "I thought we should design our tunics together so each of them can be distinctive. I have purchased this lovely blend of cotton and silk and am assured it is of the finest quality. Do you not agree?"

Prima approached the fabric with a skeptical air, but her expression softened when she saw how the fabric flowed over her open hands. "It is exquisite," she murmured. "From Egypt?"

"Of course." Mother gestured to the woman from the fuller's guild. "Prima, please tell the designer what sort of tunic you would like to wear to the banquet."

As unmarried women, Prima and I did not have much choice in style. We would wear knee-length tunics, but for this special occasion we could also wear a second tunic that would fall to the floor. The style would depend upon our choices. The *tunica interior* could have sleeves that would be exposed if the *tunica exterior* was left open at the sides. If the under-tunic had no sleeves, they could be added to the over-tunic. Either the outer or inner tunic could feature a colored border at the neckline, and we would have our choice of colored *pallas*—rectangular pieces we would drape over our shoulders like the togas worn by male citizens of the Roman Empire.

Because Mother was married, she would cover her inner tunic with a *stola*, a longer and fuller garment with a flounce at the hemline and a fitted girdle at the waist.

"I think"—Prima pressed a finger to her chin—"I would like the under-tunic to be sleeveless and the outer to have jeweled buttons on the sleeves. Pearls or perhaps emeralds, something shiny to catch the eye."

The jeweler beamed, rejoicing in Prima's appetite for adornment. "An excellent decision, my lady."

The designer turned to me. "And you?"

I sighed. I dared not make the same choices as Prima or she would accuse me of trying to imitate her. "Why not make all the arrangements for Prima's garment first?"

Prima smiled as she went to a stack of dyed fabrics and pulled out a soft blue silk for her palla. The silk rectangle would probably cost more than her inner and outer tunics combined.

The designer lifted a brow. "You are unmarried, yes?"

Prima smiled. "I will be married soon enough."

"Then you should wear a modest tunic and a delicate palla," the designer said. "I would not overindulge in jewelry. Your adornment should be your natural beauty, not expensive baubles."

Prima turned to Mother, probably hoping she would contradict the woman, but Mother pressed her lips together and said nothing. When a warning cloud settled on Prima's features, I feared she would send someone to fetch her father.

Fortunately, the jeweler seized the opportunity to push his goods. "If you want pearls, you should have them," he said, smiling broadly as he approached her with his tray of baubles. "Cleopatra wore pearls, you know. In fact, according to Pliny the Elder, she bet Marc Antony that she could host the most expensive banquet in history. At the dinner, she plucked a large pearl from one of her earrings, dropped it in her wine goblet, and drank it down." The little man sighed. "She won her bet, but I wish she had not. Pliny estimates that pearl was worth thirty million sestertii. I would have given anything to even *hold* such a treasure."

As Prima ran her fingers over the gemstones, I looked away, unable to understand why Prima had not realized that most Romans considered modesty a virtue. Though plebeians, the newly rich, and women who sold themselves for coin were not modest, the wives of senators and women from patrician families veiled themselves in public and did not flaunt their wealth. If Prima wanted to win the admiration of this Roman senator's son, perhaps she should appear modest and retiring.

"I will choose the gems later," Prima said, motioning for Gilda to undo the brooches at her shoulders. "And the sleeves must be adorned with pearls. Shiny pearls, the largest you have."

While the jeweler bobbed in delight, Mother stepped forward. "Are you certain, my dear? Sometimes it is more attractive to practice moderation."

I glanced at Mother, but she did not see my warning look. Fortunately, Prima did not snap at my mother's suggestion.

I did not understand why Mother insisted on trying to please Prima. My stepsister tolerated Mother's presence, yet she had never heeded my mother's attempts at guidance. To Prima, my mother was her father's wife, nothing more.

In truth, I could not blame her for feeling the way she did. Though I respected Narkis and honored him as head of the household, I found it difficult to love him as a father.

Prima stepped out of her tunic and stood in her undergarments as the designer draped two short lengths of soft woolen fabric over Prima's slender frame. The designer's slave stood nearby with needles and thread as the woman knelt and sewed, but within a few moments she had basted both sides to the waist and left the top open. The slave fastened the fabric with clasps at the shoulders while the designer cut longer pieces of the silk-cotton blend. Within minutes, the flowing fabric covered Prima from her shoulders to the floor.

"We will add some ruching here," the designer said, gathering the fabric at Prima's shoulders, "and on the back as well. A gold belt will provide a nice contrast and gather up the excess length. If you will remain a moment, I will mark the spots for the pearl buttons—"

Prima pushed the woman's arm away. "My handmaid can do that later. I must attend to other urgent matters."

The designer's slave hurried to undo the clasps, then gathered the fabric in her arms as Gilda helped Prima into her house tunic. Then, with barely a glance of acknowledgment, my stepsister left the room, her handmaid running after her.

Mother looked at me. "Are you in a hurry, pet?"

I laughed. "Nothing urgent awaits me."

The jeweler lifted his tray, doubtless hoping something would catch my eye, but none of his wares appealed to me, probably because I did not want to compete with Prima. At the banquet, she would shine in the light of her father's approval; she would be witty and clever as she sparkled in the light of a dozen oil lamps. Prima's marriage would be proposed, considered, and set while I stood in the shadows.

"I would prefer to wear something simple," I told the designer. "Recently I read one of the Jewish writings—the story of Esther. Have you heard of it?"

The woman shook her head, but Mother smiled. "I have read it."

"It is an amazing story," I said, purely for the designer's benefit. "Hadassah, a Jewish girl, was forcibly taken from her family, placed in the Persian king's harem, and renamed Esther. One night the king called for a woman, and Esther's slaves debated how to display her features to their best advantage."

The designer's eyes gleamed. "Did she wear silk? Or something more exotic?"

"I do not know what fabric she wore," I answered, "but she allowed others to decide what she should wear. So"—I turned—"Mother, what do *you* think I should wear?"

Mother's eyes softened as she smiled. "You should wear the whitest wool," she said, "because your heart is pure. Your hair should flow like a river over your back. And you should wear no jewelry because your beauty needs no enhancement. Go like Hadassah and let your father's guests see who you truly are."

I turned to the designer. "Does my mother's advice please you?"

"Almost," the woman said, her brows knitting. "I applaud your mother's insight, but you should not wear your hair down. People will think you are in mourning."

I smiled, acknowledging her expertise. "What if my handmaid braids it with ribbons?"

The woman nodded. "You are young, so the style will suit you. In any case, I am certain your sister will be the center of attention. If that is so, wear what you like, and I will thank you for it."

Her smile deepened as she measured the distance from my shoulders to the floor. "You have been the least troublesome of all my clients. For you, I will fashion a tunic as white as the fuller can make it. I will create the tunica exterior of the same cotton silk as your sister's."

I lifted my head. "I have no wish to imitate her."

The words had no sooner left my lips than Prima sailed back into the room, her eyes alight. "I know how to catch the governor's attention," she announced. "I will change the color of my hair."

I blinked, certain I had misunderstood her, and Mother managed a weak protest. "Are you certain that is wise? After all, the law requires prostitutes to have colored hair, and your father would never want anyone to mistake you for a woman who engages in that sort of commerce."

Prima cast a glance of restrained disdain in Mother's direction. "The law requires those women to have *blond* hair, and that is not what I have in mind."

Then, before any of us could react, she lifted the designer's rounded blade and turned to her handmaid. For a horrifying instant I thought she would strike the woman, but instead she grabbed Gilda's braid and began to hack at it. Gilda froze, her body stiff and her eyes wide, while the rest of us stood in silent shock.

Mother was the first to react. "Prima! What are you *doing*?"

"She is my slave," Prima said, her eyes glinting with purpose. "Every inch of this woman belongs to me."

Gilda covered her eyes, her hands trembling until Prima finally held up a gleaming copper rope. "Take this to the wigmaker," she said, thrusting the severed braid at the designer. "I shall expect to receive a fashionable curled wig before the governor's arrival."

The woman accepted the hair as if it were a dead animal and silently passed it to her slave. "As you wish," the designer said. She turned to Mother. "I shall have your garments— and the wig—ready by next week."

"Do not forget the pallas," Prima called. "Because the night will be cool."

"Of course."

The designer caught my gaze as she turned, then she shook her head and led the others out of the room.

Two days before the governor was due to arrive in Corinth, I joined Mother and Prima in the triclinium, which the slaves had temporarily transformed into a spa. We lay upon dining couches, our faces lifted to the painted ceiling. The scents of fragrant oils, sulfur, and minerals mingled with the steam rising from heated bowls into which the *cosmetae*, professional beautifiers of the face and body, dipped their sponges. The wooden stands that usually supported platters of food now held jars of face creams, soaps, scrubs, oils, powders, lotions, paints, and pumice stones.

Today would be our day of preparation. On the day of the banquet, the cosmetae would return to apply paint and perfume.

The slave assigned to me had just finished scraping my right arm, which stung as a result of her vigilance. I had just lifted the limb to be sure I was not bleeding when my stepfather strode into the triclinium.

"The governor has arrived early," Narkis said, propping his foot on the end of Mother's couch. "We shall hold our banquet tomorrow."

Mother sat upright, her eyes widening in her mud mask. "But there is so much to be done, and we have only begun our beauty treatments. We have not yet had the hair from our arms removed, and Prima's brows have not been joined together—"

"Her brows are perfect for now, as is she." Narkis beamed at his daughter. "All three of you are breathtaking, and I know you have laid your plans. Now we put those plans into action." He turned to Prima. "You will send slaves with the invitations, of course. They must be delivered today."

Prima swatted at the hands of the woman intent on scrubbing her elbow. "Of course, Father. The invitations are sealed and ready. The musicians have yet to be informed of the time, but I will remedy that at once. The house slaves will begin decorating this afternoon, and the cooks shall be told so they can begin their preparations now."

"And what about your personal arrangements?" Narkis looked around our circle. "Have you ordered appropriate garments and adornments?"

Mother smiled. "We have new slippers and tunics. We will not dishonor you."

Narkis's shoulders slumped in what looked like relief. "Thank the gods I am surrounded by capable women. Tomorrow we will wake early, say our morning prayers, and set to work. I met the governor at the port today, and he is most eager to visit our home."

Since he had just stepped off a ship, I suspected Memmius was most eager to eat decent food, but I dared not voice my opinion. Narkis was clearly thrilled to have a new target for his limitless ambition, and Prima would undoubtedly shine at the event. How could she not? She had made certain that every aspect of the dinner would showcase her beauty and ability. I, on the other hand, had done little but help Mother plan the menu.

I closed my eyes and surrendered to the hands of the slave, who waited to apply chalk to my face. Like it or not, by this time tomorrow evening, our household would be put to the test by our new governor.

I sighed, relieved by the thought that I was not Prima.

❖

I was on my way to bed when I passed Prima's chamber and happened to glance inside. The marble bust on my stepsister's dressing table looked different, and when I backtracked to take a second look, I realized why—her new wig rested on the sculpted head like a flaming bird nest.

I turned my abrupt laugh into a cough and ventured into the room. Prima sat at her desk writing a letter, but she did not look up when I entered. Taking advantage of her indifference, I studied the wig. The hairdresser had arranged the copper-colored hair into a basket of stiff coils, and the open end of each coil had been plugged with an oversized pearl. Such pearls, I realized, were not inexpensive.

"Your wig," I said, my hand on my chest, "will certainly attract attention. In all my days, I have never seen anything like it."

"Of course not." Prima abandoned her writing and

turned. "No one else will have that hair color. Women who tint their curls with dust and ash have no shine to their hair, but my wig will be the exception. It looks real because it *is* real."

I gave her a lopsided smile. "I have heard that the women in Rome are fond of wigs, but I have never seen one up close until now. But I must know—did you ask Gilda if you could cut her hair?"

Prima lifted a brow. "Why should I ask? The woman belongs to me."

"But surely her hair belongs to her. I cannot imagine taking Salama's hair from her head without asking."

"Are you jealous?" Prima's eyes gleamed with some emotion I could not name. "And why would you cut *your* slave's hair? Your mousy little handmaid's hair is as dark as yours."

"I am not jealous. If anything, I am curious."

Prima picked up her stylus. "Why should my handmaid care? Her hair will grow back. She can let it grow again, maybe for a few years, and then I will have another wig made. It is a unique color and just what I wanted. Now I will look like one of those exotic slaves from Gaul or Britannia."

I smothered a laugh. "I cannot believe you want to look like a slave."

"One can always pretend"—she dipped her stylus into the ink—"but I have yearned for red hair ever since Gilda was given to me. The gods made a terrible mistake when they gave such remarkable hair to a barbarian. Now it will shine on the head of a woman who deserves it."

Unable to think of a suitable response, I backed out of her room. Would Prima and I ever agree?

I was steps away from my bedchamber when I caught the

soft sound of weeping. I glanced down the corridor that led to Mother's bedchamber, and in a recessed niche I saw Salama and Gilda huddled together on the floor. Prima's handmaid was weeping while Salama tried to console her.

My stepfather would have told me to ignore the slaves, but I could not stop myself from kneeling beside them. "What is wrong?" I asked, afraid I already knew the answer.

Gilda would not look at me, but Salama boldly met my gaze. "When you are a slave," she said, her voice trembling, "you have so little. Gilda's hair, at least, was hers, but Prima has proven that Gilda owns nothing. What will she take next, Gilda's arm? Her hand?" Salama snatched a breath as if she would say more, then clamped her mouth shut.

My heart contracted in sympathy for both women, but what could I do? All wealthy Romans owned slaves. They conquered foreign kingdoms, made slaves of the defeated people, and brought civilization to formerly barbaric lands. What victor did not take spoils from the vanquished?

And how could the empire operate without slaves? Narkis often spoke of rural villas where hundreds of slaves planted and harvested crops, kept the books, and ran the business for their owners. Even in urban households like ours, slaves far outnumbered family members. But if we did not have them, who would keep the house, cook the meals, do the shopping, and carry the litters?

Narkis frequently proclaimed that his household slaves led a better life than their primitive ancestors, and I could not disagree with him. As my handmaid, Salama had been exposed to literature, music, and good food. Though she did not own a bed, she *did* have a roof over her head and the luxury of sleeping unmolested in my chamber. As my near-constant companion, she had been exposed to the marvels of Greek architecture and Roman innovation.

If Gilda paused to reflect, she might consider the sacrifice of her hair a small thing to exchange for the life she now led.

I smiled at both women, but as I turned away, another voice in my head reminded me that Paulos said believers in Yeshua were neither Jews nor Romans, slaves nor free persons, males nor females because we were united in Yeshua. None of us was more deserving of grace than the other; none was more precious to Adonai. Though we were all uniquely different, we stood as equals before the Almighty. I admired the ideal of equality, yet I did not understand how it could work in the Roman Empire.

Still, if I wanted Salama to follow Yeshua, perhaps I could demonstrate that ideal by asking Mother if I could get my slave a proper bed.

The sun seemed to rise earlier than usual the next morning, as if it knew we had a thousand things to do and only a limited number of hours to accomplish our goals. Though Prima had gone about the work of organizing the banquet with a cool and accomplished air, she took to screaming when the rented slaves arrived late, the musicians could not find a harp player, and the doorman's guard dog attacked a messenger from the governor.

When the team of cosmetae returned promptly at midday, Mother and I were already reclining on couches in her bedchamber, but Prima was nowhere to be found.

"Do you think she has run away?" Mother whispered, a hint of laughter in her voice.

"I hope not," I answered, "because I am eager to see how our Roman guests react to her wig."

Prima appeared just as the cosmetae were preparing to shave our limbs. She dropped onto the empty couch, crossed her hands over her belly, and closed her eyes, breathing deeply. "Never again," she said, her voice brittle. "When I am domina of my own household, I will have a slave oversee all the work involved in a banquet. I have worked myself into exhaustion for no reason."

I wanted to remind her that ambition lay behind her desire to do the work, but Prima would not be pleased by the reminder. So Mother and I exchanged a glance, then we closed our eyes and settled back as the cosmetae worked their magic, rendering our skin as pale and smooth as a baby's. The third woman, who had been organizing the various cosmetics, began to work on Prima.

"Father seemed excited during morning prayers," I said, trying to remain still as a slave outlined the veins of my inner arm with light blue paint.

"I noticed," Mother said. "I believe he honestly admires our new governor."

"Father is already the most important man in Corinth," Prima said. "I do not understand why he wants to ingratiate himself to yet another Roman."

Mother shook her head. "Corinth is not the center of the world," she said, gentling her voice. "Athens is more important in many respects. And we cannot forget Rome."

"Corinth is the capital of Achaia," Prima said, struggling to speak as a slave dabbed mud on her face. "And Achaia is the most important province in the empire."

"*One* of the most important," Mother corrected. "And one

of the most peaceful, so the governorship of this city is a desirable post. But Rome esteems other provinces just as much, if not more, so do not say such things in front of the governor. You must widen your vision if you wish to impress Memmius."

I thought Prima might argue, but she did not, so perhaps she appreciated Mother's admonition.

The room fell silent as the cosmetae continued to work, applying red ochre to our cheeks and lips, a mixture of wood ash and saffron to shadow our eyes, and antimony to darken and enlarge our brows. One slave colored Mother's nails with a cream made of blood and sheep fat while another woman promised to brighten my smile by scraping a pumice stone over the visible surface of my teeth.

"One must suffer to be beautiful," Mother called as I yelped at the sensation of stone against my teeth. "And never forget what Plautus said: 'A woman without paint is like food without salt.'"

"I do not need to be beautiful," I protested, testing the slave attempting to paint my lips. "I am not the one who will be presented to the governor's son."

"You will both be presented," Mother said, "so you must both look your best."

"After the presentation," Prima called from her couch, "leave me alone so I can get to know the young man."

When the cosmetae had finished with Mother, she sat up and nodded toward the doorway. "Look," she said, "Puss has brought us a present."

The cat, one of many in the house, crouched by the wall, a dead mouse between its jaws. The animal looked at us as if trying to decide who deserved such a prize, then advanced toward Prima.

She screamed and covered her freshly painted face. "Get that thing out of here!"

Mother stood and picked up the cat, then petted it until it dropped the dead mouse onto the floor. Mother nodded at a slave, who hurried forward and took the rodent while Mother released the cat.

"I do not understand why you keep those creatures," Prima said, flushing. "None of my friends keep cats."

"Then your friends have mice," Mother replied. "But any rodent who wanders into our house will soon come to a swift end."

The cosmetae were nearly finished when Gilda rushed into the chamber, her face bright with exertion. "Domina," she said, bowing before Prima, "someone has spilled goat's milk on your new tunic."

"By all the gods." Prima sat up, her face twisting with annoyance. "Who could be so clumsy?"

"I do not know—I found the mess when I entered your bedchamber."

Despite Gilda's denial, I would not have been surprised if she was the offender. She would never confess, though, because no slave would volunteer for a beating.

"You may not have spilled the milk," Prima said, spitting the words, "but you will take the garment to the fuller's and have it cleaned at once. You will run all the way, and if you and the tunic are not back before the governor arrives, you will be beaten until you cannot stand."

Gilda's face went blank with shock, but she managed to bow and nod. "Yes, Domina."

When Prima had departed, I sat up and looked at Mother, who was lying on her back, eyes closed.

"Mother?"

She stirred. "Yes?"

I lowered my voice. "What did you pray this morning? I know you did not ask Vesta to bless the banquet."

Her lips curled in a gentle smile. "I prayed that Adonai's will would be accomplished tonight, and that I would be a reflection of Yeshua's light." She turned toward me. "What did you pray?"

"I did not know what to pray, so I asked Adonai if He would show me how to stay out of Prima's way. I told Him I was willing to be sick if that would keep me safe from Prima's ire. I do not want anything to ruin her evening."

Mother reached out and took my hand. "Ah, pet, you should not remove yourself from any situation if Adonai has clearly placed you in it." She sat up and leaned toward me. "You cannot run from difficult situations; you must meet them in the strength of the Lord. So when you enter the atrium tonight, resolve to remain true to Yeshua and ask the Spirit to lead you. That is all you need to do."

"And after that?"

"After the dinner and your presentation to the governor"—the corner of her mouth rose in a wry smile—"you may do whatever you like."

Six

PRIMA

My heart thumped with impatience as I climbed the steep path that led up the Acrocorinth to the temple of Aphrodite. Father said the path required a visitor to climb more than two thousand steps, and I had no reason to doubt him. I would invest at least two hours in this trip, hours I could not spare, but the banquet's success—*my* success—would depend on Aphrodite.

I lifted the hem of my tunic and walked carefully, not wanting to stumble and injure my ankle or, worse yet, ruin the cosmetics that had just been professionally applied. I could have visited the temple in the morning, but I wanted the goddess to see me at my best. I wanted her to know I was giving all I could to her, so she could give to me.

My shoes scuffed stones as I climbed, my labored breath whistling through my nose. Behind me, the kitchen slave I chose as an escort panted heavily, obviously unused to climbing.

I could see the temple already, the highest point of Corinth,

yet the path to its peak was a twisting testament to ineffi-
ciency. It ran parallel to the mountain slope, but the steps
were cracked and my view blocked by haphazard structures
erected by shady sellers hoping to earn a coin or two from
men and women who reeked of desperation.

Women like me. This banquet *had* to be a success . . .
my future depended on it. If the governor was not pleased,
if his son did not respond to me, I would be the laughing-
stock of Corinth, the daughter who had waited for the
perfect suitor and then been rejected. So everything had
to be perfect.

I directed my thoughts toward simpler, less urgent situations.

The musicians? Done. They had found a harp player and
would arrive before sunset.

The hired slaves were now hard at work in the house and
kitchen. I stationed five of them at the front door to make
sure the litter bearers of early guests promptly vacated the
area. I gave them permission to start a fire in the stable yard,
where they could warm themselves while their masters dined
inside.

The decorations? As soon as Hester, Mariana, and I finished breaking our fast, half a dozen slaves entered the triclinium with candlestands, feathered fans, and flowers to
adorn the dining trays. Similar floral displays had already
been placed throughout the house, even in Father's office.

My tunic? Gilda would make certain it was clean. If it
was not, she would have the designer create a new one. Both
women knew how much I had done to create a perfect evening, so neither would dare disappoint me.

"Buy an idol, lady." A man stood outside a tent shrine to

Vesta and held out a primitive carving of the hearth goddess. "She will protect your home."

"Out of my way." I did not meet his gaze; to do so would only invite another proposition. Once we passed him, I commanded the kitchen slave to walk in front, not behind me. "But keep up the pace," I warned, prodding the center of his bony back. "I do not have time to waste."

We passed several temples and hastily constructed shrines to Greek, Roman, and Egyptian gods. I ignored all of them, my heart set on reaching Aphrodite. She was the goddess of love, attraction, and fertility, and only she could supply what I needed.

Finally we reached the summit. The kitchen slave collapsed against the remains of an ancient stone wall while I walked to the shining marble temple. Standing atop its broad steps, I looked out and beheld the city of Corinth, sprawled before me like a gleaming quilt. To the west lay the sea, broad and blue.

When I could speak without gasping, I entered the temple and knelt before the imposing statue of the goddess. The sculptor had portrayed her as fully clothed, holding a staff in her right hand—probably a reference to her affair with the mortal shepherd, Adonis—and securing her draped palla with her left. One leg was exposed, her knee positioned toward the viewer as if she were about to step forward and listen to my prayer.

"Oh, Aphrodite," I whispered, prostrating myself on the cold tile, "known to the Romans as Venus, to Easterners as Ishtar and Astarte, goddess of the sea, love, fertility, and war—I call on you, knowing you will leave your golden house and come flying to my aid. I beg you, come. I beg you, stand by me tonight and captivate the man I will meet. May he be as powerless in my hands as I am in yours, golden lady. For I am yours, and yours alone."

I waited, as I always did, in case the goddess wished to reply. In all my years of worship I had never heard anything, so the flesh on my arms pebbled when a silky voice responded: "Rise, daughter. The goddess has heard your petition."

I sat up. The woman towering above me was not an immortal goddess, but a priestess. She appeared to be over the age of twenty, but her eyes were old, crinkled at the corners with knowledge and power. A golden bracelet graced her wrist, the precious metal engraved with seashells, roses, and doves, all symbols of the goddess. I had seen this priestess on previous visits, but she had never spoken to me. Was this a sign?

I scrambled to my feet and bowed my head. "How can I know Aphrodite has heard me?"

"I heard you," the woman said, her voice like the tinkling of coins in an offering bowl. "And I am Cassia, high priestess to the goddess. When I hear, she hears."

Unable to find my tongue, I nodded.

"Go your way," Cassia said, lifting my head with her fingertips. When I met her gaze, she smiled and pointed to the doorway. "And know that Aphrodite, the great mother, has nothing but good in store for you."

Too overcome to say anything else, I turned and hurried away, ready and reassured that I would find victory in the night.

Seven

MARIANA

The guests began to arrive after sunset. The city council members appeared first, the men wearing their heaviest togas and their wives resplendent in silk stolas, elaborate wigs, and brilliant jewelry. Rubies dripped from one woman's ears, and another wore a strand of gold nuggets big enough to choke a horse.

I glanced at Mother, who seemed positively modest in comparison. Her white stola was elegant, and her palla framed her face in a lovely shade of pink. Narkis would not have wanted her to dress less extravagantly than the other wives, but her necklace was a single strand of perfect pearls with matching earrings. Her hair, curled and fastened into a tower atop her head, had been sewn into position and the threads strung with seed pearls.

I embraced a special friend—Titius Justus, a council member who lived next to the synagogue. He and his Gentile household had believed in Adonai about the same time as my mother, and when Paulos shared the good news about Yeshua, Titius and his family accepted Yeshua as their Messiah.

"Mariana!" Titius stepped aside as his wife, Aurora, pulled me into her arms. "You are more lovely every time I see you," she said, enthusiastically patting my back. "Adonai has certainly favored you!"

"You are too kind," I murmured, though I could not help returning her infectious smile. "You look lovely as well."

Though Prima and I were not allowed to wear a stola, no one could deny the quality of our tunics' fabric and design. I quietly studied Prima's garment, searching for signs of a stain, but either the fuller had managed to eradicate it or her blue palla concealed it.

She need not have worried about the stain, however, because anyone who saw her would have been too distracted by her jewelry. Forgetting my mother's admonition about modesty, my stepsister chose to wear a necklace consisting of several large polished stones from which dangled chains bearing other precious gems. The ornament reminded me of something, and only after I mused for several minutes did I realize what it resembled—a fisherman's net.

Prima's frustration with the banquet had been thoroughly erased by the time the guests arrived. She stood at the door with Mother and Narkis, nodding to the council members, smiling at the compliments she received, and bowing to the older men, especially those with marriageable sons.

When she turned away from one older man, her jaw flexing in irritation, I wondered if he had said something about marrying her himself. That was the moment I realized how truly discouraged she was. Prima was two years past the prime age.

I was also past the average age for marriage, but I would have been happy to remain a virgin. Paulos always said that unmarried people could devote themselves to serving Adonai, and that idea brought me a great deal of pleasure. Marriage, I had decided as I watched Mother adapt to Narkis's household, was more challenge than convenience.

A shiver pebbled my flesh as the memory of my father's death came flooding back. I was only ten that year, so no one paid me much attention as the physician worked at Father's side, collecting blood, forcing unguents down his throat, covering him with cool cloths to bring down a raging fever. I saw Mother's panicked face and the frantic way she twisted her hands, and I heard the intense whispers of the slaves as they considered their fate. "Will we be sold?" one woman asked another. "Domina cannot afford to keep all of us."

Indeed, I soon learned, Mother could not. Not only had she lost the husband she loved, but she also lost our home.

As I followed her in the funeral procession, I noticed that several merchants joined us as the crier traveled through the city streets shouting: "Mario Albina Corvus has been surrendered to death. For those who find it convenient, it is now time to attend the funeral."

No hired musicians accompanied our procession; no choir sang dirges in praise of my father. Several slaves carried the wax masks of his ancestors ahead of the body, symbolically guiding their descendant to his place in the afterlife.

Behind the ancestors, six of our male slaves carried Father on a couch, his face uncovered and his arms folded over his chest. Mother and I walked behind with a few friends and a line of merchants that grew to a sizable crowd by the time we reached the place of interment.

Mother's face paled when she saw them. She understood what I did not: they had not come to mourn my father, but to confirm his death. They might as well have stood with their hands extended because after the days of mourning, they came to the house and demanded payment for Father's debts.

Mother had no uncles or older male relatives to take her in. She possessed only two assets: beauty and a daughter. So she did what any widow in her situation would do. She sold the house and the slaves. Then ten months after my father's death—the earliest a widow could remarry according to Roman law—she married the wealthy magistrate who had proposed to her.

That was the year I learned that life can change in an instant. People can die, creditors can demand payment, and families can be refashioned. The anxiety I felt at my father's deathbed evolved into a different kind of unease—a dread of the unknown, a fear that haunted me still.

"Smile, Mariana." Mother nodded as another council member approached the house. "We cannot afford to drift away in thought tonight."

When I had greeted the last of the city council members and their wives, I left the vestibule and moved into the triclinium, crowded now with additional couches and more trays of food than I had ever seen in one place. The early arrivals had seated themselves and begun to eat. I thought about joining them, as I had not eaten all day, yet I had never possessed a gift for trivial conversation. I walked into the kitchen, but a surly glance from one of the slaves assured me that my presence was adding unnecessary pressure to an already stressful night.

I went to the back of the house and entered the garden. The night air was cool on my arms, so I wrapped my palla over my shoulders and sat on a marble bench. I lifted my gaze to the night sky. "Adonai, I am not certain what I am to do with my life, but I am content to serve you. If it is your will for Prima to marry the governor's son, let the wedding be arranged soon so Prima will be at peace."

The sound of approaching voices caught my ear—apparently the gathering was about to spill into the garden—so I slipped out a back gate and walked toward the stables.

Mother had told me not to run away, and I had not, at least not yet. I would meet the governor at the appropriate time, and I would eventually eat with the others, but until then, all I wanted to do was hide.

Eight

PRIMA

I knew the governor had come through our doorway when every voice in the triclinium fell silent. An authoritative baritone boomed in the vestibule, and everyone turned as if drawn to the sound by an invisible cord.

I threaded my way through the gathering and found Senator Servius Memmius Lupus standing with my father. The man was apologizing for his tardiness, and Father was bobbing in obsequious humility. Hester stood beside Father in submissive silence.

"It is an honor to visit your home," Memmius said, grasping Father's arm and nearly pulling him off his feet. "May the gods bless your household for your hospitality. I am sorry my wife could not be here, but she has remained in Rome with our younger son."

He kept talking, but I no longer cared to listen. Instead, I rose on tiptoe and stared past him, searching the retinue that had followed him into the house. Several young men stood behind the governor, most wearing either plain white tunics or military garb. Then a young man of about twenty stepped out from behind Memmius's imposing form, and I knew him instantly. The governor's son wore a white tunic of fine wool with a thin purple stripe that ran from his shoulder to his knee.

Suddenly aware that I was the only woman with a flaming copper wig on her head, I ducked behind a potted palm and took several deep breaths. "It is fashionable," I whispered to myself. "The wigmaker himself said so."

Once my heartbeat had returned to normal, I took advantage of my position and peered through the palm branches, grateful for the opportunity to observe the young man more surreptitiously. The governor, whose slave must have toiled an hour as he pleated and draped the man's purple-bordered toga, was presenting the younger man to my father. I crouched behind the palm, knowing Father would summon me if he suspected I was near.

Having been granted the opportunity to study the young man before I met him—was this a gift from the goddess?—I stared, attempting to take his measure. At first glance, I saw nothing undesirable in his appearance. He had the dark curly hair common to Romans, and his smooth face featured a strong jawline and a handsome nose. I caught only a glimpse of his dark eyes, but they seemed to sparkle with wit.

"Prima! Has anyone seen my daughter?"

My heart pounded as I wiped my hands on my tunic, stepped from behind the palm, and hurried toward our guests. "You called, Father?"

Hester stepped back, allowing me to stand at my father's side.

Father's face split into a wide smile. "Governor Memmius,

I would like you to meet my eldest, Prima. If you enjoy the banquet tonight"—he spread his arm, indicating all that lay in the vestibule and beyond—"know that she has arranged everything but the dinner itself."

I gritted my teeth, wishing he had not boasted so openly and so soon about my involvement. What if the governor did not care for the seating arrangements? What if he was offended by the statuary, the musicians, or the décor?

"You have a lovely daughter," the governor said, his sharp eyes roving from the wig on my head to the hem of my tunic. "How old is this vision of loveliness?"

"Sixteen," Father answered. "And I know I should have found her a husband long before this. But in truth, none of the men in Corinth are worthy of her."

"Then I should introduce my son." The governor stepped back, revealing the young man I had been studying. "I would like you to meet Marcus, my eldest. He will be remaining in Corinth to oversee provincial affairs whenever I must return to Rome. I would appreciate anything you can do to help him learn his way around the city."

"It would be our honor and pleasure," Father said, bowing to the young man.

Marcus nodded at my father and gave me a polite smile. I returned it, grateful that my appearance had not repulsed him. I did not think it would. After all, I had taken pains to be as stylish as any woman in Rome, but one never knew what sort of prejudices occupied a man's mind.

Hester placed her hand on Father's arm. "We have another daughter," she said, smiling at the governor. "I know Mariana would also be honored to meet our esteemed guests."

"My wife is correct—this house has been overly blessed

with beauty." Father turned and searched the gathering, but Mariana had been foolish enough to wander away.

Only by the grace of the goddess did I refrain from sighing in relief. "She must have found something else to do," I said. "I, however, can think of nothing more important than meeting our noble guests."

"Prima is as wise as she is beautiful." Father placed his hand on Memmius's back. "We shall introduce Mariana later. Come, sir, and let me lead you into the triclinium. Our cooks have prepared several spectacular dishes, so I hope you brought a hearty appetite."

"By all the gods, yes." Memmius patted his ample stomach. "Lead on."

They moved ahead, with Hester following, so I walked at Marcus's side. "Is this your first time in Corinth?" I smiled, suddenly grateful I'd had my teeth scraped.

"Yes." Marcus clasped his hands behind his back. "It is a lovely city. And for years I have heard about the Isthmian games, so I was pleased to discover they will be held this year. How thrilling to be able to attend the contests and concerts."

I smiled and nodded, though I cared little for the games I had attended since childhood. Every two years, hundreds of men and women came to Corinth from all over the empire to engage in competitions. In honor of Poseidon, god of the sea, men competed in wrestling, chariot races, boxing, and *pankration*, a form of hand-to-hand fighting. Both men and women were allowed to compete in music and poetry competitions.

Father had once been superintendent of the event, an honor that greatly increased his reputation, so he always encouraged me to attend. While much of the music and poetry was pleasant, I saw absolutely no purpose in watching men throw punches, slap each other, and race lathered horses for a laurel wreath. If no disputes were settled or wagers won, what was the point? I usually dozed off during such contests and marveled that anyone could enjoy such useless efforts. But most men, including my father, adored the games.

"My father was once administrator of the games," I told Marcus. "So he will be certain you are seated in a place of honor. But tell me—did you travel to Corinth by sea or over land?"

"By sea," he said, lifting a brow as if surprised to hear there was another possibility. "The port here is excellent."

"What did you think as you approached the harbor? Did you see the temple of Aphrodite atop the Acrocorinth? I believe it is truly one of the most beautiful sights in the city—"

"Marcus!" The governor gestured to his son, summoning him forward. Marcus gave me an apologetic look, then strode toward his father.

Thus abandoned, I wondered if I had done well . . . or left the young man unimpressed.

I backed away, certain that I should have been more enthusiastic about those stupid games.

Nine

MARIANA

Judging from the sudden decrease in noise from inside the house, I surmised that the governor and his party had arrived. I had promised Mother I would meet our honored guests, but no one would notice my absence during his arrival. My stepfather might call for me, but he would carry on regardless, more determined to impress the governor than to worry about where I might have gone.

I would meet the man later, perhaps when dinner was served. Until then, Narkis and Prima would do everything in their power to ensure the governor was entertained, flattered, and well fed.

I slipped into the barn, where my stepfather kept his stallion and carriage. The stall next to the stallion served as a home to Pegasus, the shaggy pony Prima had ridden in childhood. According to our stable hand, the pony and Prima were the same age, though my stepsister seemed to have forgotten about the wee horse. While I had never learned to ride, gentle Pegasus always seemed to enjoy my visits to the barn.

I stepped into his stall and pulled out a bunch of grapes I

had taken from the kitchen. He whickered, so I offered the sweet treats and laughed as his velvety lips nuzzled my palm. "You are a good boy," I said, lowering my forehead to his. When he had finished the last grape, I reached for a comb to untangle his mane.

"I have a feeling the stableboy spends more time caring for the stallion than you," I told him, working the comb through his stiff hair. "But do not worry, I will always find time to groom you. You deserve a good life, little friend."

A soft chuckle startled me. I whirled around and saw a young man leaning against the doorframe, a smile lighting his handsome face. I had never seen him before, but he could have been a new merchant or the son of one of the council members.

"You should have made your presence known," I sputtered. If this young man was given to gossip, soon everyone would know that Narkis's stepdaughter talked to animals.

"I did announce my presence," he answered, still smiling. "I laughed. And I have not been here more than a few moments."

I swallowed hard, not knowing what else to say.

"Beautiful animal," the fellow said, entering the barn. He nodded at the next stall. "That beast has the lines of a racehorse. I assume it is a stallion?"

"It is."

"He belongs to the magistrate?"

"He does."

"What about this little one?"

My hand flew to Pegasus's forelock, as if I could somehow protect him from the stranger's interest. "He belongs to my stepsister, but she never comes out to the barn. I come often—because if no one paid me any attention, I would feel terribly lonely."

"Surely the slaves care for him. He looks well fed and healthy."

"Our slaves are always rushing from one task to the next. Except for the stableboy, I doubt any of them spend even a moment of kindness on a mere pony."

The stranger propped his arms on the gate. "He seems a plucky beast. Do you ride?"

I couldn't stop a snort. "I cannot ride Pegasus. My legs would touch the ground."

The man laughed. "That is not what I meant. Do you ride *any* horse?"

"Does any woman ride? Prima lost her interest in horses the moment she realized she had slaves to carry her litter."

The man shrugged. "Given your interest in this pony, I thought you might ride for the sheer joy of it."

My face heated. "When I have free time, I prefer to read."

"Who do you read? Ovid? Socrates?"

"Mostly I read Paulos."

His dark brows slanted. "I have not heard of him. Is he Roman or Greek?"

"Neither. And you should probably return to the banquet. You are a guest, so you will be missed."

"And your absence will not be noted?"

"I am invisible. No one notices me when Prima is around."

"Ah. The girl with the hair basket."

I smothered a smile. "She wanted to try something different."

His squint tightened. "Even an invisible person must have a name."

"I suppose that is true." I shrugged. "My name is Mariana, and if you will let me pass, I should see if my mother needs anything. She will be uncomfortable if Prima has usurped the role of hostess."

"Your mother seemed comfortable when I met her—quiet but perfectly at ease."

I blinked. "And you are?"

"Marcus Memmius Lupus."

For a moment I could only stare, then realization blossomed. This was *not* a Corinthian merchant. "You are the governor's son."

"So I am told."

"Then you should *definitely* return to the banquet. I am surprised they have not sent someone to search for you."

"Why have they not searched for *you*?"

"Because tonight I do not matter."

"Neither do I." He stepped back from the gate, shaking his head. "Trust me, I've been to dozens of banquets like this one. My father will spend the night talking to the host while the host's most eligible daughter speaks of art or music or, in this case, the view from the Acrocorinth."

"You should go back. Prima will be looking for you."

"I doubt it. I excused myself because I would rather talk about horses."

I stood rooted to the spot, unable to move. I knew I ought to push past him and return to the banquet, but he had made an interesting point. Why go back when it was nearly impossible to have a genuine conversation in such a crowd? Out here, at least, I had done more than smile at the governor's son, I had actually *met* him.

"Are you hungry?" he asked. "I could fetch a tray and return so we can continue our talk. I think dinner in the barn would be much more pleasant than stilted conversation in the house."

He shouldn't have mentioned food. At the mere thought of roasted peacock, my stomach growled so loudly that I covered my belly with both hands.

Marcus laughed. "You *are* hungry."

"I have not eaten all day. We were busy preparing for the banquet."

"What do you say then? Shall I fetch us a tray?"

I closed my eyes, imagining us sitting side by side in the straw, nibbling on roasted peacock and nut cakes while the stallion snorted and Pegasus nickered for more grapes . . .

But we could not escape our responsibilities. I was a respectful daughter, and well-brought-up young ladies did not sit in barns with young men they had just met. My mother had never held a private conversation with my father before their marriage, and I had already transgressed *that* convention.

"I beg your pardon," I said, pushing past him, "but I should not be alone with you."

"The intrusion was mine."

Turning, I blinked at him in dazed exasperation. "We cannot remain here. I am honored to meet you, Marcus, but I must go back. If you are wise—and kind enough to care for my reputation—you will tell no one of this. Do I have your promise?"

His face went somber, though a twinkling light remained in the eyes that held mine. "I will tell no one, not even my father."

"Thank you. And though I enjoyed our conversation, I really must go."

Before he could say another word, I left the barn and hurried back into the house.

———————— ❖ ————————

Though I spent the rest of the evening trying to forget my conversation with the governor's son, Marcus's words and voice kept echoing in my mind. He was not at all what I thought he would be.

Because Corinth was a favorite destination for wealthy Roman patricians, we had met several senators and their families who came to enjoy our excellent entertainments, lavish temples, and luxurious public baths. During the summer months, affluent Romans filled every bench in our 14,000-seat theater, and when the men lounged in the public baths, they—or so I had been told—bragged of the beautiful women they had enjoyed at the temple of Aphrodite. While the wealthy patricians' wives shopped in our large marketplace, the men did business with our banks, which, Narkis boasted, were renowned for making solid investments and offering favorable terms.

I noticed that Romans tended to gravitate to extremes. They admired the most garish decorations, the most colorfully painted women, the lewdest mimes, and most lascivious entertainments. Those recreations would not have appealed to me even before I learned about Adonai. Even Narkis had little use for such amusements unless he needed to entertain a visiting guest.

But Marcus, who could have remained at the banquet and enjoyed the extravagant meal and dozens of fawning compliments, seemed indifferent to our attempt to impress him. He did not mention the flashy foods or lavish decorations, but instead praised Prima's little pony and accurately evaluated Narkis's stallion. Clearly, he knew about horses. He was gentle with me, and modest, not informing me about his parentage, wealth, or position. He had not even introduced himself until I bluntly asked his name.

He would make a good husband for Prima, not that she deserved him. She would probably prefer to marry someone more ambitious, but no one else in Corinth could claim to be the eldest son of a Roman senator. So she would force herself to be content as Marcus's wife. As soon as possible, however, she would urge him to move to Rome, where she could stretch her wings and fly far higher than she could in Corinth.

When the last guest finally departed, I waited until Mother had given the slaves instruction about cleaning up, then I slipped my arm around her waist and walked her to her bedchamber. The downward slope of her shoulders revealed how much the evening had drained her.

"Was Narkis pleased?" I asked.

She nodded. "With Memmius, yes. With the banquet, yes. With Marcus's attention to Prima? Probably not." She released a heavy sigh. "Fortunately, these betrothals are arranged by the fathers, so I am not worried that Marcus barely spoke to Prima during dinner. If the fathers decide they should marry, marry they will."

"So you are content?"

"Narkis is pleased, so I am as well." She stopped at her threshold and drew me into her arms. "Thank you, pet. I hope you enjoyed the evening."

I shrugged. "I spoke to Marcus for a bit. He seemed like a nice man."

"For Prima's sake, I hope he is." She pressed a kiss to my

forehead. "Now get to bed, or we shall both be only half awake at morning prayers."

I bade her good night, then walked the short distance to my bedchamber. I *had* enjoyed meeting Marcus, probably more than I should admit. He was attractive, well-formed, and comely in appearance, but I would have enjoyed our conversation even if he were plump and plain.

Still . . . I would find their marriage easier to bear if Prima and Marcus *did* move to Rome. Because even though Marcus was an idol-worshiper, his kindness and gentleness were almost irresistible, and weren't those qualities fruits from the Spirit of God? If Marcus and I were often thrust together as family members, I might find it difficult to keep a tight rein on my heart.

And I would rather die than allow love for a man to overshadow my love for Yeshua.

A week passed, a week in which Prima was as tense as a cat on the prowl and Mother worried that the governor had been unimpressed by our hospitality. Narkis tried to appear assured and confident, but he spoke with a clipped voice and constantly asked the doorkeeper if a message had arrived from the governor's house.

What was he expecting? A letter of thanks? A betrothal contract? Or a promise of undying favor?

Finally, eight long days after our banquet, a message with the governor's seal arrived while we were breaking our fast. Narkis broke the seal and unfurled the papyri in the triclinium, not caring that Mother, Prima, and I watched from our dining couches.

"Well?" Mother's brow arched. "Is someone causing terrible trouble in the province, or does he write about some other news?"

A smile wreathed Narkis's face as he lowered the letter. "This news is not even distantly related to trouble." His features softened as he looked at us, and I thought I saw the sheen of tears in his eyes. "This is the best news of our lives."

"Do not tease." Prima's voice was tight with strain. "This is not a game."

"Our prayers have been answered." Narkis braced his hand on his knee and looked at Mother. "Memmius has invited us to the governor's palace. Tomorrow night we are to dine with him and his son."

Mother's lips parted in a silent gasp, and Prima swiveled toward me. "Do you know what this means?"

"We are having dinner at the palace?"

She laughed and turned to her father. "Are we the only guests?"

Narkis glanced at the letter again. "Perhaps. No one else is mentioned."

"Then we must be." Prima pressed her lips into a tight smile. "The governor wants to settle the matter. He wants Marcus to take me as his wife."

Narkis beamed. "I had been afraid to affront the gods by voicing my fears, but from your lips to the gods' ears, may it be so!"

I listened with bewilderment. I had enjoyed a nice conversation with Marcus Memmius, but what sort of conversation did he have with Prima? I watched him during dinner, and he spoke most often to his father and only occasionally to Prima . . . but I might have missed something.

Then again, perhaps the governor made this decision on his own.

"I will need a new gown." Prima turned to Mother. "Summon the fuller's designer at once. And the jeweler—wait. I will go without jewelry. I would not want Marcus to think I already have an abundance of jewels."

Mother folded her hands and looked at me, a look of solace in her eyes. I smiled, not wanting her to think I was disappointed. I had enjoyed meeting Marcus, I found him attentive and attractive, but I never dreamed of marrying him. Prima was the natural choice.

Marcus would marry Prima, and both fathers would be pleased. When Memmius returned to Rome to visit his wife and vote in the Senate, Marcus would rule the province in his father's stead. Prima would be at his side, a queen in all but title.

Best of all, I had done my part by praying for her and staying out of the way at the banquet. Prima could never say I had not supported her.

I lifted my goblet. "To good news," I said, smiling at my stepsister. "May it soon be confirmed."

Ten

MARIANA

The following day, we women rose early, sent for the cosmetae, and submitted to the discipline of beauty. Once again we were vigorously scrubbed, sanded, plastered, and painted. As the sun dropped toward the west, we dressed in our new finery and sat before our looking brasses as slaves curled and styled our hair. Finally, we waited in the vestibule as litter bearers assembled in front of the house. Mother and Narkis rode in the first litter; Prima and I shared the second.

As slaves carried us through the winding streets, Prima peered through an opening in the rear curtains and frowned. "I do wish Father had given the slaves matching loincloths," she said. "His litter bearers look wonderful, but we have been given a mismatched set."

"Why does it matter?" I shrugged. "Only servants will witness our arrival."

"But Marcus and his father may walk us out when we depart," she said. "By that time everyone will know that our litter is carrying the future wife of the governor's son."

I looked away and braced myself for the inevitable. Prima had never been easy to live with, and I had a feeling she was about to become insufferable. If Narkis's suspicions were confirmed, within hours my stepsister would be betrothed, and she would not have to wait until the wedding to command respect. The governor might assign a guard to our house; he might even arrange for Prima to live at the palace as wedding preparations were made. She would demand new clothing, so Mother would be busy arranging for Prima's wedding garments, as well as new tunics for me, Narkis, and herself.

Life was about to become even more frantic than usual.

I pushed the unsettling thoughts aside and considered Paulos. If he were here, he would remind me of something Yeshua told His disciples: if Adonai took care of flowers and sparrows, He would certainly provide for our needs. Even our clothing.

"He is faithful," I whispered, "so we should not worry."

Prima turned. "Did you say something?"

"I was thinking aloud." I forced a smile. "About how we should not worry if we place our faith in Adonai."

Prima made a soft sound of disdain and returned to the open curtain as the governor's palace came into view. The massive house had been built on a hill that rose nearly as high as the Acrocorinth. Even from several blocks away we could see the gleaming marble pillars topped by a sculpted pediment that brushed the sky. The carved images featured on the pediment represented the major gods of Corinth: Asclepius, god of healing; Jupiter, father of the gods; Vesta, goddess of the hearth; and Aphrodite, goddess of love.

When our litter bearers slowed to manage the incline,

Prima thrust her head through the curtain. "Do not dawdle!" she snapped. "The governor is waiting!"

One of the slaves cast a resentful glance in her direction, but Prima did not notice. The slave would have paid dearly if she had.

We alighted from the litter when we reached the sprawling palace portico, and then we climbed the front steps and found Mother and Narkis waiting on the landing. A stately slave in a short tunic escorted us into the vestibule, where a burly ianitor dipped his head in greeting. Another slave hurried forward with goblets of honey water. We sat and sipped while another slave removed our slippers and washed the dust from our feet.

I sipped from the bronze cup and thought of our litter bearers, who had to be thirsty after the steep climb. Perhaps it would not be rude to ask one of the slaves to serve them as well.

"Excuse me." I spoke to the girl who had served our refreshments. "Could you supply our litter bearers with something to drink?"

The young woman blinked in astonishment while Prima huffed. "Father! She will embarrass us all."

Annoyance struggled with disapproval on Narkis's face as he turned. "These slaves are not yours to command, Mariana."

I glanced at Mother, who studiously avoided my gaze.

I returned my attention to the slave. "I apologize."

A growl crept up from Narkis's throat. "And you do not apologize to slaves!"

I lowered my voice and said, "Our slaves are thirsty."

The girl nodded and went her way—to serve our slaves, I hoped.

I thought Prima would launch into yet another criticism, but at that moment the governor came through the vestibule, resplendent in his tunic and purple-edged toga. "Welcome!" He flashed a broad smile. "Ladies, you may follow my slave to the triclinium where you will find all sorts of dainties to tempt your appetite." A slave near the entrance stepped forward, ready to lead us.

"Narkis, my friend," the governor continued, "will you come with me? There is a matter we should discuss before dining."

Mother, Prima, and I lingered while the two men walked away. Then Prima giggled in anticipation. "Can you imagine?" she whispered as we followed the slave over a tiled mosaic floor. "When you visit me here, you will have to wait in that vestibule."

"A wise woman does not presume to know the future," Mother said. "Better to wait and see what God has planned."

Prima sniffed. "I can discern the gods' will for myself. I can *feel* the truth, and the priestess of Aphrodite has affirmed that the goddess has nothing but good planned for me. I know the governor has invited us here to announce a wedding."

I remained silent, knowing better than to refute her opinion. Though I wanted Prima to marry, Marcus seemed worthy of a woman who would place his interests above her own. Yet I had no say in this matter, and neither did Prima.

We turned a corner, and I gasped when we entered the spacious dining hall. The towering walls had been painted in an ornate mural that featured fountains and verdant fruit-bearing trees. The theme continued to the floor, where talented artists had fashioned a mosaic of small tiles to resemble a forest floor, including flora, stones, and insects native to Corinth. The room must have taken months, perhaps years, to complete.

"This place is amazing," Mother said, gazing at the painted ceiling. "I could almost believe we are standing in Paradise."

"Perhaps it is meant to be the Garden of Eden," I said, thinking of the story Paulos told us about the first man and woman.

Several slaves entered with burning torches, which they fitted into gilded sconces on the painted walls. The flickering torchlight animated the vines and trees of the mural, amplifying the feeling of an exotic, living garden.

We sat on tapestry-covered couches and sampled foods from various trays the slaves offered. The food was unique, flavored with wine and spices I could not identify. After I tasted a sauce-covered dormouse, Mother saw my expression and smiled. "He must have brought foods from Rome," she said. "I have never tasted a sauce like this."

I was about to ask Prima if she knew the story of the Garden of Eden when I was distracted by the arrival of Memmius and Narkis. They were not alone—Marcus stood between them. He caught my gaze and nodded, and something in his smiling eyes made my cheeks burn.

"Welcome to the provincial palace," the governor said, opening his arms. "My son and I are honored to have you in our home."

Prima, Mother, and I bowed our heads.

The governor glanced at Narkis and rubbed his hands together. "It is appropriate that you should be the first to hear our news. The magistrate and I have agreed to arrange a marriage between his daughter and my beloved son. It gives me great pleasure to announce that in the coming month of Februarius, Marcus will be betrothed to Mariana Metelli, daughter of Narkis Avidacus Ligus."

I blinked as the room swirled around me. I stared at Memmius, convinced I had misunderstood, but the governor's smile did not waver. I looked at Marcus, saw the delight in his eyes, and felt my mouth go dry.

I had not prayed for this.

Eleven

PRIMA

It could not be true. I heard the governor's words, saw Marcus smile at my stepsister, and instantly realized he was an absolute fool. How could he have asked for her when I was far more suitable? I was blood daughter to the city magistrate and Roman ambition, bold and courageous, flowed through my veins. My father, who had once organized the Isthmian games, now *led* the city council. As Memmius's advisor, he would soon rise even higher. My father and I thought alike, we shared the same ambitions, and we would urge each other to even greater wealth and status.

How could Marcus not see the difference between me and my meek little stepsister?

Mariana could never be the wife I would be. I could urge Marcus forward, I could awaken the potential slumbering within him, and I could propel him to greatness.

Aware of the thick quiet that filled the room, I struggled to adopt a mask of equanimity. This was not the moment to rage or ask questions. This was a moment for silent reflection and careful action.

I stared, disbelieving, as Marcus stepped toward Mariana. "I hope I will be a good husband to you," he said, not taking his eyes from her face. "Because I know you will be a good wife to me."

Mariana lowered her gaze like a reluctant virgin. A blush colored her cheek, then she cast a desperate look toward her mother, who appeared as flabbergasted as I.

I closed my eyes, realization beginning to bloom. Had Memmius decreed this choice, or had Marcus asked for Mariana? If the latter, what compelled him to ask for her? She barely made an effort on the night of the banquet. She wore a gown as simple as a slave's and disappeared from the festivities. She did not ask for jewelry and only put her hair up after the designer told her it was unseemly to wear it hanging around her shoulders.

What then had he seen in her? Nothing, surely! Her head was filled with nonsense about invisible gods, and she possessed neither physical nor mental strength. She had no apparent gifts, and her only friends were vagrants, tradesmen, and Jews.

Since Mariana could not possibly have attracted Marcus, something must have bewitched him. Perhaps she had entranced him by some strange magic from the Jewish God.

I opened my eyes as Father began to speak. "This will be the most important wedding in Corinth," Father was saying, oblivious to my pain. "Know this, Memmius—we are honored to join our family to yours."

My father was *honored* by this? My mind darkened further, and thoughts I had not considered rose up, an ugly swarm of them. *I* was his daughter, not Mariana. I had been ever loyal to him, I had always loved him, I would do anything for him, and he had not protested this announcement?

Memmius reached for a cup of wine and lifted it toward Father, then drank deeply. After lowering his cup, he urged us to partake of the foods spread throughout the dining chamber. I could barely hear over the roar of disbelief in my ears, but I could force myself to be a good guest. In Aphrodite's name, I could even humiliate myself for a while, knowing that the goddess had promised me victory.

I lifted my wine goblet toward the groom. "To Marcus!"

When he looked in my direction, I raised my cup higher. "To you and your bride—may Aphrodite rain blessings upon your household."

Marcus lifted his goblet and drank, then he sat and smiled at Mariana.

I drank, too, but tasted hate—foul, burning, and rancid.

But no matter. I would have to be patient, I might even have to formulate a plan, but I would be Marcus's wife . . . in time.

Twelve

MARIANA

Back inside my chamber, I sat on the edge of my bed and reached for the looking brass on my nightstand. What aspect of my appearance had attracted the governor's son? I was not as clever as Prima, nor was I beautiful like my mother. I did not possess Prima's wit or sociability, and I did not worship Roman gods. Narkis was my father in name only, so I had inherited nothing of his nature or his talents.

So why had Marcus chosen me? And how could I marry him?

I tensed when the door opened, fearing Prima would storm in and accuse me of mischief, but Mother stepped inside and crossed the room. She glanced at the spot where Salama lay sleeping on her cot, then she sat next to me and took my hand, holding it between her own. "You were surprised, no?"

I nodded.

"And now you are wondering why he chose you."

"I am."

She blew out a breath. "You have never been able to see yourself as you truly are, pet, so I am not surprised you do not see your gifts. But you are a lovely girl, and you are genuine, which is more than I can say for most women of our acquaintance. When you met young Marcus at the banquet, you must have impressed him. Perhaps Adonai has allowed this because it is His will. Or"—a teasing smile overtook her features—"perhaps Prima's wig so repulsed him that he chose you instead."

Her unexpected comment made me laugh. We both knew Prima would have surrendered her front teeth to impress the governor's son.

"But how can I marry him?" I asked, my voice wavering. "He is an idol-worshiper. Truly, I did not try to entice him. I did not know who he was until after we talked."

Mother lifted a brow. "You talked with him quite a while, did you?"

"I was bored with the banquet, so I went out to the barn. He came in and asked about the stallion. We talked about horses, and only later did I learn I was speaking with the governor's son."

"What else did you talk about?"

I shrugged. "Nothing of importance. But when he suggested that we remain in the barn and continue our conversation, I realized that would be improper, so I went back inside. I would not say we spoke together at length."

"Long enough, it would seem."

Mother slipped her arm around my shoulders. "And now we are faced with a dilemma. I know Paulos encouraged us not to be unequally yoked with unbelievers, yet you are required to obey your paterfamilias, and he is set on this union. As the head of the family, he could severely punish you if you disobey his wish." Her grip on my shoulder tightened.

"Narkis would not be happy to hear that you do not want to marry the governor's son, so I would advise you to keep those thoughts to yourself."

"What would he do?"

I asked because I already knew what Narkis *could* do. As the head of our household, he held the lives of his family and slaves in his hands, and he had a dangerous temper. My stepfather was usually reasonable, but I had seen him beat slaves until they vomited blood and their backs were black with bruising.

No, I did not want to anger him. To refuse the marriage would not only make his temper flare toward me, but toward everyone I loved.

Mother shifted her focus to some interior field of vision I could not see. "I do not know what he would do. I *do* know he intends to please Memmius in everything."

"So, for him to please the governor, I must please his son." Mother sighed. "Yes."

Guilt swept over me, suffocating me with its weight. "Then I suppose I must marry Marcus, even if doing so will displease Adonai."

"Will it? Adonai might want you to obey your father. And consider the many people, including me, who chose to follow Adonai *after* they married an unbeliever. So perhaps the situation is allowable in certain circumstances—especially if you have no other choice."

I hesitated, wavering between conviction and desire. "I must confess, Mother, the idea of marrying Marcus does not displease me. He was excellent company and seems to be an honorable man. As we spoke, I could not help noticing that he was kind and gentle—not at all what I expected."

"But he asked you to remain in the barn with him."

"In all innocence, surely. He wanted to eat, nothing more."

Silence stretched between us, then Mother cleared her throat. "I shall write Paulos. I am not sure my concerns will reach him before the wedding, but perhaps God will speed my letter and bring a quick response."

"And if Paulos says the marriage should not take place?"

"If that is our situation, perhaps we can persuade Narkis to offer Prima instead." She lowered her head to catch my gaze. "If the young man truly cares for you, he will not force you to marry if you do not want to be joined with him. But do not be afraid, pet. Pray for wisdom and ask the Spirit to guide you. Is that not what the Scriptures tell us to do?"

I rested my head on Mother's shoulder, remembering the many times I had sat beside her at the temples of Vesta, Jupiter, and Asclepius. Before we met Paulos, we worshiped like all other Romans, reciting prayers as priests sacrificed bleating sheep and goats in an effort to entreat the gods.

What a waste those hours had been. So much innocent blood spilt after the divine Son shed His blood for any Jew or Gentile willing to receive the salvation He came to offer.

Narkis and Prima had ignored us when Mother and I told them about the Jewish rabbi in the marketplace, and our attempts to explain our enthusiasm for Adonai fell on deaf ears. Narkis listened to Mother for a while, then told her to be silent and never speak of the Jewish rabbi again. Prima said nothing to me, but the disdainful look in her eye warned me away. If I pressed and continued to speak of Adonai and His Son, she would tell Narkis, who might hold Mother responsible for my words.

After our life-changing encounter with Paulos, Mother continued to be a good wife to Narkis and mother to Prima, so they did not remark on any outward change in her. But even a blind and deaf mute would have realized that Paulos's message elicited a dramatic change in our attitudes.

Mother and I began to look at our slaves as people whom Adonai loved. No longer could we consider them beasts or property, and no longer did we ask them to perform a task without considering their ability and welfare.

I also began to see Narkis, Prima, and the people of Corinth from a new perspective. I watched them spend hours at their temples, bowing before carved images, muttering powerless incantations, and cutting themselves in a frenzy, and for what? They were praying to created beings, not to the almighty God. If only they would hear the truth!

But who was I to tell them? I had so much to learn about worshiping Adonai and following Yeshua. When Mother and I slipped out to meet with the ecclesia on the first day of every week, we received the Word gratefully. The people there were good teachers, but no one had ever been able to explain the things of God as well as Paulos. Though he was no longer with us, his letters brought new insights and knowledge every time I read them.

"How can that be?" I once asked Mother. "I have read this letter before, but now the words carry a deeper meaning."

"I think that is the Spirit of Adonai at work," Mother had answered. "Yeshua said the Spirit would be our teacher."

I needed a teacher now . . . I needed an answer. Or perhaps I needed an escape.

"If God should grant you peace about this marriage," Mother said, her voice a hoarse whisper, "could you learn to love the governor's son? Does Marcus seem like the sort of man who could make you happy?"

Her hands, which had been stroking my hair, stilled as she waited for my answer.

"Yes," I finally said. "He is a good man. In fact, before tonight I had envisioned Marcus as my brother-in-law and wondered how I could conceal my affection for him."

"Then perhaps the Lord will work through this." Mother squeezed my shoulder. "So pray, pet. And speak not of this marriage to anyone until the Lord lets you know how to proceed."

◆

Any other woman would have been thrilled to be betrothed to a man like Marcus, but I could not agree to the marriage with a clear conscience. Several reasons stood in the way of my happiness, and chief among them was the knowledge that a believer in Yeshua should not marry a man who worshiped strange gods, as Marcus surely did. Added to my concern was Prima's obvious bitterness. She had counted on marrying the governor's son, and for several days after the announcement, she did not venture from her room. When she finally joined us at dinner, she did not speak to me.

My relationship with Prima had never been close, but until Memmius's announcement I did not think she hated me. Now I did not doubt it.

But what could I do about it? Yeshua commanded me to love everyone, and in all our years together, I had loved Prima by staying out of her way. Now she hated me for something I did not do, and keeping my distance would not make things better.

And what could I do about the impending marriage?

If I did not voice my reservations, by the end of the month I would find myself married and possibly outside the will of Adonai. If I *did* object, Narkis would be furious with me, but at least he would have another daughter to offer in my place.

In the aftermath of the banquet, Mother and I decided to do nothing but wait for a reply from Paulos. As we waited, I tried to behave as normally as possible, but how could I when my life might soon be upended? I vacillated between overwhelming fear and a not completely unpleasant nervousness at the thought of living with Marcus. I liked him and believed he had seen something worthwhile in me. Yet whenever my heart was tempted to take flight in visions of marital bliss, I recalled Paulos's admonition. How could I marry a man who did not know Adonai?

I reread Paulos's letter to the Romans, searching for words that might speak to my heart. At the beginning he had written, "For I long to see you, so I may share with you some spiritual gift to strengthen you."

If only Paulos were in Corinth! I had never needed his wisdom and encouragement more.

Mother and I shared many whispered conversations during the month of Februarius. She sent the letter to Rome right after the betrothal announcement, but we knew we might not receive an answer until after the wedding. We would probably have to make this decision with guidance only from each other, believing friends, and the Spirit of God.

During the struggle, one question haunted me. If Marcus had been old and unattractive, or if he had insulted me when we met in the barn, would I be struggling with this choice?

Would it be easier to obey Paulos's instruction if I loved Yeshua more and Marcus less?

As the days slipped by, I watched each sunset and wondered what the month of Martius would bring. Would I be a bride or an outcast from my family? Would I be a wife who had disappointed Yeshua, or a homeless outcast with a clear conscience before Adonai?

Floundering in a sea of anxious indecision, I prayed at morning, midday, and evening. I begged Adonai for wisdom, yet I received no clear guidance. My mother prayed, too, as did the members of our ecclesia, and the dawn of each new morning reminded us that we were running out of time. Soon Mother and I would have to face Narkis and tell him about my reservations . . . and brace ourselves for the outcome.

For days I prayed about the wedding, about Marcus, and about Prima. I heard nothing from the Spirit until late one afternoon.

I was reading Paulos's letter to us, the ecclesia in Corinth, when a familiar passage seemed to take on a new meaning: "If I speak in the tongues of men or of angels, but do not have love, I am only a resounding gong or a clanging cymbal."

If I lived in Prima's house and called her *sister*, but did not speak to her about the matter that had come between us, how could I say I loved her?

I sighed and lowered the scroll. "So be it, Lord," I whispered, bowing my head. "I will talk to her."

I found my stepsister in the garden, cutting back the canes of bare rose bushes. "Prima," I said, noticing that she flinched at the sound of my voice. "I would speak to you."

She did not lift her head. "What troubles you, Mariana?"

"This . . . betrothal."

She turned, frowning with cold fury. "Is Marcus not important enough for you? Wealthy enough?"

I shook my head. "I did not seek this. I am not sure I want to ever marry."

"Then why do you not tell Father so?"

"Because I do not want to disobey him."

"How convenient for you."

She gave me a hard, cold smile and turned back to the roses.

I drew a breath and began again. "What I want to say is that I will always consider you a sister. I do not know if I will marry, but if I do, you will always be welcome in my home. Adonai brought us together, so that promise stands whether I am married or not. You are my sister through marriage, and I will always honor our connection."

A cold wind blew past us with a soft moan. Prima lifted her head. "Anything else?"

"That is all I wanted to say."

"Good." She snipped another dead branch. "But know this. The gods have not settled on this betrothal of yours. Your marriage may not happen."

Her comment brought a wry smile to my lips. "For once, Prima, I absolutely agree."

Thirteen

PRIMA

In the days following the governor's announcement, I felt as though I were being chopped up and fed to fearsome sharks, one agonizing bite at a time. I thought Mariana would be ecstatic at the thought of marrying Memmius's son, but though I expected her to gloat, she did not. Instead, she walked around with a preoccupied and slightly anxious expression, as if she'd been offered the keys to a glorious palace but was afraid to claim it.

I decided my stepsister was not only dull-witted but also foolish. Only a fool would hesitate to marry the governor's son, especially when the young man was handsome, charming, and certain to inherit his father's Senate seat. I would have married him if he were sixty, bald, and obese because I could always close my eyes when he approached my bed. But somehow Mariana had won the affection of the best prospect in Achaia and did not have enough sense to appreciate her good fortune.

My suspicions were confirmed the day she came to me and stated that I would always be welcome in her home—as if I, having been thus rejected, would never marry at all! Only through sheer force of will was I able to resist the urge to spit on her.

But why had my prayers to Aphrodite gone unanswered? I was not overly concerned about remaining unwed. I knew Father would soon find me a suitable match. But even if I married a wealthy Corinthian merchant, my husband would never be on an equal footing with the son of a provincial governor.

I would never be Mariana's equal, and surely the Acrocorinth would crumble before the gods would allow her to rise above me.

I found myself adrift in a sea of self-pity and discouragement with no one to trust. I did not seek my father's counsel because he would have told me to accept my sister's betrothal with grace, as if I should delight in disappointment. For the week following the announcement I spent most of the day in my chamber, sleeping until midday, then waking and commanding Gilda to bring a flagon of wine. In countless cups I drowned my sorrows until I was too numb to feel the sharp stings of jealousy. Hester often came to my door and asked for permission to enter, but each time I sent her away. Why would the mother of the victor want to see me? She and Mariana had won, leaving me no choice but to settle for a second-rate prize.

My frustration was not lost on my handmaid. Gilda remained a careful distance from me in the early days of my grief, but the slave must have begun to pity me. Because I would speak to no one else, she replied sympathetically when

I moaned about life's unfairness and remained nearby in case I wanted another bottle of wine.

Frustration finally loosened the woman's tongue. "Domina, you forget yourself," she scolded when I slept through morning prayers for the eighth day in a row. "It is not suitable for you to lie abed and drink your sorrows away. What will your father think?"

With difficulty, I sat up and struggled to focus on her blurry image. "I should have you beaten for speaking to me that way."

"But you will not," she answered, straightening her spine, "because you need to hear someone speak plainly. Since you will not let the mistress into your chamber, you have only me. I do not speak bluntly out of disrespect, but out of concern."

I stared at her. "You think I *need* you?"

"I think," she said, a look of implacable determination on her face, "that you have forgotten yourself. You are Prima, the beloved daughter of the chief magistrate. So why do you lie abed and drink yourself into a stupor? What happened to the bold mistress I often admired?"

I blinked, stunned by her appraisal. She was right—I *was* a bold woman, not a defeated one. And as I noted her trembling lower lip, I realized our relationship was about to change.

She was a slave, no more, no less, but over the past week she had hovered over me as if melancholia was a life-threatening disease. Though I had nearly been overcome by defeat, I enjoyed her solicitous care. And what was the harm in allowing her to speak openly in private? She was not usurping a parental role. Since our return from the governor's palace, my father had not even knocked at my door, probably because he was busy making arrangements for the upcoming wedding. My place in his heart had been usurped by Mariana and Marcus, and now he thought only of them.

I decided to submit to Gilda's care, but only to a point. She could address me as openly as she wished, but only when I allowed it and only in my chamber. I would not have the world know of my vulnerabilities . . . or that I would drop my guard, even briefly, before a mere slave.

I patted the empty space on the side of my mattress. "Sit," I said. "Tell me what you are thinking."

She sat, albeit gingerly, and directly met my gaze. With only a slight squint to indicate her awareness of the risk she was taking, she drew a deep breath. "Be grateful I am willing to speak the truth because no one else has the courage to confront you."

I closed my eyes and considered her answer. She was correct. Everyone else in the family—including Father—seemed terrified of my black mood.

"So . . ." I swallowed hard. "What would you suggest I do?"

"Anything." Gilda stood and pulled a fresh tunic from my trunk. "Get up, get dressed, let me do your cosmetics and arrange your hair. Leave the house and show all Corinth that you are a woman of great worth. You are not a quitter, so why would you act like one? The governor chose someone else to marry his son. Does that mean your life is over? Of course not. And Marcus and Mariana are not yet married, are they?"

A smile tugged at my mouth. "Even if they were, marriage does not last forever, does it?"

In answer, Gilda stood and picked up a comb.

I rose and moved to the chair before the dressing table. By all the gods, the slave was right—I had choices. Unless some jealous goddess had stolen my beauty during my time of mourning, I was still attractive. I remained the eldest daughter of the most powerful magistrate in Corinth. And if I was careful and clever, I could wield the power of my father's name and the gods to find an answer to this vexing situation.

"Is it a market day?" I asked, trying to recall how many days had passed since I took to my bed.

Gilda nodded. "It is."

I sat and ran my fingers through my mussed hair. "Make me presentable," I commanded. "We are going to the temple of Aphrodite."

❖

Gilda dressed me in one of my best tunics, did my hair, and painted my face. Then I summoned the litter bearers, and we set out for the Acrocorinth. My handmaid did not ride in the conveyance with me—no slave ever rode with her mistress—but walked beside the litter to remain close in case I needed her.

The litter bearers grumbled as they climbed the mountain, but when I mentioned the possibility of a beating, their tongues stilled. I had ordered Gilda to wait at the base of the mountain. She did not need to accompany me to the temple, and her presence would have made travel more cumbersome on the narrow path.

I alighted at the summit and hurried up the marble steps.

I genuflected before the statue of Aphrodite, then looked around for Cassia, the priestess I had met weeks before.

I found her in a small chamber at the side of the building, surrounded by several other priestesses. Her graceful brows rose when she spotted me, then she motioned me forward.

"You have come again, Prima." Her voice wasn't much louder than a whisper, but the shock of hearing my name made it seem as if she had shouted in my ear.

"You know me?"

"Of course." A smile ruffled her wide mouth. "Why do you seek Aphrodite today?"

I knelt before her. "There is a man, I want to marry him, but he is betrothed to another. I do not know what to do."

"Pray to the goddess, and she will show you."

"I have prayed, many times, and Aphrodite does not answer."

"Then make a sacrifice. A proper sacrifice will demonstrate the sincerity of your request."

A sacrifice? I frequently sacrificed pigeons, wine, and food, so what more could I give?

Cassia's gaze lowered, and only after a moment did I realize she was staring at my necklace—the one I had worn at our banquet to welcome the governor.

My hands rose to undo the clasp. "I will sacrifice this. It cost my father twenty denarii."

Cassia's smile broadened. "Leave it on the altar. I am sure the goddess will approve."

"Will she answer my prayer?"

"Here is your answer." Cassia leaned forward until her lips were only inches from my ear. "When an obstacle lies in your path," she purred, "the answer is simple: remove it."

❖

How to remove a human obstacle? I went to the market-place to find an answer.

Once we arrived at the bustling market, I ordered the litter bearers to wait until I returned. Gilda followed me until we found the apothecary, then I bade her stay outside while I entered the booth.

Inside I found shelves loaded with a vast array of jars containing herbs, seeds, insects, and dried berries. On a wooden counter the merchant offered crystals, carved idols, and incense. But right in front, next to the man's coin box, I found the item I sought—a stack of *defixiones*, or curse tablets.

I picked up one of the thin layers of gold. "How much?" I asked the merchant.

"You must have a powerful enemy." He gave me a crooked smile. "The copper sheets are less expensive."

"Is the gold more powerful?"

"Of course."

"Then I will have gold."

"As you wish." The merchant crossed his arms. "Have you cursed someone before?"

"Not with a tablet. But in this situation, I do not think mere words will be strong enough."

A smile gathered up the wrinkles by his tanned mouth. "This is what you must do. Write out your curse, list everything you want your enemy to suffer, and invoke the gods to do your will. When you are finished, roll the curse tablet tightly, secure it with a nail, and leave it near your enemy. Hide it where it will not be discovered or disturbed. If you do these things, the gods will hear and obey."

"And how much for all this?"

The man looked me over, noticing my spotless tunic, the jewels at my ears, and the slave standing outside. "For you, three sestertii."

I knew he would charge others less, but I did not lack coin. I paid what he asked, then took the tablet.

"Anything else, my lady?"

"Not today," I said, looking over the rest of his wares. "Perhaps later."

❖

Upon returning to my chamber, I followed the merchant's instructions exactly. Using a stylus, I wrote out my prayer, calling on Aphrodite and imploring her to destroy Mariana's beauty and shrivel her womb so she would never bear children. I commanded the goddess to wrinkle my stepsister's face, make her bald, and break her back. Then I commanded Jupiter to make Mariana's breath smell like dung and cause her skin to erupt with painful boils. Finally, I begged Asclepius to fill Mariana's days with misery and her nights with terror.

When I could think of nothing else, I used a stone to pound a nail through the rolled curse tablet. The nail bit easily through the thin layers of gold, so even if the tablet were discovered and opened, no one would be able to read my words.

I handed the nail-pierced tablet to Gilda. "Take this and bury it outside the wall of Mariana's chamber. Make certain the ground does not appear disturbed."

Gilda frowned. "Should I dig with my hands?"

"I do not care if you dig with your teeth, as long as you bury it at once."

As Gilda hurried away, I stretched out on the bed, aware that the cloud surrounding me had already begun to lift. If the curse worked, I would owe Aphrodite, Jupiter, and Asclepius a sacrifice. If it did not, they would owe me.

Fourteen

PRIMA

For two days I listened for sounds of distress from Mariana's room. I had cursed her limbs with weakness, but she walked and moved with surprising agility and grace. I had cursed her skin with suppurating sores, but her complexion remained clear. The only effect that might be attributed to my curse tablet was a surprising look of anxiety on her features, but that look had occupied her face ever since the betrothal announcement.

"What brings a frown to your forehead today?" I asked one morning as we gathered at the lararium.

Mariana's brows drew together. "I have received a letter from Marcus," she said, her cheeks flushing. "He said he is looking forward to being my husband and will do his best to please me. I did not expect to hear such things from him . . . I did not expect to hear anything before the wedding. Mother says his attitude is unusual, especially for a Roman patrician."

I swallowed the bile that had risen in my throat. "Did he say anything else?"

She nodded. "He and his father send greetings to all our household. They are looking forward to the wedding." The lines on her forehead eased. "Thank you for asking, Prima. I am grateful for your concern."

I looked away and tried not to scowl. The curse tablet had not worked at all.

❖

The merchant lifted his brows when I said I was disappointed in his wares. "My nemesis thrives," I told him, my voice as cold as spring water, "despite your instructions. I did exactly what you told me to do, yet my enemy persists in her plans against me."

"Where did you bury the curse tablet?"

"Outside her bedchamber, in the earth."

He grunted. "The tablet would have had more power had you placed it in the room where she sleeps."

"But it was only inches from her head. So why did it not work?"

The merchant tugged on his ear. "What gods does your enemy worship?"

"Why would you ask?"

"Perhaps she worships a deity greater than the gods you summoned in the curse."

"I summoned Aphrodite, and there is no greater goddess. Does Aphrodite not rule over our city from the Acrocorinth?"

"She does, but she is female, and Jupiter has far more power. Does your enemy worship Jupiter?"

I frowned. I had never told anyone that Hester and Mariana worshiped the God of the Jews because I did not want the news to blight my father's reputation. But this merchant did not know whose daughter I was.

"She worships an invisible God," I finally said. "A foreign God of the Jews. He does not have a temple in Achaia or even Rome."

The merchant stroked his beard. "I have heard of this God . . . and I have heard He is worshiped by others in Corinth. Not many, to be sure, but He has devoted followers."

"Surely He is not more powerful than Jupiter, father to all the gods."

"The Jewish God cannot be more powerful than Roman gods. The gods are strongest in the land of their birth, and Judea is far away." The merchant cocked a brow. "How much damage would you like to inflict upon your nemesis?"

I drew a slow breath and glanced at Gilda, who stood a few steps away. "I need an obstacle to be removed."

"Do you want her removed from your life . . . or banished to the underworld?"

I closed my eyes. Killing Mariana seemed extreme, but I could not think of another way to stop her marriage to the man who should be *my* husband. If she died, especially if she died from some mysterious ailment, no one would know I had anything to do with it.

"Slave," I commanded, "wait for me outside."

Gilda glanced at the merchant, then turned and walked out of the shop. After looking around to be sure no one would overhear, I leaned closer. "I was thinking some sort of poison might be useful . . . something that is easily administered yet brings powerful results."

The man nodded. "I have the remedy you seek."

He turned to a row of glass bottles and lifted several lids until he came to a jar filled with light brown powder. He set the jar in front of me. "A potent blend from a poisonous mushroom. It never fails to send the man or woman who ingests it to the grave."

"And how does it work?"

"It must be swallowed." His yellowed fingernail tapped the cork. "Sprinkle it on a dish or into a cup of wine. The odor is barely noticeable, and it has no taste—at least no one has ever lived to complain about it."

I lifted the bottle and studied its contents. "Do I use all of this or just a bit?"

"Every particle," he said, "if you want it to be effective. Then your problem will be solved."

"And how much will this cost?"

His eyes narrowed as he smiled. "Ten sestertii."

"That is robbery."

He shrugged. "It is a fair price for removing an obstacle."

I gave him the coins, took the jar, and went to meet my slave.

❖

Though I trusted Gilda as much as any woman can trust a slave, I did not tell her about my purchase. I kept the sealed vial hidden within the folds of my tunic as we traveled home, then carefully tucked it under my bed pillows after we returned.

I would administer the poison myself.

The next morning, I went to the kitchen and asked the cook to prepare a small loaf of almond bread. "On a platter, for Mariana," I said, smiling. "I want it to represent my wishes for a sweet marriage."

The cook nodded. "I will have it ready."

"Make sure you glaze the top with honey," I added. "Send someone to fetch me when it is ready because my sister loves to eat it warm from the oven."

I went back to my chamber and stretched out on the bed, feeling content for the first time in weeks. Marcus would be distressed, of course, to learn that his intended bride had died mysteriously, but Father would rectify the situation by suggesting that Marcus marry me. If Marcus balked, Memmius—who clearly wanted to create a firm relationship with my father and the council—would insist that the marriage proceed.

Perhaps *we* would marry on the twenty-eighth of Februarius, since the date had already been declared auspicious. Perhaps, if the garment was lengthened, I could wear the tunic and the orange veil Hester had ordered for Mariana . . .

In midafternoon, a servant rapped on my door. "The cook sent me to tell you the dish is ready."

I rose quickly, then hesitated, deciding it would not be appropriate to appear overeager. "Fetch the dish from the kitchen," I commanded my handmaid. "I have ordered something special for Mariana."

Gilda shot me a questioning glance, but she did not protest. A few moments later she returned, carrying the almond bread on a stone platter, the loaf gleaming with honeyed nuts. "It smells delicious," Gilda said, inhaling deeply. "Is this not Mariana's favorite?"

"It is. Now fetch a pitcher of honey water and two cups. Quickly, before the bread cools."

Gilda hurried away. As soon as the door closed, I took the vial from beneath my pillow, uncorked the stopper, and tapped the side of the bottle, sprinkling the contents on the almonds and sweetbread. The poison settled on the thick honey, looking like an innocent sprinkling of cinnamon, an aromatic spice our cook favored.

I could not stop a smile. The loaf was enough to feed two people or one with a hearty appetite. Knowing Mariana's fondness for the dish, she should finish the entire loaf tonight, even if she shared it with her handmaid. By morning the platter would be empty, the bread gone, and my obstacle removed.

When Gilda returned with the pitcher and two cups on a tray, I carried the tray and bread to Mariana's chamber. Salama opened the door, her eyes widening when she saw me.

"Mariana," I called, striding past the slave, "I know you love honeyed almond bread, so I had the cook prepare this for you." I set the tray on the table by her bed. "And now we shall drink to honor your upcoming marriage."

Mariana blinked in apparent confusion. "In truth, this brings me great pleasure," she said, her chin quivering as she stood. "And you must know—I fully expected Marcus to choose *you* as his bride."

I waved her words away. "The gods have declared what shall be, so let us drink together."

Mariana took a cup and gestured toward the bread. "Would you like a piece? It smells wonderful."

I lifted the pitcher and filled our cups. "I have an appointment with the fuller's designer. I want a new tunic for your wedding."

Before she could protest again, I took a sip of honey water, then smiled and left the room, leaving her to enjoy the fruits of my labor.

Fifteen

MARIANA

I stared at the almond loaf, baffled, then shot Salama a questioning look. "Could I be dreaming?"

Salama's puzzled expression relaxed into a smile. "Perhaps her father threatened to cut her allowance if she did not treat the governor's future daughter-in-law with more respect."

I made a face. "Perhaps. Still, this took planning, and I cannot recall Prima ever planning anything for me. And that bread does smell wonderful . . ."

I set the warm platter on the bed and sat next to it while Salama scooted to the other side. I was about to break the loaf into pieces when I heard a slave call from the hallway. "Mistress Mariana! You have a guest."

I glanced up. "Who has come?"

"Marcus Memmius, from the governor's palace."

Marcus?

Forgetting about the bread, I stood and brushed wrinkles from my tunic, then glanced in the looking brass.

"Your hair looks fine," Salama said, scooping up my *himation*. "Please remain still while I position this."

I obeyed, standing erect while my handmaid draped the colorful fabric over my shoulder and pinned it in place with a brooch. When she agreed that I looked presentable, Salama pinched my cheeks, patted away the pain, and gestured toward the doorway. "Your future husband awaits, my lady."

Would Marcus be my future husband? Narkis was determined he would, but Adonai might yet have other plans.

I hurried toward the vestibule. Marcus stood in the entry, dressed in a spotless white toga.

"Mariana."

I blushed as he bowed. "This is an unexpected pleasure. Shall we sit by the reflecting pool?"

"If that is your wish."

I led the way to the atrium and sat on a bench at the edge of the pool, folded my hands, and looked into the water. When I saw my worried reflection staring back at me, I closed my eyes, embarrassed. *Adonai, please slow the beating of my pounding heart . . .*

"I could not wait until the wedding," Marcus said, flushing as he sat next to me. "These past few weeks have felt like a dream, and at times I wondered if you were a figment of my imagination. I-I suppose I wanted to come and see if you are as I remembered."

"And if I am not?" I snatched a fleeting hope. "If you do not want to marry me, I will not protest. Because I must be honest with you—I am surrendered to the will of God in all things. If He does not wish me to marry you, I will be content."

"Do you not *want* to marry me?" Marcus's eyes widened in what appeared to be honest alarm. "I would not have asked my father to speak to yours if I did not believe you would be agreeable to a union between us."

So I was *his* choice, not the governor's. Perhaps that made sense.

"In truth, Marcus," I began, "I find you most agreeable. I even told my mother that if you were to marry Prima, I would be disappointed that you did not ask for me. But I am determined to follow God's will. If He should not be willing that I marry at all, I would happily agree to remain as I am."

"I am glad to hear you are devout," he said, a glint of eagerness in his eyes. "I, too, want to follow the will of the gods in all things. And I am glad I came today. Hearing you say you are truly willing, that you would have been disappointed if I had not . . ."

He leaned forward and kissed me. His action was so unexpected that afterward I could not catch my breath to speak, and I still had many things to say.

I knew I ought to tell him that I did not worship the gods he worshiped, but if he told Memmius that I worshiped the God of the Jews, Memmius might cancel the wedding. Narkis would be embarrassed, possibly to the point of punishing me and my mother.

Before I could speak or even think further, Marcus stood. "I will leave you now," he said, giving me a dazzling smile. "I will see you again on the day of our betrothal ceremony."

An unwelcome surge of excitement zipped through me as he turned and walked away. I knew I should restrain my emotions until Adonai had given me peace about the situation, but in that moment my feelings had a mind of their own.

As I made my way back to my chamber, I encountered Salama in the hallway, where she had been eavesdropping from behind a pillar. Giggling like a young girl, she took my hand and squeezed it, and together we went back to my room.

She gasped when we crossed the threshold. There on the bed lay the sticky remains of the almond loaf . . . and three sleeping cats.

"Oh no!" Salama cried. "They have eaten all your bread."

"I should not have left it on the bed." I walked forward and picked up one of the cats, then froze when I saw its eyes. The cat's eyes were open and opaque, utterly lifeless.

I dropped the cat and stepped back, my heart pounding hard enough to be heard across the room.

"What?" Salama asked, coming closer. "Domina, what—?"

"It is dead." I pointed at the remaining cats. "They are all dead."

Salama picked up another cat, shook it slightly, and lowered it to the bed. "Prima has finally done it. She has finally found a way to kill your mother's cats. A shame, though, that the animals ate your almond bread before the poison took effect."

I stared at the unfortunate cats. "You think she poisoned them?"

"Probably." Salama shrugged and picked up a basket. "I only hope your mother won't be too upset." She picked up the cats and placed them in the basket. "I do not know how Prima killed them, but she will deny it."

"Of course she will." I peered into the basket, my eyes

welling with tears. "But Mother will only get more cats. I would not be surprised to find a nest of kittens out in the barn."

"I will look," Salama said, pulling the soiled covering from my bed, "after I have cleaned up this mess. Then I will ask the cook to make you another almond loaf."

Sixteen

PRIMA

"Are you expecting someone, Domina?"

I pulled my head back inside my bedchamber and closed the door. "No, no one." I pasted on a smile and moved to the couch.

"Should I bring something for you to eat?"

"No!"

When the slave flinched, I forced another smile. "I was wondering if Mariana enjoyed the nut bread I brought her. I have heard nothing since I took it to her room."

"She had a visitor," Gilda said, nodding. "The governor's son came to see her."

I blinked. "Is he still here?"

"He left some time ago." Gilda picked up her embroidery. "He did not stay long."

"And Mariana?"

"Went back to her room with her handmaid."

"Ah. Well, good. I hope she enjoyed her bread."

Gilda shot me a curious look, then shrugged. "I would not know, Domina. But if you would like me to ask her—"

"Perhaps I will ask her myself."

I rose from my couch and sailed toward the door, my heart beating double-time beneath my tunic. How should I react when I found her? Shocked? Dismayed? Perhaps I should display a range of emotions—shock first, then denial, and then, after a great deal of protestation, a few tears. Perhaps Father would take me to the palace when he delivered the sad news to Memmius. I would stand by, sober and silent, then pull Marcus aside and offer my condolences.

I rapped on the door. "Mariana? I came to see—" I opened the door and halted, my words strangled by a suddenly tightened throat. I had expected to find Mariana and her maid dead, but they were sitting side by side on the couch, their laps filled with sheets of papyrus.

Mariana looked up. "Yes, Prima?"

Words failed me. I glanced at the bed, but the loaf had disappeared, as had the platter. "I came to see—" I stopped and swallowed—"if you enjoyed the bread."

Mariana laughed. "I appreciate your thoughtfulness, sister, but we were not able to eat a single bite. Unfortunately, Mother's cats helped themselves to it while I was out."

"The unfortunate cats," Salama said, looking at me with narrowed eyes, "died soon afterward. One would think they had been poisoned."

I was stunned by the implied accusation as well as the slave's tone, but Mariana seemed to think nothing of the girl's insinuation. "I know you do not care for cats," Mariana said, "but they are dear to Mother, so I hope you will not attempt to kill them again. Some poor beggar might find and eat the poisoned scraps, and I know you would not want a man's death on your conscience."

"No," I whispered, barely able to speak. "I would not want that."

The handmaid lifted a brow. "I am only a slave and therefore foolish, but I wondered if the bread had been poisoned."

"Salama!" Mariana shot her slave a look of rebuke. "You do not know what you are saying!"

"Forgive me." The slave hung her head. "I spoke without thinking."

"Prima is my sister. I cannot tolerate such disrespect for her."

The slave stood and came toward me. "Forgive me, Domina. I meant no disrespect."

I lifted my chin. "Do not accuse me of such things again."

"Never, Domina."

Mariana smiled. "There. All is well. Try to see the good in Mother's cats, Prima, and learn to appreciate them. And thank you again for the bread. I was truly touched."

I closed the door and stood in the hallway, still stunned beyond words. Either Aphrodite had completely failed me, or Mariana's invisible God was far stronger than I imagined.

In either case, one thing was clear: Mariana was as naive as her mother.

Seventeen

MARIANA

The morning of our betrothal ceremony, Mother slipped into my chamber early, found me in bed, and squeezed my hand. "Now," she whispered, a tremor touching her smooth lips. "Before morning prayers, you and I must go to Narkis and explain why this marriage should not take place. Your stepfather will not be shamed as long as we speak before the betrothal is arranged. I have been praying and am convinced this is what we should do."

I nodded, suspecting that she was right, but her confidence did not settle my heart. I knew a believer should not marry an unbeliever. I had only to look at my mother's marriage to realize how difficult that situation could be. Because every morning Mother had to kneel before a pagan altar and go through the motions of worshiping dark gods, she was not at peace within herself.

Neither was I.

Narkis knew, of course, that Mother and I worshiped Adonai and His Son. He knew we attended meetings of the ecclesia and read accounts of those who had walked and talked with Yeshua.

But he did *not* know that we had completely turned our backs on the ancient gods who desired to usurp Adonai's place in the hearts of men. How could he know the depth of our devotion to Adonai when every morning we knelt before images of false gods?

"I need some time," I told Mother. "To prepare." I glanced at Salama, who was staring at me from her bed. "Apply cosmetics, please, so I will find favor in my stepfather's eyes."

"I will wait for you," Mother said, releasing my hand. "But hurry."

I got out of bed, dressed, and sat before the looking brass. As Salama powdered my face, applied kohl to my brows and lashes, and brightened my cheeks, I prayed that Adonai would give me courage, a quality I always lacked when facing Narkis.

"There." Salama stepped back. "I am sure the master will be pleased with your appearance."

I moved into the hallway and found my mother waiting. She wore a simple white tunic, and her face bore no trace of cosmetics. I did not know if she wanted to emphasize her vulnerability or if she had simply chosen not to adorn herself.

"Come." She gripped my hand. "With the betrothal in only a few hours, we cannot delay."

I usually avoided the bedchamber Narkis shared with my mother, so my cheeks heated when we entered and found him sitting on a bench. His dresser was adjusting his tunic while another slave shaved his face and neck. With his head tipped back, Narkis eyed us with curiosity, then waved the slaves off. "Leave us."

The slaves left the room as Narkis wiped his damp neck with a towel. I was afraid he would not appreciate my unusual appearance in his chamber, but instead he gave me an approving smile. "Has the bride come to ask a special favor before the betrothal ceremony?"

When Mother sank to the floor and knelt before her husband, I followed her example.

"Narkis," she began, bowing her head, "I have come before you in all humility to present a possible problem with the marriage. But I have also come to offer a solution."

Narkis's face went the color of a thundercloud. "What possible problem could there be? And why have you waited until the day of the betrothal to speak of this?"

"I thought something might happen." Mother's face twisted in misery. "I thought Marcus might change his mind."

A cold, suspicious expression settled on Narkis's face. "I hope you are not about to tell me that your daughter is not a virgin."

"Of course not." Mother stiffened. "The problem does not lie with Mariana's virtue, but with her beliefs. The governor's son worships different gods."

"Why should it matter?" Narkis snapped, obviously vexed. "There are enough gods in the pantheon to satisfy anyone. He may worship any of them, as long as he includes Caesar."

"But Mariana worships none of the Roman gods," Mother whispered. "Nor does she worship Caesar. This . . . could present a problem."

Narkis cast Mother a disdainful look, then stood, crossed his arms, and glared at me. "I suppose your daughter has followed your example and worships the God of the Jews."

"She does."

Narkis shrugged. "Then I fail to see a problem. As long as she is able to remain by her husband's side as you remain by mine, why should it matter? As head of the household, Marcus will conduct the prayers and sacrifices. What she does in private is her affair. As long as she is discreet—"

"She does not want to be false to him—or to her God." The syllables seemed to slip, unbidden, from Mother's lips. Her face flooded crimson as her words echoed in the room.

"She does not want to be *false*?" Narkis focused his glare on Mother. "Are you saying you have been false to me?"

"I have not been unfaithful." Mother lowered her head again. "As a wife, I have been loyal and true. But I cannot pray to false gods, nor can I worship them. I have tried to be obedient and please you in all things, but I would be lying if I said my actions at your family altar were sincere."

Without warning, Narkis slammed his fist into Mother's face, sending her to the floor. Surprise squeezed the air from my lungs and left me gasping.

"Mariana," Narkis said, his voice ragged as he turned toward me, "know this. I will give you to Marcus Memmius regardless of your choice of gods. If you value your mother's life, you will not protest. As long as you remain in my house, you will say nothing of this invisible God to the governor or his son, and you will not broach the subject with anyone in this household. Do you understand?"

Trembling, I met his gaze and nodded.

"Excellent." Narkis rubbed the reddened knuckles of his right hand and gave me a grim smile. "Help your mother up and see to her face. And know that I will not tolerate another discussion about this marriage. It *will* take place in one week."

I hesitated, hoping he would regret his brutality and aid his injured wife, but Narkis stood like a tree, his bare feet rooted to the floor. I ducked beneath his hot glare, gathered my unconscious mother into my arms, and dragged her from the chamber.

❖

Salama helped me place Mother on my bed, then she applied cold compresses to my mother's swollen nose and cheek. When Mother stirred and groaned, I hurried to her side.

"Morning prayers," she whispered, trying to sit up. "He will expect me at the lararium."

"Not this morning." I pressed against her shoulder, guiding her back to the mattress. "I will join the others, but you will remain in my chamber where Salama will take care of you."

She moaned and closed her eyes.

I went to morning prayers, where I stood silently and stared at nothing. Narkis performed his ritual without variance, praying for peace, love, happiness, and prosperity. I remained silent and still, and when he had finished, I hurried back to my chamber.

Mother was sleeping when I returned. "She will be fine," Salama said. "I have seen many women with such bruises. We will apply cosmetics, and all will be well."

Would it?

I opened my trunk and pulled out my copy of Paulos's letter to the Romans, then skimmed the text until I found the passage I sought: "I urge you therefore, brothers and sisters, by the mercies of God, to present your bodies as a living sacrifice—holy, acceptable to God—which is your spiritual service. Do not be conformed to this world but be transformed by the renewing of your mind, so that you may discern what is the will of God—what is good and acceptable and perfect."

The Spirit's answer to my dilemma came through Paulos's words. If I were an independent woman, I would not marry an unbeliever, but in this circumstance I had no choice. I would therefore present myself as a living sacrifice because I loved Adonai . . . and because my mother had just given herself as a living sacrifice for me.

Surely this would be the good and acceptable and perfect will of God. My marriage might not be ideal at its beginning, but I would trust Adonai to make it so . . . in His time.

❖

At midday on the twentieth of Februarius, Marcus, his father, and the chief priest at the temple of Jupiter arrived at our house. Mother did not appear at the ceremony, but Narkis explained her absence by saying she had taken ill.

Like an obedient daughter, I did not dispute him.

Prima was likewise absent, but Narkis did not comment on her whereabouts.

In the atrium, Marcus and I faced each other and joined hands. Narkis stepped forward and promised Marcus that I would become his bride on the twenty-eighth day of Februarius.

No proper betrothal could take place unless the bride brought her future husband a dowry. Narkis assumed this responsibility and presented Marcus with a vineyard outside the city.

Then Memmius, as paterfamilias to Marcus, presented me with a gold ring. Marcus slipped it on my third finger, where a nerve was said to lead directly to the heart.

In conclusion, Marcus and I signed the written agreement proffered by his father, then we kissed, a physical symbol of our union. I was now his *sponsa*.

As the priest of Jupiter held his hands over us and prayed for the god's blessing, I bowed my head and asked Adonai to give me courage, strength, and resolve . . . because I could see no way out of this wedding.

Part of me, I must admit, was glad of it.

Eighteen

MARIANA

I did not sleep the night before my wedding. In the privacy of my chamber, I knelt and prayed until my knees ached, then I climbed into bed and begged God to bless my arranged marriage. Surely Adonai would not cast me off because I married an idol-worshiper. After all, He blessed Esther when she was subjected to an arranged marriage to a pagan king. Though she was only one woman, Adonai used her to save thousands of Jewish lives.

"You can stop the wedding," I told the Lord, "but if you do not halt the proceedings, I will marry Marcus out of obedience to my stepfather. I will place my trust in you, I will remain true to Yeshua, and I will remember what Paulos taught about living with an unbeliever. If Marcus ever wants me to leave him, I will go. If he wants me to remain, I will stay by his side. I will strive to be a good and righteous wife because I want to lead him to you."

When the eastern sky brightened to a lovely shade of lilac, I rose from my bed, determined to follow the course Adonai had set before me. I filled a basin with cool water from the pitcher on my bedstand and glanced at the cot where Salama slept. My wedding tunic lay on my trunk, along with my orange veil and matching slippers. As soon as she woke, Salama would use the *hasta caelibaris*, the celibate spear, to braid my hair in the traditional arrangement of six braids.

I splashed the puffiness from my face, grabbed a towel, and nudged Salama's shoulder. "Wake," I whispered. "Today we move into our new lives."

Her eyes flew open. "I was dreaming," she said, her eyes wide. "I saw you standing before Nero, and he did not look happy."

I chuckled. "Then we should be glad he was not invited to the wedding. What did the emperor look like?"

She sat up and shuddered. "He was most unattractive, with ginger-colored hair and a beard that covered only his neck and the sides of his face. His nose—something about it seemed odd, as though it had been flattened."

"Your imagination has distorted the image on our coins," I told her. "And I do not believe in dreams unless they are sent by God. Since I am not likely to meet the emperor any time this year, rise and help me with my hair."

Salama had almost finished the last braid when Mother knocked and stepped into my chamber. She carried the garland I would wear over my veil and set it on my trunk as she looked at me, her eyes welling with tears.

"You will be a beautiful bride," she said, a quaver in her voice. "I prayed that I would be able to dress you for your wedding day, but I did not imagine a situation like this."

"I am at peace, Mother." I gave her a confident smile. "Now, is it not time to begin?"

I studied her face as she moved toward my bridal garments. The purple bruise below her left eye had nearly faded, and Salama had done a commendable job of straightening her nose. With a proper styling of her veil, she might be able to conceal the physical damage Narkis had done.

But I feared he had damaged far more than her face.

"We have prayed, pet, so do not be afraid." She lowered her voice and lifted my interior tunic. "Since God has not prevented this marriage, let us trust that He knows what He is doing."

I lifted my arms as she dropped the tunic over my head. This tunic was ankle length and fell loosely over my frame. Salama fastened it at the shoulders while Mother picked up the outer tunic, which possessed a sheen rarely seen in wool. Again I lifted my arms to accept it, then Mother and Salama used pearl-encrusted brooches to hold the material at my shoulders.

The other tunic was much longer, as long as the stola I would henceforth wear as a married woman.

"And now your girdle." Mother fingered the woolen cord that ended in a series of strings, then looped it around me and tied it in the traditional knot of Hercules. "Only your husband is allowed to untie this." She tapped the knot for emphasis.

I smiled. "I know."

Mother pulled the length of the tunic up and over the girdle, then hesitated as tears slipped from beneath her lashes.

"I will be fine." I squeezed her arm. "Have you not said so?"

"I will pray for you every day, asking God to protect you and keep you safe. But more than that, I will ask Him to bless you with true joy."

I hugged her and swallowed the lump in my throat. "I suppose we should put on the veil."

Mother picked up the gauzy square and let it fall over my braids. Then she added the final piece—the wreath I had fashioned with greenery from our own garden. "This should be made of roses," she said, fussing with it.

"Hard to find roses in Februarius," I reminded her. "Except in a hothouse. The greenery is fine."

Mother stepped back for one final look. "May the Lord bless and keep you," she said, swiping wetness from her eyes. "May Adonai make His face shine upon you and give you peace."

She kissed both my cheeks, then we left my chamber together.

❖

I stepped from my chamber into a wedding wonderland. Our slaves had worked throughout the night, decking the house with tree boughs, woolen bands, and elegant tapestries. Mother and I went to the lararium, where my stepfather and several slaves were waiting. Narkis began his morning prayers, but he had no sooner addressed Jupiter than the doorkeeper announced that our wedding guests had arrived. Narkis cut his prayers short and ordered the doorkeeper to admit our guests. At once the vestibule flooded with the governor's retinue of guards, advisors, priests, family, and friends.

I searched the crowd until I spotted Marcus and was surprised to feel the tightness in my chest relax. He smiled at me, and in his eyes I saw eagerness and affection. Surely he would never be like my stepfather. Perhaps I could be myself with him, as I had been when we met in the barn. Surely, after the wedding, I could be honest with him about Adonai.

My bridesmaids—two of our neighbor's young nieces—giggled in excitement as everyone moved into the atrium. Memmius had brought a priest of Jupiter, who gestured to a slave carrying a yearling lamb across his shoulders. He lowered the animal to a stone bench and cut the beast's throat, then opened the belly. The priest examined the entrails and announced that the liver was perfect, so Jupiter had accepted the sacrifice.

Then everyone turned toward me.

Blushing under the scrutiny of so many pairs of eyes, I stepped forward in my ivory tunic, orange shoes, and orange veil. One of our neighbors filled the role of a matron married to her first husband and joined my hands with Marcus's.

I whispered the traditional words of consent: "Where you are Gaius, I am Gaia."

Marcus responded, "Where you are Gaia, I am Gaius."

The priest handed us a stylus, and my groom and I signed the marriage contract. We two had become one.

While the guests murmured in approval, Mother led us inside to the family altar, where a small flame blazed in the brazier. When she nodded, I removed my garland and lifted my veil, which Mother placed over both our heads. Marcus took my hands, and we remained motionless while Narkis recited a prayer to Vesta, goddess of the hearth, for our happiness.

While he uttered the traditional words, I closed my eyes and prayed as I had never prayed before. *Adonai, let me be a servant to this man, and may I lead him to the truth.*

My mother approached, her hand trembling as she broke

a fresh loaf of spelt. Marcus and I each took a bite, then smiled at each other as the hardy wheat crunched between our teeth. With the traditional first bite swallowed, we kissed, and Narkis broke the silence with a shout. "Time to celebrate! I have prepared a feast!"

The guests found seats on couches spread through the house as slaves paraded an array of festival foods past us: platters of roasted goat served with pears, chicken stuffed with plums, honey-basted peacock, boiled dormouse, and stewed beef served with walnuts and pomegranates. My stepfather had spared no expense—not to impress me, but Memmius.

While the guests ate and drank copious amounts of food and wine, Marcus and I shared a couch. At first I focused on the guests, too self-conscious to even look at my new husband, but when he took my hand I finally found the courage to meet his gaze. "Greetings, wife," he said, a smile twinkling in his eyes. "I am glad we are finally together."

I smiled but could not suppress the desire to ask a question that had nagged me for weeks. "Before we begin this new life," I said, "I must know why you chose me. Why not Prima, who is far more suitable for you?"

"Who can explain the way love works?" His smile deepened. "But I believe the gods whispered to my heart the night we met in the barn. I have met a hundred women like your stepsister, but I have never met anyone like you."

He kissed me again, and several onlookers cheered. Marcus released me, then stood and lifted his goblet. "I do believe," he said, looking to the bright sky visible through the opening in the roof, "it is time to take my bride home."

The diners roared their approval as Marcus grabbed my

hand and led me through the vestibule and onto the street. I waved to Mother and Narkis. I looked for Prima but did not see her. I did manage to smile at Salama, who would join me at the palace.

Many of the celebrants followed as we walked through the streets. They cheered as hired musicians marched with the *sistra* and cymbals, drawing people to their doors to cheer the wedding procession.

Finally, we reached the governor's palace, where the wedding guests followed us up the chiseled steps and into the building. We climbed a marble staircase, traversed a long hallway, and finally stopped before an ornate pair of double doors.

"And this," Marcus said, grinning as he turned to address our noisy celebrants, "is where you leave us."

He lifted me into his arms and carried me over the threshold, ensuring that I wouldn't trip and fall. In the eyes of the assembled guests, such clumsiness would have been a bad omen indeed.

Nineteen

PRIMA

My breath burned in my throat as I watched the newlyweds depart. I knew I should be among the guests, throwing flowers and cheering, but I did not want anyone to see the emotions that had to be evident on my face. I sent Gilda to the wedding banquet in my place, knowing that anyone who saw her would assume I was nearby.

When the wedding party had gone, I went into the atrium, which had emptied of everyone but several slaves who were mopping up splashes of sacrificial blood.

"It should have been me," I declared.

The slaves ignored me, but my statement startled a pair of pigeons, who flew away as if indignant that I had disturbed their rest.

Something had shifted in the heavenlies. Aphrodite had failed me, the curse tablet had been a waste of time and coin, and the fates had somehow managed to save Mariana from a deadly poison. I had heard—from Gilda because slaves heard everything—that Hester had even spoken to my father about the folly of Mariana's marriage, yet he refused to withdraw his consent.

Why had *everyone* failed me? Marcus should have been *my* husband, not Mariana's. I was destined to be part of a noble family; I was destined to live in Rome.

A smiling slave entered the atrium, her eyes focused on the handsome youth holding a mop, while I seethed with anger and humiliation. I walked over and slapped the girl, hard, and narrowed my gaze when she retreated in shock, her hand covering her cheek.

"Why should you be happy?" I snapped. "Leave this room at once."

The girl fled, and I sank to a bench, burning with frustration.

Why was I, the pride of Corinth, sitting alone in a grotesquely decorated atrium while my stepsister celebrated a marriage to the man meant for me? I curled my hands into fists and pounded the bench, not caring that the rough plaster bloodied my knuckles. Why had Aphrodite not answered my prayers? I had done the work. I had arranged the banquet, hired the servants, designed my clothing, and worn the most striking wig in Corinth, and yet all of my efforts only seemed to propel Marcus toward Mariana.

How could the gods disappoint me? Mariana's God could not be stronger than Aphrodite, Jupiter, and Asclepius. She had one God; I had dozens. Impossible that one foreign God could have prevailed against the gods of Rome. Because Rome pleased its gods, Rome ruled the world. The Jews could not even rule themselves.

I blew out a frustrated breath and lowered my head into my hands. All the slaves had disappeared; I had only my thoughts for company. As I watched shadows lengthen across the room, an unformed thought teased my mind. What was it, a memory? Or was Aphrodite trying to tell me something?

I lifted my head. If Aphrodite had a message for me, Cassia would know what it was.

I went to my chamber, pulled a veil and cloak from my trunk, and gestured to a slave I caught creeping through the hallway. "You," I said, pointing toward the front door. "Summon the litter bearers. I am going out."

<hr />

I climbed the torchlit steps to the temple of Aphrodite and stopped for a moment to turn and take in the view. Seen from above, at night, Corinth seemed a scattered collection of lights, an almost insignificant community.

Perhaps that is why the builders chose this lofty place for a temple. At this elevation, the problems of life seemed inconsequential, and the gods close.

I walked into the smoky interior and lowered my veil from my head to my shoulders. Images of Aphrodite, her husband Hephaestus, and her lovers Ares and Adonis shimmered in the torchlight, as if they had come to life with the advent of darkness. Around the altar, reclining on couches, reclined at least a dozen temple prostitutes, available to help a worshiper enact the goddess's gifts of passion, pleasure, and fertility.

But I had not come to the temple for such reasons; I wanted answers. I walked over to a priestess and asked for Cassia.

The woman pointed toward a gilded couch. "Have a seat. I will see if Cassia is available."

For an interminably long time, I watched a pair of women dance in a pantomime of lust. I sighed and looked away, not wanting to think of Marcus and Mariana on their marriage bed.

The high priestess's sultry voice cut through the velvety shadows. "Prima, daughter of Narkis Avidacus, why have you sought me?"

I turned and saw Cassia standing behind me. She wore a sheer tunic that would have made Hester faint. Apparently, Cassia had never heard that noble women valued the virtue of modesty.

"I have come," I said, standing, "because Aphrodite has failed me. My sacrifices and prayers, even a curse tablet, did not persuade the gods to help me. I was supposed to marry a certain man, but he chose to marry my stepsister. I want to know why my prayers were not answered."

Cassia sat on my couch, then patted the space next to her. "Tell me, daughter—do you love this man?"

I frowned. "*Love* him? I do not even know him, but I know I am more suited to be his wife. He is a patrician, and I am the daughter of an important Corinthian official. He is Roman to the bone, and I was raised in the home of a Roman citizen. He is from a wealthy household, so am I."

"And why do you feel your stepsister is not worthy of this man?"

I barked a laugh. "Mariana is not worthy of being associated with our family name. If my mother had not died—" My voice caught in my throat, and I had to wait a moment before I recovered the ability to speak. "If my father had not been widowed, he would never have looked at Hester. But she was poor and pretty, and when she smiled at him, Father lost his common sense. He married her as soon as he could and received a mousy stepdaughter in the process."

162

Cassia examined my face with considerable interest. "Does this girl have nothing in common with you?"

I snorted. "We might have found common ground, but not long after the marriage, Mariana and her mother began to follow a Jewish rabbi and his foreign God."

"Ah." Cassia smiled, her dark eyes creasing in an expression of admiration. "How clever of you to avoid the same temptation. I am certain they tried to lure you from the old gods."

"They did." I lifted my chin. "But I would not listen. I vowed to remain true to Aphrodite, Jupiter, and the others, but Aphrodite has not been answering my prayers. How could that be?"

Cassia smiled, her eyes bright with speculation, her smile sly with knowledge. "Perhaps you are focused on the wrong result," she said, her voice low and seductive. "What if Aphrodite did *not* fail? What if she refused to do your bidding because she has a better and more profitable plan for you?"

I snatched a breath, utterly astonished. "You mean something better than having my desire *now*?"

"You are young," Cassia said, her cheek curving in a smile. "You have much to learn, and I am honored to teach you. Perhaps you cannot imagine anything better than having the man you want today, but tomorrow still waits for you. You must learn to acknowledge your desires, Prima. You must determine to bring your goals into existence."

I frowned as her words tumbled in my head. "I do not understand."

She leaned closer. "Ask yourself what you want more than anything. Then every morning when you rise, state your desires as if they had already come to pass. When you sit to eat at midday, tell your household what you long for. In the evening, as you go to bed, agree with the goddess that this yearning *will* be fulfilled."

My head swirled with doubts. "But he belongs to someone else."

"Aphrodite is the goddess of love and pleasure," Cassia purred, running her fingertip down my arm. "She wants her followers to have what they want. Become acquainted with her ways, and you will be prepared to beguile any man who suits your purpose. Serve her, follow her ways, and then return and tell me the goddess has failed you."

I was at the point of agreeing with her out of sheer discouragement when a small dose of defiance dribbled out of me. "But what good will this do? The governor's son has already married my sister."

Cassia tipped her head back and laughed. "You are such a child," she said, standing. She walked away, her lean body rippling beneath her tunic, but her parting words echoed in the space between us: "Every chain has a weak point, Prima, so find it and stress it. Trust me, the chain *will* break. Marriage does not last forever."

Twenty

MARIANA

"Good morning, wife."

I opened my eyes to discover Marcus smiling at me, his face only inches from mine. I scarcely knew how to react, but since we were alone and still basking in the newness of married life, I obeyed a heartfelt instinct to slide my arms around his neck and kiss him, silently thanking him for his gentleness.

He drew me closer, and we lay together, flesh against flesh, in the soft light slanting through the clerestory windows. "Do you feel different," he asked, "now that you are a married woman?"

I exhaled a contented sigh. "I feel happy. And a little unsure of myself."

"Why?" he asked, his voice rising in surprise. "Have I made you feel uncertain?"

I patted his chest, amazed that I had the right to do so. This man was *mine*. My husband.

Resisting a wave of shyness, I met his gaze. "You have been wonderful. But until last night, I had never slept with a man. I have never been a wife. I have never lived in a palace. Everything is new to me."

"Much is new to me, as well," he admitted, drawing me closer. "But now I understand Ovid's poetry about the joys of love."

My cheeks burned. "I have never read him."

"'When, look! here comes Corinna in a loose ungirded gown,'" Marcus quoted, "'her parted hair framing her gleaming throat, like lovely Semiramis entering her boudoir—'"

I placed my fingertips over his lips. "You embarrass me, husband. I am not a poem."

"I disagree—you are very much like the fabled Corinna." He kissed me, then sat up. "You must be hungry. Shall I send for food? Would you like to break your fast in bed?"

"That sounds terribly indulgent," I said, sliding out from beneath the bed linens. Suddenly shy, I found my inner tunic on the floor, stepped into it, and fastened it at the shoulders. "Do as you please, husband, and I will be happy with whatever you decide."

He stood and clapped. His *atriensis*, or personal slave, entered the room and slid a clean tunic over my husband's head, then picked up the toga Marcus had carelessly discarded on the floor.

"Jason"—Marcus gestured to me—"meet your new domina. Mariana, Jason is now in your service. If you need anything, he can procure it."

"And my handmaid—where is Salama?"

Marcus lifted a brow and looked at Jason.

"Your handmaid slept in an antechamber," Jason said, bowing to me. "Shall I fetch her?"

I shook my head. "Not yet."

I relaxed on the bed and watched Jason carefully fold Marcus's toga and drape it over a trunk. I was glad women did not wear togas—the arrangement of a woman's palla was child's play compared to the art of draping a toga with the proper number of folds and pleats.

Marcus picked up a scroll that had appeared on his desk during the night, leading me to admire Jason's discretion. Marcus read the message and scowled. "I must leave you after morning prayers," he said, furling the scroll. "But if the gods permit, I shall return soon."

I was curious to know where he was going but did not want to ask. Did a wife have a right to know her husband's schedule? Though I had seen nothing but kindness in Marcus, my stepfather had also been kind when he first sought my mother . . .

When Jason had finished combing my husband's hair, Marcus nodded at the slave. "Have food delivered to this room after prayers. And on your way out, find Salama and have her report to her mistress."

As Jason and Marcus left, I sat up, suddenly realizing that I would need to be dressed for my first appearance at the palace lararium. The entire household would be present, including the governor.

I rolled out of bed just as Salama tiptoed into the room, her brows uplifted. "Well?" she asked, an impenitent grin on her face.

"Marriage is wonderful," I told her. "But today my new life begins. Marcus wants me to join his family at the lararium. After that, you and I will come back here to eat."

Hearing the urgency in my voice, Salama opened my trunk

and peered inside. "I had nearly forgotten. You must now wear a stola."

I blew out a breath, realizing I would never again wear the short tunic of a virgin. The tunics in my trunk were edged with a wide border, the *instita*, and would display my status as a respectable married woman.

"I hope I do not trip on my way to the lararium," I muttered as Salama studied the garments in the trunk. "I am not used to wearing such a long garment."

Salama pulled out a new tunic and helped me into it. The long garment fell to the floor, then she tied a girdle around my waist.

"I hope you will eat more now that you are married," Salama fussed as she knotted the girdle. "You are as thin as a stick."

She fastened the garment at my shoulders with a pair of gold brooches, a wedding gift from Mother. Then she pulled the length of the tunic up through the girdle until the lower edge of the instita barely cleared the floor.

"What do you think?" Salama asked, turning me toward the looking brass.

I stared at my reflection. The deep color of the crimson border at my feet was repeated in a band at the neckline, and the color made me look paler than usual. The fullness at my waist made me feel like a girl playing dress-up in her mother's garments.

"I look like a child," I whispered, "but I suppose I will grow into it."

"You will," Salama said with a confidence I did not feel. "Your mother has filled your trunk, so you need not worry about having nothing to wear. Now, let me do your hair."

She sat me on a stool as she combed my hair, pulled it up, and held it off my shoulders with a trio of pearl-encrusted hair combs, another wedding gift from Narkis.

"My stepfather certainly spared no expense," I murmured as Salama pushed the combs into place. "He wanted to impress the governor."

"Have you ever considered that he might be fond of you?" Salama asked.

"I am certain he was thinking of Memmius, not me."

When Salama had finished applying my cosmetics, she draped a silk himation over one shoulder and around my neck, then stepped back to study her work. "Oh," she said, breathless. "You are every inch a lady."

I glanced at my reflection in the looking brass. Odd, how the stola and uplifted hair made me appear to have aged overnight.

"Since I have no plans to see anyone but Marcus and his father," I said, barely recognizing my own voice, "I would say you have done well. Now, help me find the palace lararium . . . because I am lost in this place."

❖

My clever Salama had already located the palace lararium, so we found it without wasting time—a fortunate happenstance, since Marcus was waiting beside his father when we arrived. Memmius stood in front of a smoking brazier in the wall niche, his chief attendants behind him.

Salama took her place behind me, and Jason stood behind Marcus. My husband gave me a quick smile as Memmius covered his head and began to pray. "O Jupiter, hear my words. We ask you to warm our home, warm our hearts with your flame, and guard my family, including Mariana, Marcus's new wife."

A small flame burned in a clay bowl on the altar. To this Memmius added a sprinkle of incense, which smoked and filled the ornate chamber with a spicy scent. "O Jupiter, I welcome you to our home. I ask you to look down with favor upon our family. I ask for your blessing, and in return, I give thanks and the gift of incense."

The governor smiled at me as he continued. "I ask you to look with favor upon my son's wife. I ask for your blessing on their marriage. You have given me a pleasant wife, so I pray you will bless my son in the same way. You provided me with a lofty position, and you have given all of us good health. With great thanks, we pray to you. Protect our family today and strengthen our marriages."

Without speaking, Memmius extended his hand toward a slave, who pulled a dead pigeon from a leather pouch. The governor set the bird on the brazier, surrendering the sacrifice. "Through prayers and duty, we give you an offering of a pigeon in recognition of your many blessings to us."

Fear blew down the back of my neck when the governor turned to me, a look of expectation in his eyes. I knew he was waiting for me to offer a prayer to Vesta, the goddess of wives and mothers. I could not do such a thing, so I did what I could.

With a quick glance at Marcus, who watched with undisguised curiosity, I lifted my arms, palms outstretched, and looked toward my Father in heaven.

"Great Adonai," I prayed, "thank you for bringing me a kind and gentle husband. Bless him today and protect all his family from evil. I thank you for your goodness to me, and for the many blessings you bestow on people everywhere, even those who do not know you. Thank you for the gift of your Son Yeshua, for it is through His name that I approach your throne and offer this petition."

I lowered my hands, and from the corner of my eye I saw that Marcus's face had twisted with confusion. Memmius stared at me with a frown between his brows.

The governor recovered quickly, however, and murmured a final prayer before pulling his toga from his head. When he did not look at me or Marcus, I sensed he was waiting for his son to address the unconventional prayer from the newest family member.

I was not surprised when Marcus caught my hand and led me away.

"I have never heard," he said, his voice low, "of this Adonai. Is He a god of the Greeks?"

"He is God to anyone who seeks Him," I answered, struggling to match his long stride, "and though many do not acknowledge or even know Him, He is God of the universe."

"But what people does He serve?" Marcus asked, insistent. "And how did you hear of Him?"

"He does not exist to serve us," I answered, "for He is the Creator of all. We serve Him. As to where He is worshiped, He chose the Jews as his favored people and directed them to establish His Temple in Jerusalem."

When we reached the door to our bedchamber, Marcus turned me to face him, his eyes soft and serious. "Rome allows people to worship whatever god they please. Would you like my father to build a temple for Adonai in Corinth? Many Jews live in this city, so they might appreciate being able to make sacrifices without traveling all the way to Judea."

"No, husband." I smiled, touched by his thoughtfulness. "Adonai no longer dwells in a temple, but in the hearts of those who worship Him. The Jews in Corinth do not sacrifice here. They gather in synagogues to study their holy writings. Some of them believe in the Son of Adonai, as I do, but others do not. They cannot accept that His Son, Yeshua, came as a man to live and die—"

"Dominus." Jason appeared in the hallway and pointed over his shoulder. "Your father is waiting for you."

"I must go." Marcus lifted my hand and kissed it. "I have a meeting with my father, then we must meet with Narkis. The work of the city keeps us busy, so I am relieved to hear the Jews will not want me to build them a temple."

I managed a weak smile and wriggled my fingers in farewell. Marcus pulled me close and kissed me again, then turned and strode away.

Clearly, my husband did not know much about Adonai or Yeshua . . . but perhaps that was a good thing. He did not know enough to object, and I had begun the first day of our married life with the truth about my God.

An auspicious beginning.

Twenty-One

PRIMA

The day after Mariana's wedding, I woke and did not know what to do with myself. Ever since Father told me the governor had a son who needed a wife, I had centered my thoughts and actions around the conviction that Marcus was fated to be mine. I spurned my friends, reckoning that I would soon be above them in station, and abandoned all other interests.

So what was I to do now? The wealthy families of Corinth—the only families that mattered—would now think of me as the sister who had been rejected. Father would have to search among the merchants to find me a suitable husband, but none of them would outrank the governor's son, and none of them could lay claim to a palace in Corinth, a villa in the Italian countryside, and an elegant domicile in Rome. When I considered how far I had fallen beneath my undeserving stepsister's status, I found myself yearning for a different kind of life, one in which marriage did not matter and rank meant nothing.

But such a world did not exist. So I was trapped in a place

where no one valued me—not even my beloved father—and I had no hope of achieving my goals.

I rolled over and buried my face in my pillow. I tried to return to the phantom-filled world of dreams, but my mind roiled with memories of the wedding, where I saw the governor's son regard my stepsister with an expression that looked like love.

How could he love her and not me?

The high priestess of Aphrodite had told me to pursue my desires with all my heart, relying on the goddess and acting in confidence that she would hear my prayers. I did my best—after making sacrifices at the temple that night, I climbed into bed, stared at the ceiling, and confidently spoke aloud, "I will marry Marcus and be his wife."

From her mat on the floor, Gilda had chuckled.

"Domina?" Gilda tapped my shoulder, bringing me back to the present. "Your father will soon expect you at the lararium."

I sighed and got out of bed, then dropped into the chair by my dressing table. "I should have been born a plebeian in the Roman slums," I muttered, planting my chin in my palm as Gilda began to comb my hair. "I could have been arrested for thievery and sentenced to a *ludus*. I could train to be a gladiatrix and spend my days driving a sword into stumps painted with Mariana's face."

"If that were your destiny," Gilda replied, "you would not know Mariana, so what would be the point of hating her?"

"I would hate her instinctively. Just as I hate all those who follow her foreign God. If her Adonai is responsible for this situation, those who worship Him should be executed."

"I do not think you would enjoy life in the ludus," Gilda said, ignoring my comment. "I hear the same food is served every day, you would not have a comfortable bed, and you would have no slaves. If you wanted your hair curled, you would have to heat the rod yourself."

I glared at her in the looking brass, but she only smiled. "I am speaking the truth, Domina," she said, combing through another hank of hair. "Sometimes I think you do not realize how bad things could be if you had been born into another family."

"I will tell you how bad things could be—tomorrow I could sell you at the market. Then *you* would discover how bad things could be."

Gilda fell silent, but only for a moment. "I came to this house from the slave market. I have already lived a wretched life, so I do not complain about this one."

"You are a slave. A slave should be grateful for anything she receives."

"I am grateful because in this house I have food to eat and a roof over my head. And sometimes, when the occasion suits her, my domina can be pleasant."

I scowled at the mural on my chamber walls. Amid a thicket of green vines and tall trees, half-naked gods and goddesses romped in playful pursuit of one another. So why was no one pursuing me?

"I need a diversion." I sighed. "Yesterday I had to endure that wedding. Today I want to enjoy myself."

"You could go shopping," Gilda suggested, tying off the end of a braid. "You might find something interesting and—"

"I could go to the arena." I stared past Gilda, fascinated by the idea.

My handmaid's mouth curled in distaste. "You could not go to such a place alone. It is not proper."

"You will go with me."

The slave shook her head. "I do not enjoy violence. If you force me to go, I will close my eyes during the fighting."

"So be it," I said, slapping her hand away from my head. "My hair is fine, do not fret with it further. After morning prayers, we are going to watch the gladiators. If I look like a wanton woman, who would possibly care?"

When I walked toward the door without my veil, Gilda looked at me as if I had suddenly grown a second head. "You cannot go out uncovered. It is unthinkable."

I would have ignored her, but when the slave threatened to tell my father of my intentions, I stopped and allowed her to drape a palla over my hair. I hissed in irritation when she covered her own head. "Now you are putting on airs. Slaves have no reason to wear a veil."

"I do," she said. "If someone recognizes me, they will know who my mistress is, and that would not be good for either of us."

"I do not care if anyone sees me."

"Your father would care. And he might have me beaten—or worse—for not reporting your plans."

Because a mist had chilled the outside air, Gilda draped my mantle over my shoulders and drew a deep breath. "If we must go to the arena, let us be away. The sooner we return, the better for everyone."

Feeling more alive than I had in weeks, I led Gilda through the house and exited by the kitchen door. If all went well, my father need not know I had gone anywhere—not that he would care. Why would he when he had been blind to my agony and indifferent to my needs? He should have insisted that I be Marcus's bride, that his blood daughter be married first. He prided himself on being a good negotiator—so why hadn't he negotiated a marriage for me instead of Mariana?

I had asked myself that question a hundred times, and his betrayal cut more deeply with each repetition.

We had walked only a short distance when I spotted a tavern on the corner. Perhaps a libation would ease my anxiety about venturing into the arena.

"There." I pointed. "We will go inside and have a drink."

Gilda halted. "Domina, well-bred women do not visit taverns. Those places are filled with thieves, gamblers, runaway slaves—"

"Perfect." I lengthened my stride and marched toward the wide counter that spanned the front of the building. The tavern was filled with tables for those who sought privacy, but I did not care if anyone saw me at the bar. Why should I care? Father had cared nothing for me.

I pulled out the purse I had tucked inside in my tunic. "What is your best wine?" I asked the bald man behind the counter.

He squinted as if he would see behind my veil. "Opimian wine is very fine," he said, shrugging. "Falernian is also popular."

I pulled out a sestertius and slid it toward him. "Is that enough for a drink?"

His brows rose. "Lady, that is enough for a pitcher."

"Then that is what I will have. At once."

The man shook his head, then pulled a brass pitcher

from beneath the counter. He carried it to an amphora, then watched as a stream of red wine splashed into the vessel.

He jerked his head toward the back of the tavern. "Will you want a table?"

Given the size of the pitcher, I thought it best to accept his suggestion. I went inside, stepped over an unconscious man on the floor, and strode toward the first empty table. Gilda followed, her face twisting in disgust, then we sat and stared at the pitcher, its contents shimmering in the light of a flickering oil lamp.

"Wine for two," the man said, setting two cups on the table. "Enjoy yourselves, ladies."

When he had moved away, Gilda lifted her veil and met my gaze, her eyes blazing. "If we drink all this," she said, "we are not ladies."

"You were never a lady," I said, filling my cup. "You are a slave."

I sipped the wine and found it tolerable, then tipped the cup back and drank as if I were dying of thirst. Gilda's eyes widened, but she remained silent as I drained the cup and filled it again. "What?" I arched a brow. "Will you not drink with me?"

"One of us must keep her wits about her," she said, eyes flashing. "Though I am tempted, one of us must make sure you return safely home."

I laughed, already feeling more carefree. I was no stranger to fine wine. For years Father had allowed me to drink during banquets and on other special occasions, but never had I enjoyed the liberty to imbibe as much as I wanted. Though certain Roman leaders—Caesar and Augustus came to mind—had been praised as sober men, most Romans drank like parched camels. Nero, our current emperor, was reportedly never too ill to enjoy his wine. Marc Antony, who had favored Dionysus, the god of winemaking, had been accused of drinking from morning until night, and even traveled with special golden goblets.

"Did you know?" I held up the tavern's plain metal cup. "I do not think Hester has ever had more than a single cup of wine at dinner. She is the Caesar of our household. Like him, she overthrew my mother while completely sober."

Gilda heaved a sigh. "You should not speak ill of your father's wife. Your mother died long before he married again."

"He should have remained true to her," I whispered, the memory of my mother tightening my throat. "She was the only woman who ever showed me kindness."

"Not so. Hester has been more than gracious to you."

I slammed my cup to the table, splashing wine in every direction. "Do not dispute me, slave. You did not know my mother."

Gilda sighed, a tear slipping from beneath her lashes. I did not care. The wine had fortified my flagging spirit, and I would drink another cup, and another, until I had summoned enough courage to fulfill my current desire.

"Had enough yet?" A masculine voice startled me. I looked up to see a man at my side, a working man in a plain toga and worn sandals.

"No," I answered, a thread of irritation in my voice. "Leave us, so we may drink in peace."

"I thought you might like a little company." The stranger bent and attempted to slide onto my bench, an action that sent a snake of anxiety through my bowels.

Before I could react or speak, Gilda stood, picked up the

pitcher, and slammed it against the man's head. He recovered, but quickly gathered his wits, drawing back his hand as if to strike her—

"Do not move," I said, speaking directly into his ear. "If you do, I will summon the governor's men and you will die in a prison cell."

The fool lowered his hand and stood, wine dripping from his face and tunic. "You know the governor?"

"I know Servius Memmius Lupus very well," I answered. "We are connected through marriage."

The tavern owner peered over my assailant's shoulder. "Is this fool giving you trouble?"

I glanced at Gilda, then forced a smile. "Not so much. But we have spilled most of the wine."

He shoved the intruder aside, then nodded and hurried away, returning a moment later with another pitcher.

I glanced at Gilda, who trembled across from me, her empty cup in front of her. I filled it and lowered the pitcher to the table.

"When this vessel is empty," I told her, filling my cup again, "we are going to the arena. I hear Atrox is fighting today."

Gilda did not meet my gaze, so I bent forward and forced her to look at me. "Did you hear what I said? According to the drawing on yonder wall, the great Atrox fights today."

"I do not know who that is."

"He is a champion," I answered, amused to hear a slur in my words. "What more do we need to know? They say he is the greatest, strongest, most attractive gladiator in the empire. I have prayed to Aphrodite, telling her that I should experience love just as Mariana has. Why should she lie in a man's arms while I lie alone?"

I sat back and smiled, delighted by the way I had confidently stated my desire.

Aphrodite—and Cassia—would have approved.

❖

The games had nearly finished by the time I arrived at the arena. Gilda had to help me through the gate because I stumbled and giggled every time I misjudged a step. Clasping my arm with an iron grip, she led me to a box where we sat on stone seats and looked out on the arena, its bloodstained sands littered with scattered weapons.

I had never witnessed a gladiatorial contest. With wide eyes, I looked around, overcome by the riot of color and sound. Above us, crimson awnings snapped in the chilly breeze while a faint stink rose from beneath our seats. I crinkled my nose. What was that smell? Blood? Beer?

The Corinthian arena was not particularly grand, but from Father I knew it had proved adequate to meet the city's need to execute escaped slaves and criminals. Encased by a wall about ten feet tall, the elliptical field of combat lay at the bottom of a hollow. Thirty-five rows of seats surrounded the ellipsis. The lowest seats were carved marble, the middle seats rough stone, and the highest seats wooden planks. A wide terrace separated the stone and wooden seats, and a row of small boxes occupied the front edge. Though several women watched from the enclosed boxes, the bottom two tiers were occupied only by men.

Despite my blurry eyes, I recognized the man who sat in the administrator's front row box. He was a city council member and well acquainted with my father. The burly fellow rested his elbow on his marble chair and supported his chin with his hand, his eyes intent on the action.

On the sand, two men stood with their backs to us. The largest man wore a loincloth and an iron helmet. His shoulders seemed as broad as a street, and dark hair, tightly bound, streamed down his heavily muscled back. I could see nothing of his face until he turned toward the other man, a small fellow wearing a dirty tunic. With both hands he gripped a huge sword and pleaded for his life.

I could not hear his words through the noise, but when the administrator lifted both arms to the crowd, asking if the man should die immediately, the onlookers responded with a rhythmic cry of "Fight, fight, fight!" The administrator nodded and jerked his chin at the imposing gladiator.

"The little man must be a criminal," Gilda said, her voice tight. "This is not a proper contest."

"It is a feast . . . for the eyes," I said, struggling to form words. "Yonder gladiator is an amazing specimen."

Gilda gestured to a picture someone had painted on the inner wall. "Is that the same man?"

I read the name beneath the drawing. "This must be the renowned Atrox," I said. "He is undefeated, but if he is only fighting thieves and runaway slaves, I am not surprised."

Gilda shook her head. "If he does well here, they will send him to Rome."

When I stared at her, amazed she would know such a thing, she shrugged. "I have spent time in a slave market. From where do you think the best gladiators come?"

As one, the crowd leaned forward when the action began. The smaller man extended his sword and ran toward the gladiator in a reckless rush. Atrox swatted the sword away and sent the little man sprawling face forward into the sand. For several minutes the gladiator played with his opponent like a cat with a mouse, then the smaller man dropped to his knees, lowered his blade, and bowed his head.

The crowd hissed. They thirsted for a spectacle, not an execution.

When the smaller man lifted his chin, a hush fell over the crowd. I leaned forward, straining to hear what the man would say.

"Kill me, please." The words, though spoken with the heaviness of defeat, somehow reached our ears. "By all the gods, I beg you to show mercy and kill me now."

When the gladiator glanced toward the administrator's box, I followed his gaze and gasped. Memmius now sat in the gilded chair, with my father at his side.

For a moment my heart stopped, then I slowly exhaled. Father need never know I was here. I was veiled, and so was Gilda. He would never suspect.

Memmius stood, met the gladiator's gaze, then slowly extended his arm. Then, in a dramatic gesture, he flattened his hand and dragged it across his throat.

The gladiator moved swiftly. Before the criminal could snatch another breath, Atrox's sword swept through the air, cleanly separating the condemned man's head from his torso. The crowd cheered, the governor smiled, and Gilda groaned.

I leaned forward and vomited.

❖

The arena had nearly emptied by the time I felt steady enough to stand and walk. Though I had never attended a gladiatorial contest before, I knew what happened in the arena. I had heard stories of executions and extreme violence, but I could not explain my visceral reaction.

Yes, the death was horrible, but surely that aspect paled in comparison to the glory of victory, the swiftness of the fight, and the thrill of conquest. Some gladiators, even those who had been plebeians, freedmen, or slaves, could rise to great heights and surprising wealth if they survived long enough to attain victory in Rome. Wealthy women, even noble wives, regularly bribed guards at the ludus in order to visit gladiators in their subterranean chambers. So despite what many imagined, gladiators did not suffer *complete* deprivation.

When my head had cleared and my stomach settled, I stood and squared my shoulders. "He is gone," Gilda said, nodding at the box where my father had been watching with the governor. "Though I wondered if he would ever depart. A dozen men were vying for his attention."

"Sycophants." I shook my head. "Now that he is related by marriage to the governor, everyone wants to be my father's best friend. I would not be surprised if several were trying to negotiate a marriage between me and their sons."

"Would that not be a good idea?" Gilda gave me an overly enthusiastic smile. "If you had your own home and children, perhaps you would no longer think so much about your stepsister."

"I will always think about her." I lifted my chin. "As long as she has the man I want, I will despise her."

My handmaid lifted a brow, doubtless intending to argue, but I would not hear another word. "You do not know what happened in the meeting between my father and Memmius," I said, stepping into the aisle. "Even if Marcus preferred Mariana, he is not the paterfamilias of his household. If the governor wanted me for his son, I would be married to Marcus. But he chose Mariana. Only the gods know why."

I pressed my lips together, resisting another rise of bile in my throat. The blame for my situation did not belong to Memmius alone. He might have given his son the freedom to choose, but *my* father had lacked the courage to suggest I was the better choice. I could not deny the hard reality—my only parent had betrayed me and honored my stepsister instead.

But I would waste no more time on regrets; I would find my own way to achieve my goals. With the help of Aphrodite, I would strike back at Father, Memmius, Marcus, and Mariana, making all of them suffer the consequences of their mistake.

Still unsteady on my feet, I gripped Gilda's arm to negotiate the stone steps. "Now," I told her, "take me to the rooms where the gladiators are kept."

She blinked, her features hardening in a stare of disapproval. "Domina, you cannot visit that place."

"I know what happens after the games." I glared at the empty administrator's box. "And I know what the usual price is. Why should I be any different from other women who long for a gladiator's attention?"

Gilda stood like a post, her arms rigid. "You cannot be serious. You have had too much to drink, and you are not yourself. I will take you home, but I will not take you down—"

"You will obey or be beaten," I said, digging my nails into her arm. "Lead me to the gladiators' chambers, or I will lead you to the slave market."

Gilda looked at me and blinked hard, then she lowered her head and led me down the steps. I leaned on her, occasionally glancing at her face, but she would not meet my gaze.

So be it. I would let her sulk, but she should not have lectured me. I had been far too lenient and should never have taken her into my confidence. "Slaves," my mother once told me, "should never be treated as equals, or equals they will imagine themselves to be."

Most of the crowd had dispersed by the time we walked through the tunnel and reached the arena's exit. Gilda led me out into the sunshine, then she nodded toward another set of stairs that led to an area beneath the stadium seating. She pressed her back against a pillar, and I knew she would not take another step.

I squared my shoulders. I would not go to this gladiator as a rejected woman, I would go as a daughter of Aphrodite. I was the firstborn child of an important magistrate. If my stepsister's invisible God had not cursed me, I would be the governor's daughter-in-law.

I walked toward the guard station at the opening to the gladiators' quarters. Aphrodite wanted me to experience pleasure, I told myself. She wanted me to know how it felt to lie in a man's arms.

I would know soon enough.

Father, Hester, Mariana, Marcus, and Memmius had prevented me from having the things I desired and deserved, but with Aphrodite's help I was going to regain control of my life.

Twenty-Two

PRIMA

Shivering despite the heat, I fastened my tunic at my shoulder and stumbled in my effort to stand. Atrox sat cross-legged on the edge of the dirty mattress that served as his bed, his back to me.

"If you would like to visit again," he said, his voice unnervingly flat, "I could use the coin. If I am victorious in Rome, I will retire to a villa in the country. They are not cheap."

I opened my mouth, wanting to say that no respectable Roman would sell a villa to a brute, but I could not summon the breath to speak. I lurched for the iron door of his cell.

Gilda, who had reluctantly decided to follow me into the dungeon-like basement of the ludus, saw me through the small window in the door. "Guard! My mistress would like to leave."

I pressed my hands to the heavy door as the guard strolled over. He studied me through narrowed eyes as he turned his key. I managed to stride through the doorway with my head high, but as soon as we left the subterranean prison, I crumpled in Gilda's arms.

"Domina, are you well?" She bent to look at my face. "Did he hurt you?"

Hurt me? The humiliating experience had shattered me, but I could not let her know how callously I had been handled. Going in, I had considered myself a strong and independent woman, but within two minutes of entering that chamber I knew I had made a terrible mistake. The stench of his breath, the rough strength of his grip . . .

The gladiator was as indifferent to me as he had been to his opponent in the arena, and if that act was part of marriage, I wanted nothing to do with it.

I whimpered at the memory. "Gilda?"

"Domina?"

"Take me home."

She pulled my rumpled veil over my face, then tightened her grip on my shoulder. "Do not worry. We will slip through the garden gate, and I will tell your father you are ill. You need not face him or anyone else tonight."

I uttered words I had never spoken to a slave: "Thank you."

❖

When the bruises on my arms and legs had faded, I returned to the temple on the Acrocorinth and asked to see Cassia. This time the images of Aphrodite and her lovers did not charm me. Instead, I seethed with barely suppressed rage.

When Cassia emerged from an inner chamber, I stood and met her gaze without flinching.

"You instructed me to determine what I desired," I told

her. "You said the goddess would help me if I learned Aphrodite's ways. I did, but I did not enjoy the experience."

Cassia's curious expression softened to sympathy. "And who did you seek to teach you of love?"

"A gladiator," I said, the word leaving a vile taste on my lips. "A man so rough that for days my body bore the marks of his hands."

Cassia's brows drew together in an agonized expression as she led me to a couch. "That was not love," she said, her voice soft with compassion. "And you chose a violent teacher. Let me lead you to someone who will teach you more appropriate ways to seek pleasure. Aphrodite gives strength to those who are willing to persevere."

I laughed to cover my annoyance. In truth, I never wanted to visit the ludus again.

A thoughtful smile curved Cassia's mouth. "I see a flame of defiance in your eyes," she said, "and I know you will not abandon your desires. Come with me, Prima. Come learn lessons from the goddess."

Bewitched and bewildered, I rose and followed her deeper into the temple.

Twenty-Three

MARIANA

I had never imagined that living with a man could make a woman utterly happy. Marcus was almost everything I had hoped he would be—kind, attentive, and gentle. I did not expect him to have a sense of humor, but he often made me laugh when he described situations and people he had met throughout his day. His descriptions of foreign places made me long to see them, and his retelling of stories left me spellbound.

I was honored when I realized he trusted me. One morning we awakened and remained in bed, enjoying the quiet moments before the servants entered. Marcus turned to me and asked, "Are you happy?"

The question caught me by surprise. "I am."

"Good." A quick smile crossed his face. "I am happy as well. I have said it before—I have never met a woman like you."

I resisted the urge to shrug away his compliment. "Marcus, I am nothing special. I have no great talents, no special abilities—"

"You are perfect."

I laughed. "Indeed, I am not."

"I have never seen a flaw."

"Perhaps you have not looked closely enough."

In response, he leaned over me, bringing his nose to mine, a boyish grin on his face. "I am as close as I can be, but still I do not see."

"Now you are being silly." Playfully, I pushed him away, then rolled onto my side to face him. "Seriously, Marcus, you should know that I have no courage. I used to watch Prima, who has never feared anything, and felt like a timid mouse in comparison. I was not always this way, but after my father died, I could not help fearing the unknown. Even after Mother married Narkis, I worried about whether he would keep us, if he would like me, or if I would upset him." I pressed my hand to Marcus's bare chest, grateful for its warmth and stability. "Adonai tells His followers not to fear because He will defend us, yet sometimes I forget. I wish . . . I wish I were braver. You deserve a courageous wife."

Marcus's eyes, which had softened while I spoke, now glimmered in the morning light. He rested his hand in the gentle curve above my hip, reassuring me with his touch.

"Roman men are supposed to be brave," he said, his gaze drifting away. "The sons of senators are taught to wield a sword and spear, to ride and give speeches. My brother and I had Greek tutors who taught us oratory in the morning and wrestling in the afternoon. We are supposed to represent the ideal, you see. The son of a senator should be a perfect Roman man."

I searched his face. "You have always seemed ideal to me."

He sighed as his gaze moved into mine. "I have fears, too. Chief among mine has always been the fear that I will disappoint my father. Though I took pains not to show it, I was terrified when we landed in Corinth. I knew Father expected—and still expects—great things of me. I had to find an ideal wife."

"At least you have done that," I teased.

He grinned, but his eyes remained sober. "He expects me to learn how to rule so I can control the city in his absence. He wants to know that I will be capable of stepping into his shoes when he departs this life. Now that we are married, he will begin to leave the city. I will be in control of the province, and each of his trips will be a test. If I fail or if something goes wrong—" he swallowed hard—"if I do not fulfill my father's expectations, he will feel that I have been a waste of his time."

"Surely not!" I clenched his arm. "No one is truly perfect. Accidents happen, and often things are beyond our control."

"Men of my age are not allowed to make mistakes," Marcus said, his mouth tightening. "And the art of governing is the art of maintaining control. So when you pray for me, pray that I will not disappoint my father. Even the small mistakes of rulers loom large in history, and that thought is what terrifies me."

I wrapped my arms around his neck and drew him closer, hoping my embrace would provide the encouragement he needed. How could I, an anxious girl, teach a Roman anything about courage?

In such moments of honest vulnerability, my attraction to Marcus deepened into fondness and then affection, yet our relationship was not all I hoped it would be. Though I often spoke of Adonai, my husband remained an idol-worshiper. He seemed to take pleasure in the idea that Rome was great because the empire allowed its people the freedom to worship any god, but how could a false god lead anyone to freedom? Freedom was found in truth, and truth was found only in Adonai and His Son.

At our wedding, I prayed that Adonai would help me serve my husband and lead him to the truth. I still wanted to do that but would step carefully. I could not forget the look on Narkis's face when he told me never to speak of Yeshua in his household. What if Memmius felt the same way?

But Marcus was curious about Adonai and Yeshua. When he could not sleep, he often asked me to read to him, so I would light the lamp and read sections of Paulos's letters to the Corinthians or the Romans. Eventually, Marcus slept. And though I waited for him to comment on or question the papyri I had read, he never did.

Still, our young marriage filled me with great joy. I envisioned an endless succession of blissful days and cozy nights, an existence that could be improved only if Marcus chose to follow the God who had given me peace and purpose.

❖

About three months after our wedding, I woke with an oppressive feeling of malaise. I thought of the idol-worshipers around me and wondered if someone had dispatched an evil spirit to devour my energy.

As I sat up and reached for Marcus, my stomach lurched. Overcome with urgency, I ran to the chamber pot and vomited, then clutched my belly and sank to the floor, sweat oozing from every pore.

"Mariana?" Marcus sat up, his face contorting with concern. "Should I call a physician?"

I wanted to tell him not to worry, but I could not banish my fear. Had I been *too* happy? Had some dark spirit descended to shake my faith in Adonai?

"Send for my mother," I whispered. "She will know what to do."

❖

My weakness had abated by the time Mother arrived, and I felt well enough to meet her on the front steps of the palace. As she alighted from her litter, I pasted on a smile and embraced her, apologizing for disturbing her morning.

"No need to worry about me," she said, pushing loose curls from my face. "The messenger said you were ill."

I shrugged, not wanting to worry her. "I must have eaten something that did not settle properly."

"Are you tired?" She placed her hand to my forehead, then lowered her voice. "Are your breasts more tender than usual?"

I blinked. "Did . . . did the Spirit inform you of my condition?"

She laughed and slipped her arm through mine. "Daughter, you are not ill, you are with child. Tell me—how many days since your blood last flowed?"

I stared in bewilderment, then understanding dawned.

"It has been more than a month. So these signs are portents—"

"They are symptoms of pregnancy," she said, her voice light. "Your body is changing to meet the needs of the baby within your womb. About eight months from now, you will bring a child into the world."

I stopped on the top step, my mouth agape. "Truly?"

"I would not mislead you about such an important matter."

I embraced her again, my heart singing with delight. "I cannot wait to tell Marcus."

"Will the news please him?"

"Why would it not?"

Mother shrugged. "A few men are not happy with such news, but Marcus seems to truly care for you. I am sure he will be pleased—and so will the governor."

I smiled, imagining the pleasure on Marcus's face, but my smile flattened when a shadow of concern twisted Mother's brow. "What?"

She shook her head. "Nothing that need worry you, pet. I was only thinking of Prima, who has not been herself since your wedding. She has become quite . . . preoccupied."

"She has always been distant with you and me."

"This is different—a darkness has settled over her. I am concerned."

I forced a smile. "Perhaps my good news will cheer her."

Mother patted my hand. "We can certainly hope for the best. But for now, give your husband the news and ask a physician to confirm my suspicions."

"Will you come inside?" I asked, suddenly remembering my manners. "I am certain Marcus would like to see you."

"I should go." Mother squeezed my hand. "You will not want an audience when you give him this wonderful report."

Twenty-Four

PRIMA

Hester shared the news at dinner, the joy in her smile echoing in her voice. Father realized the significance of her report almost at once and immediately ordered a slave to bring more wine. "Servius Memmius and I will share a grandson," he said, his eyes dancing beneath heavy lids. "This occasion will bind us together for years to come."

I stared at my father, not bothering to disguise my disdain, but he did not even glance in my direction. Without eating a morsel, I quit the triclinium, leaving him to celebrate with Hester. In my bedchamber, I threw myself on the bed and wept angry, frustrated tears while Gilda crouched silently on the floor.

Why had the gods failed me so spectacularly? I had asked Aphrodite to make Mariana barren and shrivel her womb, but apparently the goddess did the opposite. Why would she betray me after I did so much to prove my loyalty to her?

When I lifted my head, I saw that Gilda had slipped out of the room. I sat up, swiped tears from my face, and was staring at nothing when my handmaid returned with a tray of sweetbreads and wine. She left these on a table and retreated to a corner. I ignored the food awhile, then turned and stared at the tray. "My stepsister is pregnant," I announced, reaching for the wine. "Hester and my father are overjoyed."

Gilda finally spoke. "The governor must be thrilled as well."

"Must you pour salt on my wound?"

"I am sorry, Domina."

Silence stretched between us until I realized I should not waste an entire evening feeling sorry for myself. What had Cassia said? Perhaps Aphrodite had *not* failed me. Perhaps she refused me because she had a better and far more profitable plan. Perhaps she wanted me to worship her in word *and* deed.

"Rise, slave," I commanded. "Arrange my hair and apply my cosmetics. I am going out."

A warning flashed in Gilda's eyes. "Have you forgotten what happened the last time you went out? You were sick after you returned home, miserable and—"

"I have grown wiser since that day."

Indeed I had. So many horrible things had occurred, situations beyond my control, but I was not powerless. I could still make my own choices. I could visit the ludus. I could feel a man's arms around me. I could commit acts that would shame my father, demonstrating that if he did not care for my reputation, neither would I care for his.

I met Gilda's gaze with determination. "This time when I go to the ludus, I will teach that brutish Thracian a thing or two about pleasure."

"What Thracian?"

"Atrox."

Gilda flexed her jaw. "It is a miracle of the gods that your father did not learn about your activities. Another visit to the ludus will only increase your risk of discovery. Surely you cannot mean to humiliate your father as well as yourself."

"My father has scarcely spoken to me since Mariana's betrothal." I moved to the chair before the looking brass. "And what he does not know will not affect him at all."

❖

Since Aphrodite had not heeded my previous curse tablet, I decided to personally alert the goddess to the next one. I stopped by the apothecary shop and purchased a blank tablet and a nail, then Gilda and I climbed the mountain to reach the temple of the goddess. The marble structure glimmered in the slanting rays of the setting sun as I strode upward, with Gilda struggling to keep up.

Once inside the temple, I paid a priest for a pigeon, then took the bird to an altar and twisted its neck. I beat the air with the dead bird, flinging its blood on the altar, and dropped the carcass onto the heated brazier. As the feathers flamed, I sat on a nearby bench and used the nail to inscribe the copper sheet with the horrors I wanted Mariana to experience.

Within her temple, I would beg the goddess to fulfill my desires. Surely she could not ignore me here.

"O mighty Aphrodite, goddess of love and lust, pleasure and passion, fertility and procreation, act upon my will today," I wrote, speaking each word aloud so the goddess would be sure to hear. "May Mariana's breasts wither and dry up. May her child rot within her. May her eyes turn red and her feet swell with sores. May her breath repel her husband, and may her appearance cause others to turn away in horror. May her God be vanquished, and may she go weeping to her grave, with no hope for happiness in the afterlife."

Gilda hissed in disapproval. "Would you be so cruel to your own sister?"

I ignored her. Since taking my handmaid into my confidence, the boundary between slave and mistress had become far too relaxed. I had not minded her maternal admonitions, but of late she had begun to scold.

"She is not my sister," I replied, rolling the thin tablet into a tight spiral. "She is not of my family's blood. She and her mother are usurpers of my father's affection and intruders in our home. May Aphrodite curse them both, but especially Mariana!"

I carried the tablet outside and used a rock to drive the nail through the center.

"Where will you put it?" Gilda asked, her eyes wide. "The merchant said it must be close to the victim."

I smiled. "It will be." I slipped the coil into a fold of my tunic. "I will make certain of it."

❖

"Ah," Gilda said, finally recognizing the magnificent house at the top of the hill. "You did not say we were going to visit the governor."

"We are not visiting him," I answered, peering out the litter's curtain. "We are calling on Mariana to share our congratulations."

Gilda lifted a questioning brow.

"And while we are there," I continued, "you will seek out

Salama because she is your friend. You will ask to see her mistress's bedchamber. When you reach that room, you will distract Salama with some task, then you will slip the curse tablet under Mariana's mattress. If it needs to be near the cursed one to be effective, then it shall be within the bed where she sleeps."

Gilda flushed. "How am I supposed to distract Salama?"

"Are you entirely worthless? Ask her for a glass of water—anything to make her leave the room. Prove your worth and hide the tablet on Mariana's side of the bed."

I slapped the curse tablet into Gilda's palm and gestured for her to conceal it in her girdle. "You must be quick. I do not intend to stay long."

"If I am caught, what do I say?"

"Only a fool would be caught," I snapped. "But know this—if you are discovered, I will declare I knew nothing of your actions, so you will be beaten and on the auction block within days. So take care and do not disappoint me."

Twenty-Five

MARIANA

I was reclining on a couch in the peristyle, enjoying the sun and a tray of honeyed figs, when one of the palace slaves came running. He bowed before me and offered a sealed scroll with both hands. "An epistle for you, my lady."

For a moment I wondered who would possibly send a letter to *me*, then a memory arose. Could it be?

I accepted the scroll, eagerly broke the seal, and began reading.

Paulos, called as an emissary of Messiah Yeshua by the will of God, to my young sister Mariana: Grace to you and shalom from God our Father, and our Lord Yeshua the Messiah!

How I thank God for you and your mother. I was surprised to receive her letter, and even more surprised to hear that you were about to marry an unbeliever. But I am well acquainted with your situation. I know you are subject to your mother's husband, whom she married before she believed in Messiah Yeshua.

I have prayed for you and trust that the Spirit of the Lord

205

gave you guidance. And now, whether you are married or living with your mother, I would encourage you to live in harmony with everyone. If, as I suspect, your stepfather insisted on the marriage, do not be proud in your lofty position, but be willing to associate with all people, rich or poor, free or slave. Be careful to do what is right in the Lord's eyes. Do not be overcome by the evil that permeates this present world but overcome evil with good.

Love your enemies, always remembering the example of Yeshua, who prayed for those who betrayed Him.

If you have married, remember that a wife must not separate from her husband. If your unbelieving husband is willing to live with you, you must not divorce him, for your unbelieving husband will be sanctified through your godly example. But if he leaves, let him do so. A believing woman is not bound in such circumstances. God has called us to live in peace.

Luke tells me I must blow out the lamp and go to sleep, but I cannot finish this letter without warning you about coming afflictions. Yes, dear one, they will come. Even when we were with you, did we not tell you that we would all suffer persecution? Trials will come to all who believe because Yeshua's kingdom is not of this world, and we belong to Him.

Always remember: you were bought at a price, so do not become a slave to anyone but Messiah Yeshua. I will continue to pray for you.

The believers in Rome send greetings to you and the ecclesia in Corinth. Luke sends his greetings, as do Aquilla and Priscilla, who love you like a daughter.

The grace of Messiah Yeshua be upon you. My love to you and your mother.

A tear slipped from my cheek as I furled the scroll. According to the most recent rumors, Paulos remained a prisoner, yet his letter contained not a single word of complaint. How like him to be more concerned about me than about himself!

I wanted to write and assure him that Marcus treated me well. I should also inquire about Paulos's health and tell him I was praying for him, but I could not be certain my letter would reach Rome. And if I wrote, I would not want to confess that despite Marcus's tolerance of my belief and his affection for me, my husband remained an idol-worshiper. Thus far my prayers and example had done nothing to change his heart. As an emissary for the Gospel, I was a failure.

I handed the scroll to Salama. "Place it in a safe spot," I whispered. "I will want to read it again."

She lifted a brow. "Will you reply?"

"Not yet. Perhaps later." I sighed. "I am ready for a nap. Wake me if Marcus returns, but otherwise let me sleep. I am exhausted."

"Certainly, Domina." She took the scroll, and together we walked toward the comfort and security of my chamber.

❖

"Wake, little one." For a moment I thought Marcus was speaking to me, but when I opened my eyes, I found him bent over my bulging belly, a wide smile brightening his countenance.

I yawned. "I think the baby is still asleep." I rolled to face my husband. "Last night the child was fluttering under my skin, but now it is sleeping."

Marcus kissed my belly, then grinned at me. "How long before the baby arrives?"

"A few months." I held up five fingers. "The child must grow until Ianuarius."

"Then I should let you rest." Marcus propped his head on his hand. "I do not know how you can sleep with our son dancing inside your womb."

"Our *son?*" I gave him a teasing smile. "What if the little dancer is a daughter?"

Marcus blinked as if astounded by the possibility. "I suppose we *could* have a daughter . . . but first a son, to continue the family name."

He wrapped his arm around me and drew me close. "Have I told you how happy you have made me? I have heard only a few men refer to their wives as companions. But you, Mariana—you have become that rarest of all things."

"And that is?"

"A friend." He looked away, a soft smile curving his lips. "Apart from my father, I have never had a true friend. Most of the men who seek my companionship are only searching for a way to get close to my father. They care little for me, and long only for power." He looked into my eyes. "But you see me. And you saw me in that barn, even before you knew who I was."

I felt the weight of his gaze, his dark eyes gentle and soft like the sea at dawn. In that moment, like so many moments before, I wanted to tell him about the reservations I'd had before our wedding and of how I had prayed that Adonai would make His will clear. I wanted him to know that I wrote to Paulos for advice. I wanted him to understand that Narkis threatened me and my mother to force the marriage. And then, if Marcus became upset or angry, I wanted to quickly assure him that I consented to the marriage in *faith*, trusting the Lord to work within a union that had been arranged for political reasons. I wanted him to *see* how Adonai could work within our lives . . .

I wanted him to know I loved him.

I never expected to love him. I thought we could be good friends and work together to raise a family. I expected to honor him, obey him as my husband, and serve him to the best of my ability. I hoped, with Adonai's help, to lead him to the truth of the Gospel.

But I had not expected to thrill to his presence, to feel my heart pound at the sound of his voice, or to feel a surge of excitement when he touched me.

Could this love be the will of God? To make certain, I had been asking myself, *If Marcus asked you to leave, could you go out of obedience to Adonai?* With each passing day, I found it harder to say yes, but now I took comfort in my pregnancy. Once our child arrived, Marcus would never want me to go.

But though I had fallen in love with my husband, I was not so sure of his love that I could tell him everything. As my husband, he was my head and authority. He could divorce me with a word; he could confine me to the house on a whim. Some Romans believed husbands should hold the power of life and death over their wives and children—such was the belief in the days when kings ruled Rome—but calmer heads now prevailed.

Yet Marcus was not my only authority in the palace. As part of the governor's household, Memmius was our pater-familias, and would be until Marcus and I set up a household of our own. Fortunately, the governor seemed to hold me in genuine affection and had been extremely pleased to learn that we would soon present him with a grandchild.

Still, living at the palace had taught me that one could never be too discreet in a Roman family. Only the emperor, I supposed, could live completely free from intimidation because previous emperors had unflinchingly murdered their wives, mothers, and siblings for reasons known only to them.

So no matter how much I loved my husband, restraint urged me to behave respectfully in his presence. When we were with the governor, I carefully considered every word that proceeded out of my mouth. Even when we were alone, I kept a guard on my lips, lest I offend with some ill-considered word.

I was not cautious for my life alone. Now that I carried an innocent child, I was also cautious for the baby's sake.

After Marcus went into the bath to dress and shave, Salama entered to prepare me for the day. She dressed me in a silk stola, chuckled when she tied a shimmering girdle around my expanding waist, and draped a beautiful green palla over my shoulder. Then she picked up a sheer veil to cover my hair.

"I saw a similar veil the other day," she said, sewing the delicate lace to a tight curl. "It can hang over the back of your head when you are in your chambers, but you can pull a second layer forward to cover your face when you go out."

"Clever." I groaned when the little one moved within me. "I believe the child has kicked a rib." I winced. "I believe Marcus is right—the child must be a boy because his kicks are powerful."

When I was dressed, Salama followed me to the lararium for prayers. Because Memmius had made his sacrifice earlier that morning, only our small family would pray at this hour. Marcus tossed a handful of incense on the fire, covered his head with his toga, and prayed to Vesta and Jupiter. Then he lowered his arms and waited for me to offer the traditional wifely prayers.

But instead of praying to the goddess of the hearth and home, I lifted my heart to Adonai. "Father," I prayed, "how I thank you for your goodness to us. Your will is perfect, and your path leads through the most pleasant places. Protect my husband today and make his path smooth. Guide Servius Memmius as he works for the province; may he establish justice and do your will among the people. Bless the emperor and lead him in paths of understanding for your name's sake."

Marcus cleared his throat. "Do not forget the baby."

I smiled. "And please bless our child, Father. May he or she grow within me until the appropriate time, and may the birth be a blessing to all. I offer this petition in the name of Yeshua, my Savior and Lord."

I lowered my hands as Marcus enveloped me in an embrace. "I hate to leave you," he said, smiling into my eyes, "but since Father has gone to Athens, I have much to do in his stead."

Ah, the first test. Memmius had taken a short trip, and Marcus was certain to be anxious about doing a good job in his absence.

"Do what you must do but come back quickly." I rested my folded hands on my belly as he and his slave left the chamber.

"Domina?" Now free to speak, Salama looked at me. "What are your plans for the day?"

"I think we shall read," I answered. "Then the baby and I will take a nap."

"Will your mother come to visit?"

"She has not mentioned it."

"Will we see Prima or Narkis?"

I snorted a laugh. "I have not seen Prima in weeks, and Narkis is with Memmius in Athens, so we should have hours to read and relax."

Salama nodded. "I cannot think of a more perfect day."

❖

On the last day of the summer month of Sextilis, Marcus and I stood on the palace steps waiting for the governor to return from Athens. Marcus had done a good job of ruling in his father's absence, and I was glad to see his confident smile. I should have been happy to know Memmius would soon lift the burden of responsibility from my husband's shoulders, but for the last two days I had been shadowed by a cloud of apprehension. I had not felt the baby move, not once, during those days. Though the physician assured me that babies needed rest, too, I could not help being worried about our child.

I had not mentioned my unease to Marcus, and apparently he had not noticed the worry in my eyes. As we waited on the steps, he smiled and took my hand, which I squeezed in gratitude. Perhaps he *had* noticed.

A moment later we heard the music and shouts of the *anteambulones*, slaves who cleared the way for traveling dignitaries. "Soon I will have you to myself again," I said, squeezing Marcus's arm. A moment later the governor's carriage, flanked by mounted guards in full Roman armor, entered the open area in front of the palace. Marcus stepped forward, eager to greet his father, and I smiled, happy to welcome Memmius home.

My smile flattened when a sharp pain twisted in my gut. I clamped my teeth together, not willing to make a scene, but I could no longer stand erect. As I bent at the waist, my knees threatening to buckle, Salama's arm slid around my back. Without making a fuss, she pulled me away from the other officials.

A moment later we were in the palace vestibule, where the doorkeeper stared at me in alarm.

"But the governor . . ." I muttered through clenched teeth.

"At this moment, he does not matter," Salama whispered, then she caught another slave's attention. Together they carried me to my chamber and placed me on the bed. While I sobbed and curled around the agony in my womb, Salama sent the slave for a midwife.

"It is too soon," I protested between sharp breaths. "The baby cannot come yet."

"The midwife will have an answer," Salama said. "Lie still, Domina, and try not to worry. Pray to Adonai for comfort."

I *did* pray but found it hard to form words when my voice sharpened into shrieks every time the pain rose like a wave, cresting, crashing, and sending currents of agony in every direction. I stopped trying to speak when every coherent thought centered on two words: *Adonai, help!*

Nearly an hour passed before the midwife arrived. By the time she entered my chamber I was drenched in sweat and the sheet beneath me wet with blood. The woman looked at me, placed her hands on my stomach, and peered between my legs. "The baby is coming," she said, her voice flat and final. "You will have to push it out."

"Is the child alive?"

She shook her head. "I do not believe so. But perhaps your gods will be merciful and allow it to take a breath."

I prayed again. Lying flat on the bed, my hand gripping Salama's wrist, I begged Adonai to show mercy to me and my unborn baby. The pain continued, but because I knew the governor had important people inside the palace, I locked my screams inside my teeth and stared at the ceiling, unable to watch the midwife or her blood-slick hands at work.

When Marcus finally burst into the chamber, I had no words for him. I could only grit my teeth against the pressure that threatened to rip me apart.

Marcus beheld the bloody bed linens and the fragile form in the midwife's hands.

"Your son," the woman told him, "has gone to live with the gods."

Her announcement, delivered so calmly, shattered me. I rolled onto my side and sobbed as Marcus sank to the mattress and cradled my head, his tears mingling with my own.

And though he did not speak of it, I knew what he was thinking. If Adonai, God of the Jews, was all-powerful and worthy of my exclusive worship, why hadn't He saved our baby?

Twenty-Six

PRIMA

News of the untimely birth reached us before sunset. Father's hands trembled as he lowered the sealed papyrus.

Hester clutched at his arm. "The baby?" She crumpled at his answering nod.

Though I attempted to appear as though I shared their grief, my heart danced at the news. After countless sacrifices and prayers, the goddess had *finally* responded to my curse tablet.

Mariana the Perfect had been found wanting. She was not an acceptable wife, and she would not be giving Marcus a son. The goddess had acted powerfully on my behalf, and the much-anticipated baby was no more.

During my weeks of waiting, Marcus had exhibited an almost unmanly excitement when he beheld Mariana in her expectant glory, so he would be crushed. And Memmius, who had already bragged about the potential for three generations of family governors in Achaia, would be keenly disappointed.

I excused myself and went to my chamber, where I found

Gilda mending one of my tunics. She read my expression and lifted her brows. "You have received good news?"

I flattened my smile. "Mariana's baby has died. And yes, I am not as grief-stricken as the others. Father had hoped the child would bind him to Memmius forever, but apparently the gods have other plans."

I dropped onto a couch and reached for my empty cup. "Fetch a pitcher of wine."

Gilda stood, her expression shifting from curiosity to disapproval. "You want to celebrate such news?"

I forced a smile. "Does wine not gladden the heart of the sorrowful?"

I was about to tell her to fetch it at once, but a sudden thought occurred. Marcus was grieving, and so was his household. Since I was now related to the entire family, I should offer my condolences.

I sat up. "Forget the wine. I wish to go out, so make me presentable. Do my hair and bring the scented oil—the one with fenugreek, marjoram, and sweet yellow clover."

Gilda sighed. "I do not know why you bother to dress in finery and put on perfumed oil; no one in the tavern is sober enough to notice."

"I am not going to the tavern, nor to the ludus," I said, winding a wayward curl around my finger. "I am going to pay my respects at the governor's palace."

❖

I stopped in the palace vestibule to ask the doorkeeper where I could find my brother-in-law. "I do not wish to disturb my sister, who needs to rest," I added, giving him what I hoped was a sad smile. "But despite the late hour, I would like to extend my condolences to Marcus. I will not stay long."

"The governor's son is in the lararium," the doorkeeper said. "I will have a slave escort you."

Mindful of Mariana's unusual concern for slaves, I gestured toward the door. "My handmaid waits outside with the litter bearers. Will you send someone with a cup of water for her?"

The burly man's eyebrows lifted, but then he clapped. When another slave appeared, he jerked his thumb toward Gilda, who waited outside in the torchlight. "Water," he said. "For all of them."

"I will summon another slave," he said, looking faintly apologetic as he turned, "to take you to the governor's son."

I smiled, reassured of my status within the governor's household.

A moment later I followed another slave to the lararium, where the scent of incense tinged the air. A niche, taller and wider than any I had ever seen, had been built into the wall, its interior elaborately painted with images of Jupiter, Aphrodite, and Mars. An altar stood at the back of the niche, supporting a brazier and a half dozen candles. Above the altar hung several death masks of the governor's ancestors, the wall's red paint gleaming through their hollow eyes.

"Every chain has a weak point," Cassia had told me, "so find it and stress it." Marcus was the weak link in his marriage. He and Mariana were both suffering, but he would be weaker than my stepsister.

I expected to find him standing before the altar, but Marcus lay prostrate on the floor, his elbows bent to support his head, his hands clasped in fervent prayer . . . to Jupiter, no doubt.

I dismissed the escort and walked forward, then knelt beside the man who would soon be my husband. "Marcus."

When he opened his eyes, startled, I placed my hand over my heart. "I have come to pray with you."

He took me at my word and resumed his prayers, his eyes closed and his lips moving soundlessly while I remained beside him and prayed to Aphrodite.

When he sighed, I lifted my head and gave him a sorrowful smile. "My heart has broken for you," I said, grateful for the soft glow of the candles. In their golden light, he might not notice that my eyes were as clear as spring water. "I have done nothing but weep since I heard the distressing news."

"The gods give, and the gods take away." A rueful smile twisted his mouth. He pushed himself up and sat crossed-legged on the tiles. "The physician said we will have other babies."

"Still." I lowered my hand to his bare arm. "I wish Mariana was stronger. I have heard Hester confess to losing several babies before my sister was born. The women from that family seem to inherit a weakness of the womb."

Marcus looked away, a dark tide creeping up his throat.

"Forgive me." I sighed. "I know men do not like to talk about women's matters. Men prefer to speak of war and politics and horses. My father is no exception." I tilted my head and sought his gaze. "Did you know I have seven uncles? My father's line is strong; their daughters give birth to healthy babies. I expect to bear a dozen children."

A groan rose from Marcus's throat—born from grief or frustration, I could not tell which.

"Again, I am sorry." I squeezed his wrist, hoping to leave a trace of my perfume on his skin. "If the gods are displeased with you, I hope you will do whatever is necessary to regain their favor."

With a small smile, I stood and left him alone to ponder my words.

Twenty-Seven

MARIANA

The knowledge that I would have a child introduced me to a new kind of joy . . . but when our son experienced birth and death in the same moment, I plumbed depths of grief I had never imagined.

Marcus grieved as well but would not express his feelings to me. I intuited most of them—not only did he grieve for his son, but he also felt as though he had failed his father by not providing Memmius with a grandson. That realization struck at his core, wounding the most vulnerable spot in his heart.

I suspected he remained silent to spare me pain, but nothing could intensify my loss. I felt as if there were cold hands on my heart, slowly twisting every trace of joy from it.

So we lived together, each of us wrapped in a cocoon of despair, individual shells of silence. We spoke only of trivial things and did not mention the loss we shared. What would be the purpose? I would want to talk about Adonai, but Marcus did not believe in Him.

While I poured my heart out before Adonai, Marcus spent hours praying to gods I did not know.

Neither of us received comfort. Despite my many prayers, I remained alone and sorrowful, sick with despair. Adonai had failed me.

As summer melted into autumn, Mother came every morning to sit with me. She would spin or do embroidery while I knelt by my couch and prayed or read copies of Paulos's epistles. Sometimes we would sit in the atrium, but neither the breathtaking mural nor the beautiful fish in the reflecting pool could soothe my ravaged heart. Grief had numbed my spirit, leaving me helpless to do anything but pray, breathe, and exist.

I would have spent those months in bed, but Mother's daily visit forced me to rise and greet her. But though she talked of various topics, her words seemed to hang in the air, never reaching me. I knew she meant well—everyone did, from Mother to Memmius, who visited me the night of my son's death, bowed his head, and said he did not blame me for "this accident of the gods."

Was it an accident? Was Adonai asleep while my unborn child perished?

My prayers tasted like gall. Even as I prayed, I knew my grief was nothing compared to the agony Yeshua endured to save sinful people, yet His agony was beyond my limited comprehension. My agony was human and sharp.

During the five months of my pregnancy, I had imagined a future revolving around my husband and my child. At the end of our first year of marriage, I would have held our son's hand as he toddled around the atrium pool. After two years, I would have assigned him a tutor so he would learn Latin, Aramaic, and Greek. After three years we would have taught him to ride a pony. After ten years, he would have been the image of his father, and after fifteen years, he would have donned the white *toga virilis* of manhood and joined Marcus in his work. After twenty years, Marcus would have found our son a wife, and a few years after that, we would have made time to play with our grandchildren . . .

But those dreams vanished the hour my son arrived, a blue-gray replica of what a child should be. Though the physician assured me I could have other children, I could not release my dreams for my firstborn.

How could any woman abandon such dreams? I had conceived a child that lived and moved within me. It was part of me, and when I lost my baby, I lost part of myself—a part I could never regain. Marcus did not know how that felt . . . and neither, I suspected, did Adonai. He had never lost a child.

One afternoon Mother and I were sitting in the atrium when one of the household slaves entered and knelt before me. "Excuse me, Domina, but a woman called Rachel is waiting in the vestibule. She asks for an audience."

I shook my head. "I do not wish to see anyone."

"Wait, pet." Mother leaned toward me, her eyes bright with compassion. "I asked Rachel to come."

"Whatever for?"

"She is a Jewish believer. I met her at the ecclesia, and she knows the holy Scriptures better than I do. I think she can comfort you in a way I cannot."

I did not want to be comforted, and, truth be told, I had grown weary of my mother's company. But she would be hurt if I did not see this woman, so I nodded at the slave. "Bring her in. But I am tired, so she must speak quickly and go."

Mother squeezed my arm as the slave hurried away. "Thank you. I know you are not in the mood for company."

I closed my eyes and pressed my hands to my empty belly. I did not look up until I heard the soft sounds of sandals scuffing the tile.

"Shalom," the woman said. She was plain, this Rachel, and near my mother's age. Her tanned skin and leathery hands indicated her lowly status, but her eyes shone with peace.

I did not return her greeting.

"Mariana." Mother's voice held a note of reproach. "Rachel has taken time away from her work to speak with us."

I gestured to a nearby chair. "Make yourself comfortable."

The woman sat and modestly tucked her feet beneath her tunic. "I have come, my lady," she began, "to offer condolences on the loss of your child. I have also lost a baby. Though each woman's loss is unique, I am somewhat familiar with what you are feeling."

I nodded, though I found it difficult to imagine that we had much in common. She had lost a son, but I had lost a son who would have become a Roman senator. The difference between us was immeasurable.

"I understand," she said, her voice dropping to a conspiratorial tone, "that you are a believer in Yeshua."

Uncertainty filled the woman's voice, so I nodded. "Yes. And I am struggling to understand how Yeshua could know what I am feeling. He was not a woman and He never carried a child. How can He understand this exquisite pain?"

Rachel slipped from the chair and sat on the floor at my feet. "Yeshua is God," she said, her face shining as though lit from within. "He was present when Adonai created the world, and through Yeshua all things were created—the animals, the plants, and our first parents, Adam and Eve. They were His children, and He lost them to sin. He understands more than you realize."

"But He did not actually *lose* them. They repented and died much later. I cannot understand why . . ." I looked away, unable to continue. I would be sobbing in a moment and did not want to lose control in front of a stranger.

Rachel's mouth curved in a soft smile. "Are you familiar with the account of King David and Bathsheba?"

I blinked, trying to remember if Paulos had ever mentioned the story. I glanced at Mother, who seemed as ignorant as I was.

"You will find it in the Jewish scriptures," Rachel said. "David was a man after God's own heart, and Adonai loved him greatly. But David lusted after a woman and took her. When she became pregnant, David had her husband killed so he could make her his wife. David married Bathsheba and longed to be happy with her, but Adonai said that as a result of David's sin, Bathsheba's baby would die."

"Horrible," I whispered, wondering why this woman felt I needed to hear this story.

"The baby was born and languished for days," Rachel continued. "David fasted, prayed, and put on sackcloth, but the Lord did not heal the child. When the child died, David dressed and called for his dinner. When his servants asked why he was not mourning, he replied, 'While the child was yet alive, I fasted and wept, for I thought, "Who knows? Adonai might be gracious to me and let the child live." But now that he has died, why should I fast? Can I bring him back again? It is I who will be going to him, but he will never return to me.'"

Her final words, echoing in the atrium, ignited a ball of

anger in my chest. "Why do you feel it necessary to remind me that my child will never return?"

Rachel shook her head. "You did not heed *all* my words. David said, 'It is I who will be going to him . . .' At the end of this life, my lady, you will go to your son, who is waiting for you. He is an innocent, and you are a believer in Yeshua. So though you mourn him today, one day you will see him and shout with joy. Those who trust in the goodness of Adonai will not be disappointed."

I looked at Mother to see her reaction to the story, and her eyes were shimmering with unshed tears. She had drawn comfort from Rachel's account . . . and since it came from the Jewish holy writings, Paulos, if he were here, might have chosen the same words of comfort.

"Though you are grieving, Adonai has not left you alone," Rachel said, a smile trembling over her lips. "He is also known as *Yaweh Shammah*, which means *the God who is there*, and as *El Roi, the God who sees*. He is here, and He sees you. Always."

I grasped at those assurances and held them tightly. As I clung to the holy names of my God, my indignation and despair began to melt away.

"Adonai is the author and giver of life," Rachel said, looking directly into my eyes. "You have trusted Yeshua with *your* life, so why do you hesitate to trust Him with your son's?"

Why? Because I was selfish. Because I wanted my son with *me*.

"I have another reminder for you," Rachel said, her voice brimming with compassion. "From the words of Yeshua himself. Speaking of those who have died, Yeshua said that Adonai is 'God not of the dead but of the living, for to Him they all are living.'" She smiled. "Your son is not dead. He is living with God."

A thrill shivered through my senses. My little boy . . . was alive. With Yeshua. What better place could there be?

A cry of relief broke from my lips. "Thank you," I said, reaching for Rachel's hands. "You have given me hope."

Rachel blushed. "Our hope lies in Yeshua."

With a shiver of vivid recollection, I whispered words from Paulos's last letter to our ecclesia: "If we have hoped in Messiah in this life alone, we are to be pitied more than all people. For since death came through a man, the resurrection of the dead also has come through a Man. For as in Adam all die, so also in Messiah will all be made alive."

"Yes." Rachel squeezed my hand. "Our life on earth is only a season. The best is yet to come."

A sob rose in my throat, preventing further speech. So I patted Rachel's hand, smiling in teary gratitude as Mother stood to escort her out.

"I will leave you now," Mother said, bending to kiss me on both cheeks. "Know that I am praying for you and trusting in the goodness of Adonai."

I watched the women depart, tears spilling over my cheeks in an overflow of emotion. I believed every word from Rachel's lips, but my heart had been severely battered by grief. Healing would take time.

For me . . . and for Marcus. I wanted to share everything I had heard with him, but if he did not believe in Yeshua, what assurance and comfort could he find?

Twenty-Eight

PRIMA

I was still abed, my eyelids heavy from the effects of a late night spent visiting a tavern and the ludus, when Gilda shook me. "Domina, you must rise and dress."

I opened one eye and glared at her. "I will have you beaten if you touch me again."

She backed away, arms raised. "But, Domina, Marcus is here and waiting to speak to your father. Do you not want to see him?"

I sat up, instantly awake. "Marcus is *here*?"

She nodded.

"Without Mariana?"

"Yes."

I shook my head. "He probably comes on business. The governor must be traveling."

"Marcus has never come to this house on business; he has always summoned your father to the palace."

Gilda might be a slave, but she was no fool. Marcus would not come here unless he wished to discuss something personal . . . like Mariana. Or me.

"Do not stand there, slave, get my tunic! I will wear the one with gold trim."

Gilda opened my trunk and rummaged through garments while I staggered to the pitcher and basin. I splashed my face, gasping as the cold water struck my heated skin. I had to appear calm, as though I had spent the morning . . . I turned to my handmaid. "What excuse did you give my father at morning prayers?"

"I said you were praying," she answered, not looking up, "for your stepsister."

"Good."

Gilda helped me into my tunic, put leather slippers on my feet, and draped a palla around my neck and shoulders. She smoothed my hair and pinned it up, then stepped back and judged my appearance with a critical eye. "Not the best you've looked, but not the worst either."

"It will have to do."

I left my chamber and hurried toward Father's office. Before entering, I stopped in the hallway to calm myself with deep breaths. I could hear Marcus's voice and the deep rumble of Father's reply. Rather than rushing ahead, I decided to see if I could learn why Marcus had come.

I crept closer, positioning myself just outside the door. A slave walked by and gave me a curious look, but I ignored him. A woman could do as she pleased in her father's house, as long as her father approved. But my father, thank the gods, had no idea what I had been doing of late. Unless . . .

Panic tingled my shoulder blades and crept down my spine. Had Marcus come to tell my father about what I implied the last time I visited the palace? Or had he heard about my late-night adventures?

I had returned to the ludus several times, not to watch the games, but to see Atrox. I had learned many things during my time at the goddess's temple, and now when I visited Atrox I did not play the part of victim, but victor.

Soon I would wield my power over Marcus as well.

I pressed my ear to the door and thrilled to the sound of his voice.

"I am concerned about Mariana," Marcus was saying. "She has not fully recovered from her grief, and I want to lift her spirits. I would like to take her to our family villa outside Rome, but I wanted to ask your opinion first. Would this truly please her, or would she miss her mother too much?"

Father cleared his throat. "I have not had an opportunity to personally tell you how sorry I am," he said, "but I was grief-stricken to learn of your loss. Perhaps—and I hope I am not out of line to suggest this—you should set Mariana aside. Any man whose wife cannot carry a child should consider divorce. You would not be left alone. I could offer my other daughter, Prima, who is strong and healthy. She would serve you well."

I caught my breath. Would Marcus avail himself of this opportunity? Roman men thought nothing of divorcing their wives and often gave no reason.

I waited, hearing nothing but the rapid beat of my heart, then Marcus answered. "Thank you for your suggestion," he said, "but I pledged my loyalty to Mariana, and I am not willing to renounce that pledge."

"Not yet," Father answered, a smile in his voice. "But time might change your mind. If she loses another baby—"

"Gods forbid," Marcus said, his voice flat. "But what say you to the idea of taking Mariana away? I think the country air would do her good."

"She is your wife," Father answered, a hair of irritation in his voice, "for as long as you will have her, but I think you should remain in Corinth. Mariana will want to stay close to her family, and we want to be close to her."

I closed my eyes and sighed. Good. My clever father would keep Marcus from leaving the city. He would remain at the palace with his mournful wife, and I would be able to visit him.

Furthermore, I noted with some surprise, Father had apparently abandoned Mariana's cause. Now he was firmly on my side and would remain so as long as Mariana did not produce an heir.

Aphrodite be praised—she had arranged everything for my benefit.

Twenty-Nine

MARIANA

Four months after the death of our son, the emperor summoned Memmius to Rome. He would travel to the imperial city during the cold, wet days of December, leaving Marcus and me alone in the palace. My husband would face another test, and I would do my best to support him.

We waited on the marble steps, shivering in the damp air, as the guard assembled for the journey.

"Son." Memmius gripped Marcus's shoulders, his eyes crinkling with concern. "If you have any problems while I am away, send a letter by the *cursus publicus*. I will receive it within two days."

"I do not anticipate any problems." Marcus gave his father a weary smile. "Go to Rome, speak to the Senate, accomplish all the emperor asks of you. And do not worry. I will take care of everything here."

"Feel free to call on the chief magistrate if you need advice," Memmius said. "Narkis is eager to be of service." My father-in-law's gaze settled on me. "And do not forget to take care of your beautiful wife."

"I would never forget that."

I returned my father-in-law's smile, grateful for his affection and support.

Marcus squared his shoulders as his father climbed into the *carpentum*, a luxurious closed carriage that would take him to the port, from whence he would sail to Rome. We did not know how long he would be away.

A guard closed the carriage door and signaled the mounted escorts at the head of the caravan. With shouts and the click-clack of horses' hooves, the governor's party set off, leaving Marcus and me as interim master and mistress of Achaia.

Turning me to face him, Marcus linked his arms behind my back. "Well," he said, giving me an indulgent smile, "how does it feel to be domina of an entire province?"

"Not good," I admitted. "I would much prefer to be domina in one ordinary house."

"Which house would that be?"

I slipped my head into the cozy space between his chin and chest. "The one in which you live."

I shivered as the rising wind brushed my cheeks with the touch of icy fingers. Marcus held me tighter as we watched the horizon swallow up the carpentum, then we climbed the steps and returned to our chamber.

Though Memmius had not given us many details about the purpose of his trip, several rumors from Rome had reached Corinth. Nero, who inherited the throne at age sixteen, had been a reasonable ruler in the early years of his reign, but people attributed his common sense and practicality to the steadying influence of his mother, Agrippina. But the year before Marcus and I were married, the emperor had Agrippina murdered, and Memmius now feared our emperor was no longer listening to his advisors.

Weeks ago, we heard that a Roman senator, Lucius Pedanius Secundus, had been murdered by a mistreated slave. The penalty for killing one's master was death, but in order to stanch the possibility of a slave revolt, the Senate would soon vote on whether or not to execute *all* of Pedanius's four hundred slaves. Marcus suspected that Memmius and several other provincial governors had been recalled to Rome to vote on the fate of the imprisoned slaves. Far more slaves than masters lived in Rome, and if the slaves revolted . . .

I shook the possibility of a bloodbath out of my head. I had seen too much blood in recent months and harbored too many thoughts about death.

My father-in-law had been nothing but kind during the months following the loss of our child. And though I no longer struggled to get out of bed each morning, a hollow feeling still occupied the center of my chest. Mother assured me the feeling would go away when Adonai again opened my womb, but at that moment I had no baby and only a sliver of hope. Marcus and I wanted to conceive again, but month after month my courses flowed, and Adonai delayed His answer to my prayers.

"I have a meeting with the city council," Marcus said, releasing me in the vestibule. "Would you like me to greet Narkis for you?"

"Please do. Also give my regards to my dear friends Titius Justus and his wife. I will be reading in my chamber if you need me."

"I always do," he said. "But today I will let you rest."

He hurried away, followed by his amanuensis and a pair of guards. I turned, nodding to Salama, and together we

235

climbed the stairs. I was about to go to our living quarters but paused to glance into Marcus's office. He must have left the room in a hurry because a bottle of ink sat unstoppered on the desk, and a letter lay unfinished. Quietly shaking my head, I inserted the cork into the bottle of ink, then glanced at my husband's correspondence.

The letter, addressed to his father, gave me pause. If he wanted to address something with Memmius, why didn't he handle the matter before his father departed?

I skimmed the writing:

> *You asked if I had misgivings about my choice of a wife. While the loss of our child grieved me deeply, it grieved Mariana as well, and I do not fault her for it. Narkis suggested that I divorce her and take his other daughter to wife, but . . .*

❖

My stomach twisted. Narkis had suggested that Marcus *divorce* me? My stepfather had been pleased with our marriage, so why would he change his mind?

The answer came to me at once: he had another daughter. Narkis would only change his mind if Prima was available to take my place.

And she was. Marcus and I had been married for months, but Prima had not yet been betrothed.

Comprehension seeped through my shock. Of course Narkis would suggest Prima. She was his blood and far more like him than I was. And though it pained me to admit it, I was certain Prima coveted my position. Narkis was not actively seeking a husband for her, so they were

236

biding their time, hoping and praying my marriage would fail.

I drew a deep breath and slowly exhaled. Marcus had not finished this letter, so the governor had not heard these thoughts . . . unless Marcus spoke to him before I joined them in the vestibule. Or Marcus might have decided to wait and send the letter by post because of its sensitive subject matter. He might not want to speak of divorce in the palace. With so many slaves in the house, all of them capable of eavesdropping, the news could easily reach my ears. A letter, on the other hand, could be vouchsafed with relative security.

I lowered the letter and braced myself for the possibility that Marcus might be planning to end our marriage. He did not behave like a man intent on divorce, but perhaps he meant to keep me in the dark while he laid his plans . . .

Adonai, what does this mean?

I lowered myself into the chair. Had I made a mistake? I agreed to the marriage because God had given me peace, but perhaps I mistook my longing for love as God's shalom. Had I been so blinded by my own desire that I missed the will of Adonai?

Narkis had pressured me, but he would have been equally as happy if Marcus had chosen Prima. My stepfather's first concern was pleasing the governor. After I failed to deliver the governor's grandson, his plan might have changed, but not his goal: he still aimed to please the governor above all else.

So did Marcus. His father was away, Marcus was being tested, and the governor wanted a grandson.

But what did my husband want? *Narkis suggested that I divorce her and take his other daughter to wife, but . . .*

My marriage was hanging by an unfinished thought.

———————❖———————

At first, I resolved to pretend I had not seen Marcus's letter. I would have been wise to keep that resolution, but knowledge of the letter twisted and turned inside me, leaving me unable to read or rest or even converse with Salama.

In an effort to control my frantic imagination, I opened the latest epistle from Paulos, but reading brought me no peace. So I opened the scroll written by Mark, one of the books that had recently arrived from Judea. The words of Yeshua distracted me from my troubling thoughts, but the moment I set the scroll aside, my insecurities returned.

Noticing that I was upset, Salama was unusually quiet as she dressed me for dinner—until she could no longer remain silent. "Are you well, Domina?" She frowned into my looking brass as she sewed pearls into my hair. "You seem troubled."

I shrugged, for though she knew most of my secrets, I did not want to share this one, especially if it amounted to nothing. "I am probably being foolish." I smiled in an attempt to change the subject. "Who has been invited to tonight's banquet?"

"Your mother and stepfather," she said, "and Prima, of course, along with all the city council members. The cook mentioned priests from the temples of Asclepius and Aphrodite, and Marcus has invited a sculptor who wants to create a statue in Memmius's honor. He wants your husband to sit for him after dinner."

"Why? Memmius is broad, and Marcus slim."

Salama smiled. "The sculptor says the resemblance is close enough to satisfy his requirements. I know nothing of sculpting, but I daresay the governor would rather have a slender statue than a true representation."

I shook my head. "I never imagined being daughter-in-law to a man whose likeness would stand in the center of Corinth."

"I am sure Memmius never dreamed he would be father-in-law to a woman like you." Salama sewed the last pearl into my hair, knotted the thread, and stepped back. "You are ready."

I picked up the looking brass and beheld my face, which seemed older and sadder than I remembered it.

Because Marcus wanted to affirm his father's reputation as a generous host, he had invited Corinth's leading citizens to a feast. At the beginning of our marriage, I would have been delighted to serve as hostess at a banquet as grand as the one that awaited me. With Marcus at my side, I would have enjoyed meeting strangers, knowing that he would provide the cues I needed to correctly identify and greet my guests. But would Marcus remain by my side tonight, or would he drift toward Prima?

I thanked Salama for her help, put on my slippers, and went to the top of the stairs. From my elevated position I could see that ornate guest couches had been situated throughout the enormous dining hall, candles burned on stands against the walls, and a dozen slaves stood ready to stir the air with huge feather fans. As the air moved throughout the room, an overhead net of hothouse rose petals would sway, gently raining on the diners.

The guests had already begun to arrive. I looked down on the sea of enthusiastic faces and wondered if any of them knew of Narkis's intention—when they looked at me, did they see a rejected woman? Though they smiled and nodded, did they laugh at me when they turned away?

Marcus loves you. The voice inside my head spoke firmly. *Did he not say so earlier today?*

But he did not say he loved me. He promised to take care of me . . . something he could do even if he set me aside.

I looked around—where was my husband? He should be with me; we should walk into the banquet together. But I had no idea where he was.

I drew a deep breath and realized I had a choice—I could stand at the top of the stairs all night like a coward, or I could go down alone, assuming my position as mistress of the house. Which action would win my husband's respect?

In the hollow of my back, a single drop of perspiration traced the length of my spine. Then, with my heart thumping against my ribs, I walked down the stairs. Smiling stiffly, I moved through the rose-scented air and sat on my husband's couch, nodding at the guests who came over to greet me.

Then Marcus appeared, smiling broadly and carrying a cup of wine. He sat next to me and people rushed forward, friends and sycophants, to fawn over my husband. While I acknowledged their overgenerous praise with a nod, Marcus beamed, thrusting out his arms and inviting his audience to eat, drink, and eat again.

I spotted Prima almost at once. She wore a simple tunic and elaborate jewelry that sparkled on her arms and at her neck. Her hair dripped with jewels, and heavy earrings dangled from her earlobes and brushed her shoulders. She stood with a woman I did not recognize—a tall creature who moved with a quiet air of authority. Prima did not look in my direction, but frequently smiled and whispered in her companion's ear.

I looked away, not wanting Prima to dominate my thoughts. Perhaps she did not know what Narkis had suggested. I did not think she could be completely ignorant of his intention, but I should not blame her for her father's actions.

After a sharp trumpet blast, slaves marched forward with large platters destined for stands scattered throughout the room. The cooks had prepared roasted boar, honeyed dormice, and stuffed peacocks, complete with fanned tail feathers that bobbed with every movement of the scented air. Several serving trays offered exotic flavored breads, while other slaves walked among the guests with pitchers of the finest wines.

I sipped from my glass, but Marcus drank freely, perhaps a little too eager to enjoy his temporary promotion. As I nibbled from passing platters and observed the guests, I hoped Memmius would not be angry when he received the list of expenses for this affair.

When Narkis approached with my mother, I found it difficult to meet my stepfather's gaze. I nodded at his greeting and looked away, afraid he would see the knowledge of his treachery reflected in my eyes. Did fidelity, sacred vows, and mutual responsibility mean nothing to him?

As Narkis spoke with Marcus, I tilted my head and studied the older man. I had always assumed Mother married him because she needed someone to provide for her, but I was no longer sure of her reasons. Perhaps she worried about her reputation as a woman alone . . . or perhaps she realized a woman needed a protector. If she had not married Narkis, she would have returned to her family to live under the authority of her younger brother. And though I knew my uncle only slightly, I understood why she would not want to be under the thumb of a pompous fool.

As the wine flowed, the food disappeared, and the guests grew less restrained, I became increasingly anxious. "Husband"—I touched Marcus's arm—"may I be excused? I have grown weary of these excessive delights."

He looked at me, his brows lifting. "I will not be much longer," he said, leaning closer. "I will come to you after I have spoken to the sculptor."

Would he?

I stood and crossed the crowded dining chamber, but a friendly voice stopped me. "Mariana?"

I turned to see Titius Justus, a council member and friend, looking up at me from the couch he shared with his wife, Aurora. Her enthusiastic smile faded, however, when her gaze met mine. She rose and pulled me toward her ample bosom. "What is wrong, love?" She pitched her voice for my ears alone. "What troubles you?"

Something in her voice made me want to spill all my worries and fears, but I could not speak freely at a public banquet.

"Thank you for your concern." I pulled away and attempted to smile. "I cannot talk now, but would you pray for me?"

She nodded, concern and confusion mingling in her dark eyes. "We will," she said, squeezing my hand. "Tonight, Titius and I will lift prayers for you to Adonai's throne."

Afraid I would burst into tears, I hurried away to my chamber. Salama helped me undress, then slipped my chemise over my head. I crawled into bed and closed my eyes, ready for sleep that did not come.

The palace had gone silent by the time I heard our chamber door open. I lifted my head and saw my husband's silhouette in the lamplight from the hallway. "Marcus?"

"Are you asleep?"

"No." I leaned over and lit the lamp on the bedside table.

"Ah." My husband sank to the mattress and groaned as Jason entered and removed his sandals. "Go," he said, waving the slave away. "I want to be alone with my wife."

When Jason had departed, Marcus turned toward me. "You looked beautiful tonight," he said, his lips grazing my neck. "I would have come earlier, but there were people to acknowledge and words to be said."

"I understand," I said, withdrawing from the touch of his lips. "And yes, there *are* words to be said. Words I do not want to speak, but I must."

He pushed himself upright, his eyes searching my face. "What words?"

Even though an inner voice urged me to remain silent, my fears came tumbling out. "I saw the letter on your desk—the letter to your father. I do not know why you did not send it, but I could not believe Narkis advised you to divorce me and marry Prima. Since you mentioned the matter in your letter, you must have considered Narkis's suggestion—"

"You read my letter?"

Anxiety spurted through me when Marcus pulled away, his eyes flashing. "Why were you in my office?"

Heat flooded my face. "I did not intend to read it, but I saw the open ink bottle and thought to tidy your desk. The letter was in front of me, practically begging to be noticed."

"And now you are sorry you read it."

"I am sorry you considered divorcing me. I am sorry my

stepfather suggested the idea. And I am *very* sorry he thinks Prima would make you happy. She is completely different from me, so if she could make you happy, clearly I have made you *unhappy*."

"By all the gods, I will never understand the mind of a woman!"

Marcus stood, shoved his feet into his sandals, and strode to the door. There he turned. "As you noticed, I did not send the letter, nor have I made any plans to divorce you. But to know you thought I would—or could—now causes me to wonder if we are as well suited as I thought."

I reached for him, anguish searing my soul. "Marcus, I am sorry. I should not have doubted you, but to read your words on the page . . . was unnerving."

"Good night, wife." He spoke not with anger, but with weariness as he reached for the door. "Tonight we will sleep alone, and tomorrow we will agree never to speak of this again."

Thirty

PRIMA

Father, Hester, and I stood outside the governor's palace waiting for our litter bearers. My father was talking with another magistrate, a conversation from which we women were pointedly excluded.

"I am ready for bed," Hester said, unsuccessfully stifling a yawn. "I had no idea a banquet could continue so long."

I snorted softly, wondering if she realized that half the guests had visited the vomitorium to empty their stomachs and eat again. My stepmother had been the picture of moderation: picking at the food, drinking only one cup of wine, and generally remaining quiet unless someone addressed her. Father, on the other hand, enjoyed himself immensely, eating, drinking, and gossiping with other city leaders. Information gleaned at such banquets, I knew, could prove useful if he needed an advantage over an opponent.

While Father played politics, Cassia and I reclined on a couch and greeted those who addressed us. I ate like a lady, drank only a wee bit more than I should have, and smiled at any man who looked in my direction. If Marcus noticed me, he would have seen a woman who could make guests feel at ease in any situation, a woman who would bring him honor. The perfect politician's wife.

Cassia left early, and when no one approached to take her place at my side, I leaned back and studied my handsome brother-in-law. Obviously delighted with his new responsibilities, he reveled in the part of generous host until the hour grew late, then he took his leave and went to meet a sculptor who had been engaged to create a statue of Memmius. "But Marcus will not sit tonight," Father told me, slurring his words. "The hour is late, and the young man is weary."

I might have followed Marcus, but common sense overruled the idea. What could I say to him in front of a sculptor?

Yet as we waited for the litter bearers, I saw Marcus stumble down the palace steps, his face turned toward the outbuildings. Where was he going at this hour?

"Tell Father I went to see Marcus," I told Hester. Knowing Father would not question me, I took off, my slippers barely skimming the paving stones. I followed Marcus around the side of the main building and down an alley, then caught the scent of horses and manure. A barn stood in the courtyard, and torchlight shone through the open doorway. I darted forward and spotted Marcus inside a stall, his head down. What was he doing? No one went riding at this hour.

Realization struck in that instant. He should have been in bed with his wife, but he was not. Surely that was all that mattered.

Great Aphrodite, goddess of desire, empower me now . . .

I crept forward, moving soundlessly over the pavement. Marcus must have been planning to go for a ride. He had saddled a horse and was struggling with a strap.

"Do you need help?" At the stall's gate, I braced my arm on a beam so that my sleeve dropped, exposing the pale flesh of my shoulder. "You should summon a slave."

He startled, recognized me, and turned back to the horse. "The slaves are asleep."

"How fortunate for us."

I met his narrowed eyes with a smile and stepped into the stall, then took his hand and tugged him away from the stallion. "Let me help," I said, inhaling the aromas of wine and incense. He tried to push me away, but I moved closer.

"I do not need your—"

"Yes, you do."

My time with Atrox had not been wasted. If I had been an innocent girl, I would not know what to do, but the gladiator and Aphrodite had taught me well.

"I think," I whispered, leaning forward until my lips brushed his ear, "you do not need to go riding. You are too drunk, and the hour is too late. What if you fell off the horse? With no guards and no slave in attendance, no one would help you. Better to remain where you are . . . with me."

Marcus swayed on his feet. "Prima. It is not proper—you should not be here."

"Who can say what is proper?" I pressed myself against him. "I have also had too much to drink, but who could blame me? The banquet was festive, and my host *most* charming." When he retreated, I wrapped my arms around his waist, pushing him back until his shoulders hit the wall. The stallion whickered uneasily.

I ran my palms over Marcus's chest, but he caught my hands and turned to evade my lips. "You should not be here."

"Neither should you," I answered, interlacing my fingers

with his. I smiled at our entwined hands. "You should be with your wife, but you are not. And see how perfectly we fit together? The son of the governor and the true daughter of the chief magistrate. We should have been married months ago, but you were bewitched. Mariana's God blinded you, but it is not too late to correct your mistake."

My mouth covered his, and for a moment his hands gripped mine so tightly I winced. He had been seized by some emotion—I could not tell if it was anger or passion—and when I tried to pull free, his fingers imprisoned mine.

"By all the gods," I said, catching my breath, "your ardor surprises me."

"It is not ardor," he said, pushing me away, "but frustration. I do not understand women."

I laughed and blocked his escape. "Women are not so difficult to understand. We are made to give and receive love and pleasure, to bear children and ensure that our husbands are honored in the afterlife. If you want those things from me, you have only to ask."

I stepped forward and laced my hands around his neck, intending to pull him into the straw, but he shoved me aside and staggered toward the gate.

"Go home, Prima," he called, his voice vibrant with what might have been passion. "By all the gods, leave me alone!" He slammed the gate and strode away.

Knowing I would not find victory in that hour, I sank into the straw and let him go. The stallion swung his head and gave me a dark look. I moved away from the beast's powerful legs, then spied a gleaming object beside the horse's hoof.

Moving slowly lest I spook the giant beast, I reached through the straw. I found a piece of jewelry, but not just any piece of adornment. Marcus had been wearing the governor's signet ring, the seal with which the senator signed letters and official documents. Marcus had worn it as his father's proxy and *should* wear it until his father returned.

But now he could not.

I slipped the ring over my thumb. Then, smiling in silent gratitude to Aphrodite, I slipped past the nervous stallion and walked to the front of the barn where all had gone quiet. When I reached the steps of the palace, I saw that my father's litter bearers had disappeared. Mine waited by the steps, as patient as statues.

I strode toward them, feeling relaxed, confident, and invincible.

Thirty-One

MARIANA

Two days after the governor's departure, Marcus burst into our bedchamber, his eyes wild and his face pearled with perspiration. "I cannot find it," he said, raking his hands through his hair. "I need it to sign documents, but I do not know if I have lost or misplaced it."

I gaped at him. "I am sorry, but I have never been good at riddles."

He looked at me as if I had suddenly grown stupid. "I cannot find my father's signet ring. I had it at the banquet; I remember showing it to Narkis. But now I cannot find it, and I cannot authorize a single action without it."

I clenched my jaw, finding it far too easy to remember the details of the banquet and its aftermath.

"My slaves would have let me know if they found the ring," I said. "But they have said nothing."

"Are you certain? I must have been wearing it when I came here after the banquet. The room was dark, so I might have dropped it or set it on a table."

"The slaves clean this room every day, and no one has seen

251

it. Perhaps it slipped off your finger. Your hands are not as thick as your father's, so—"

"The slaves have swept under the bed? Looked through your trunks? If one of them has stolen it, I will have the culprit beaten and sold."

"My slaves have thoroughly cleaned, but I will ask them to look for the ring. I myself will search, not only this room, but every step from the triclinium to this chamber. Where did you go when you left me?"

He placed his hands on his hips, then shook his head. "I will have the slaves search the entire house," he finally said, a vein rising in his forehead. "If I cannot find it, I will have the jeweler make a copy."

I wanted to ask if he had memorized the design but thought it wiser to remain silent.

Without being told, I knew Memmius would be horrified to know his signet ring had disappeared. What if someone sent the emperor a letter sealed with that ring? What if someone authorized a legal action or ordered goods or summoned a legion of soldiers in the governor's name? Losing the ring was a small thing, but the consequences could be catastrophic. A copy of the ring would help in the short term—Marcus would be able to sign documents and orders—but a replica would do nothing to stop the actions of a thief who wished to impersonate the governor.

Marcus's words kept coming back to me: *"If I do not fulfill my father's expectations, he will feel that I have been a waste of his time."*

In the days that followed, I moved through the palace on tiptoe, trying not to disturb my husband, pry into his affairs, or add to the stress of his work on the governor's behalf. I kept busy overseeing the household slaves, inviting guests for the evening meal, checking the menu, and approving foods purchased at the market. Dinner, served after sunset, was never a simple affair. Merchants, procurators, and *aediles* from throughout the province had to be served and complimented, entertainment had to be arranged and compensated, and the meals had to be the most spectacular in Asia.

And though the slaves searched the house from basement to attic, no one found the missing signet ring.

"I did find this," Salama said one morning, handing me a lump of metal. "Someone placed it beneath your mattress."

I studied the odd object. It appeared to be a coil of thin gold, pierced with an iron nail. "It was in *my* bedchamber?"

Salama gave me a grim smile. "It is a curse tablet, Domina. Undoubtedly made for you."

I pushed the object away. "It has probably been under that mattress for years. Throw it out."

"But, Domina . . . are you not concerned that someone wishes you ill?"

I hesitated. The thought that someone might have invoked the power of demons to curse me was terrifying, but . . .

"'For I am convinced,'" I said, recalling a portion of Paulos's letter to the ecclesia in Rome, "'that neither death nor life, nor angels nor principalities, nor things present nor things to come, nor powers, nor height nor depth, nor any curse tablet will be able to separate me from the love of God that is in Messiah *Yeshua* my Lord.'"

Salama gave me a crooked smile. "So you are not afraid?"

I shook my head, feeling far braver than I had a moment before. "I am not."

"Then I will throw out this worthless thing."

While I tended to the household, Marcus rose early, spent his mornings tending to correspondence, and visited the baths before the midday meal. Afterward he met with council members, where he listened to conflicting recommendations from various officials, each with his own political ambitions.

Though Marcus had said we would not speak again of the difficulty between us, he stopped sleeping in our bedchamber, retiring instead to his office, where I suspected he read official parchments until he fell asleep on the couch. I often crept out to see him, but he was rarely awake when I peeked into his office. His personal slave would open the door so I could see that he was well, but when I asked if I could enter, Jason said Marcus had asked him to make sure he would not be disturbed. The answer stung because never before had Marcus considered me a disturbance.

My mind began to embroider the difficulty between us. Perhaps Marcus's reason for eluding me had grown beyond the letter to his father. Perhaps I had become not only a disturbance, but a visible reminder of the grief we still felt and the loss we could never forget. Perhaps he had begun to regret our marriage.

I did not know how to restore my husband's affection for me, and I had no friend to ask for help. Assuming that time had healed my grief, Mother had stopped her daily visits. Salama had never been married, so she was no help, and my friends from the ecclesia did not want to visit the palace. For comfort, I had only Adonai and Paulos, so I spent most of my days in prayer or reading my scrolls.

The only good to come out of those dark days was the knowledge that Salama had decided to believe in Yeshua.

One night, as I prepared to climb into my lonely bed, Salama looked at me with a question in her eyes. "Yes?" I asked.

"Domina"—a frown appeared between her brows—"I have never heard you curse Prima, and we both know she would be happy to take your husband from you. Why do you not curse her?"

I blew out a breath. "I am not Prima's creator, so I do not have the right to judge her, only Adonai does. And Yeshua said we should pray for our enemies . . . even bless them." I shook my head. "Sometimes it is not easy to pray for Prima, but still I try."

Salama sucked at the inside of her cheek for a moment, her forehead creasing. "You do not buy curse tablets or pay a priest to curse your enemies."

"No one who truly follows Yeshua would do such a thing."

"So even if your enemy wounds you, you would not curse her."

I shook my head.

"Even if she takes your husband."

I cut a sharp look toward my handmaid. Did she know something I did not? But Salama's gaze remained clear.

"If Prima takes my husband—" my voice broke, but I forced myself to continue—"if she takes Marcus, I would be heartbroken. But I would trust that Adonai had another plan for me." I looked away, remembering my frantic prayers in Narkis's house. "In fact, before the marriage, I asked Adonai to stop the betrothal if I was proceeding against His will. I love my husband, but Adonai holds first claim on my life. He is my Lord and Master."

When I lifted my gaze, I found Salama studying me, her

eyes alive with calculation. "This Adonai . . . would He listen to a slave?"

"Of course. He listens to everyone."

"A slave can worship Him?"

"Yes. Though he is a Roman citizen, my friend Paulos writes that he is a slave to Adonai."

A corner of Salama's mouth curved upward. "Your Adonai," she said, her voice firm, "He must be the true God."

"How do you know?"

She folded her arms. "Because He is the only God who asks His followers to do what they cannot do without His help."

I did not know what to make of her answer, but as the cold month of Ianuarius bore down on us, I thanked Adonai for Salama's company. During those lonely days, she joined me as I prayed at the governor's lararium and in the privacy of my bedchamber.

And in her prayers, lifted from an eager and submissive heart, I found comfort in the knowledge that I was not alone in my season of grief.

Thirty-Two

PRIMA

Father must have wondered why my morning prayers had increased in length and fervor, but he did not know that Aphrodite had begun to answer my petitions. In response, I increased my devotion to the goddess, visiting her mountaintop temple every day.

"Aphrodite, daughter of Zeus," I prayed one afternoon, "hear my prayer. Let the sun fall on my love's skin and let him desire me as I desire him. Remove the impediments that stand between us and draw him to me as a flower draws a bee. When we are united, bless our union with children. May my womb abound with fertility and my breasts with sweet milk. May I raise strong sons to honor their mother and father. Bind Marcus to me with deathless love and passion . . ."

I hesitated, momentarily running out of words. Yet my heart overflowed with gratitude, so Aphrodite had to know how grateful I was.

The goddess had cursed my stepsister's unborn child, caused strife in Mariana's marriage, and allowed Marcus and me to be briefly alone together. My ultimate aim was finally within reach, and I would win Marcus within the year. Yet I had to proceed with caution because my plan was not without risk. "Love without risk," Cassia once told me, "is like pleasure without pain."

When the month of Ianuarius arrived, I rededicated myself to the goal of becoming Marcus's wife. I would, I told Gilda, be an example of the perfect Roman matron.

She lifted a copper brow. "Truly?"

"Watch me."

I stopped drinking and did not visit the tavern. No longer did Gilda have to glance around like a frightened rabbit when we ventured out into the streets.

But I did not stop visiting the ludus. Atrox—and my encounters with him—were a necessary part of my plan.

I was not planning to see Atrox on the afternoon Father invited me to join him at the arena. We sat in the administrator's box, and I wore a veil in case Atrox happened to appear on the sands.

The first contest featured several inexperienced gladiators against a pack of wild dogs.

"What do you think?" Father gestured toward the sand. "Too bloody for you?"

I averted my eyes, unable to stand the sight of dying dogs. "I think Corinth should increase the quality of its animals. They say Nero imports lions, hyenas, and bears. How can we expect people to be entertained by mongrel hounds?"

Father grinned and patted my arm. "This is only the opening round. The good fighters will appear later."

We watched a pair of gladiatrices, and even Father was dissatisfied with the bout. "The women do not fight to the death?" He leaned sideways to speak to a council member seated behind him. "Watching women slap each other with wooden swords is not entertaining."

"You must understand," the council member said, "the *lanista* does not want his females to die before they are skilled enough to reach Rome. They must learn, so they can live to fight another day."

Father looked at me. "What say you, Prima? Are you content to watch a training exercise?"

I gave him a wry smile. "I am. After all, dying requires neither courage nor talent."

Father chuckled. "Well spoken, my dear."

Though I took pains to maintain my composure, my heart leapt into the back of my throat when Atrox sauntered into the arena, followed by a burly Thracian known as Pollux. "Pollux will be victorious," Father announced, gripping the edge of his toga as the two men saluted those in the administrator's box.

Father, who was acting administrator for the day, gave the order to commence. The two men circled each other, and Pollux, who wore leather armor only on his arm and shoulder, seemed lighter on his feet than Atrox. He danced over the sand, armed with a net in one hand and a trident in the other. I recognized the three-pronged spear from statues of Neptune, god of the sea.

I leaned toward Father. "Why do you think Pollux will win?"

Father gestured to the bloodstained sand. "Atrox has outlived his popularity, and he knows it. Pollux is the new favorite, which gives him an advantage."

"I fail to see how popularity could settle the contest between two warriors."

Father gave me the smile one gives an ignorant child. "Pollux is playing the part of a fisherman, and Atrox is the helpless fish. If thrown properly, the fisherman's net will bind Atrox, freeing Pollux to strike."

I watched, my heart twisting as Father's prediction proved true. The length of Pollux's spear kept Atrox from getting close enough to wield his sword. Even from our box, I could see desperation on the more experienced gladiator's face.

The man had dreamed of winning in Rome and retiring in a country villa. That dream would end today because the owner of the arena had chosen Atrox to be the fish. Why would the gods allow a man's life to be so meaningless?

"This hardly seems fair," I murmured.

"Atrox is finished," Father said, crossing his arms. "Unless the gods intervene, this will be the day he dies."

Grateful for my concealing veil, I closed my eyes and swallowed to bring my heart down from my throat. I considered asking Aphrodite to protect Atrox, but what good would that do? The gladiator did not feel any particular attachment to me, nor could I feel any affection for a slave. He had never spoken a word to me about love—we had scarcely spoken at all.

❖

My father's prediction proved true. Atrox met his match in the arena that day. I regretted the loss of a skilled and handsome fighter, but I did not mourn because he had enabled me to bait a trap . . . and within a few days, I would spring it.

I waited until mid-Februarius, then feigned a casual air and asked Gilda how long it had been since my blood last flowed.

She closed her eyes to think. "A month," she said, then her fingers flew to her lips. "Wait—it has been longer."

I lifted a brow. "Has it been two months?"

She wriggled her fingers as she calculated. "The last time I prepared your cloths was before the governor left for Rome. And he departed in early December."

I smiled. "I have been praying to Aphrodite, goddess of fertility. I believe she has answered my prayers for a child."

"Domina." She recoiled from my steady gaze and shook her head. "If this is true, I do not see how this can be good."

I lifted my chin. "Go find my father. Tell him I am coming to him with important news."

While Gilda trudged away, I dripped salted water into my eyes until they burned. Then I mussed my hair, rumpled my tunic, and checked the looking brass to be certain I resembled a weeping woman who had just learned a terrible truth. Then I went to Father's office.

He stood when I entered, his eyes hard and wary. "What is so important that you must interrupt my work?" His eyes narrowed. "Why do you look as though you are ill?"

I sank into a chair, buried my face in my hands, and managed a hoarse whisper. "Father, I would do anything to avoid displeasing you. I had hoped I would not, but . . ." I hesitated.

"Speak, girl." He came out from behind the desk and sat next to me. "What is the cause of your distress?"

I opened my hand and let the heavy signet ring drop into his palm. "I suspect I am with child. The babe was fathered by the man who wears this ring."

My father's countenance flooded with emotion. I saw anger, humiliation, pride, shame, and cunning flit across his face. He lifted the gold ring and squinted at the engraving.

"Let me clearly understand what you are saying. Did *Memmius* father this child?"

I looked away, lest he see annoyance in my eyes. "Not the governor, but his son," I said. "The ring slipped from Marcus's hand when we were together. I kept it . . . because I thought I might need proof."

Father parked his chin in his hand and stared at the ring, then shifted his gaze to me. Calculation flickered in his eyes: What would be best for our family? What would be best for *him*?

Finally, he set the ring on his desk. "Have you been with Marcus many times?"

"By all the gods, no." I clasped my hands. "I would not be so cruel to Mariana. I have been with him once. We were drunk and . . . carried away by the spirit of Aphrodite."

Father inhaled a deep breath, then exhaled in a rush. "I am surprised, but this is not an insurmountable problem." He smiled at me—for the first time in months, it seemed—and I took pleasure in the small but satisfying victory.

Mariana had failed. I would win. Unless . . .

"But, Father—" I hesitated, pretending to search for words—"what if I am wrong and there is no child?"

His brows flickered only a little. "If there is no child today, who can say there will not be one after you and Marcus are married? Do not worry."

"What if he demands proof? My belly is still flat."

"I told you not to worry." The flush of color in his face reminded me that he had never been comfortable discussing the mystery of women's bodies. "We will summon a midwife and pay her handsomely. She will say whatever we want her to say."

"I am not lying, Father. It has been two months since my blood flowed, so I truly believe—"

"So much the better." He reached out and caressed my cheek. "Do not worry, daughter. Marcus will divorce Mariana and marry you as soon as possible. So tell me—when did this encounter occur?"

"The evening of Marcus's first banquet. I have not been back to the palace since that night. I have been . . . too embarrassed to face him."

"Then you have behaved honorably. I will visit Marcus to arrange Mariana's divorce and your betrothal. You will move into the palace; Mariana will return to her mother. And by this time next year, no one will remember that the younger sister was married to Marcus first."

"May I go with you?" I arranged my face into what I hoped was an expression of bewildered hurt. "I want to see him. I want him to know that my only desire is to be a good wife to him and a virtuous mother to his child."

Father studied me, probably weighing my intentions, then he nodded. "Take some time to adorn yourself. We will set out this afternoon."

❖

As Gilda prepared my best tunic, I went to the lararium and prayed. I sprinkled my most expensive oils onto the brazier, filling the room with the sickly-sweet fragrance of roses. I sacrificed a dove, recited every prayer I could remember, and offered my eternal loyalty to the family ancestors if only they would do my bidding.

I knew what I wanted—what I had *always* wanted—and I had risked everything to get it. Father would be horrified if he knew his supposedly virgin daughter had regularly visited the ludus. He would have been humiliated by my drinking and cavorting in public, and only his fixation on Marcus and Mariana kept him from learning of it. But he would have killed me—probably with his bare hands—if he knew I used an enslaved gladiator to place a child within my womb.

Now I needed the gods to *keep* the child in my womb and not let it wither as Mariana's had. I needed Father to support my cause no matter how Marcus protested. I needed Mariana to remain submissive and accept whatever happened. Most of all, I needed my secrets to remain hidden.

"Great Aphrodite, daughter of Jupiter," I prayed, clenching my jaw to stifle the desperate sob in my throat, "I have risked everything in order to honor you. Guide me now, protect me, and bring my husband to me. Bind his heart and soul to mine, and from this day forward let nothing separate us."

And then, to prove my sincerity, I drew a blade from my tunic and ran it across my palm, allowing my blood to drip onto the stone altar. "I give you my life's blood," I whispered, staring at the painted image of Aphrodite on the wall, "and demand that you answer my prayer. I have served you, so you must serve me. O great goddess, my soul is yours, and we are united forever."

And then, in a voice of delicate ferocity, I heard the goddess answer: "So be it."

Thirty-Three

MARIANA

Wounds, no matter how severe, tend to heal over time. By mid-Februarius, Marcus and I had established a tentative truce. We spoke politely to each other and even managed an occasional smile. He also returned to our bedchamber but did not enter until after I had fallen asleep.

We did not speak of having another child. We did not talk of love. And though we continued to pray together each morning at the lararium, he continued to pray to Jupiter while I prayed to Adonai.

We were together, yet in many ways we were further apart than we had ever been.

We were enjoying a light meal one afternoon when a slave entered to tell us that Narkis and Prima were waiting in the vestibule. I glanced at my husband. "Why have they come so early? Tonight's banquet will not begin until sunset."

He shrugged. "Some important council business must have arisen."

"But Prima has nothing to do with the council."

Marcus told the slave to bring our guests in, then tossed

a ball of cheese into his mouth. "I only wish Narkis could have waited until tomorrow," he said. "I am already weary, and the day is not half done."

Narkis led Prima into the dining hall, a concerned expression on his face. I sat up, surprised, when I saw that my stepsister had worn an exceptionally nice tunic—not the sort of garment one usually chose when visiting family at midday.

"Come," Marcus called, waving them forward. "We were enjoying a catch of fresh fish. You are welcome to join us."

Narkis dropped to a dining couch and ignored the food. "We have come on an urgent matter," he said, looking steadily at Marcus. "And while the consequences of this development are unknown to you, you may not be surprised."

Marcus's forehead knit in bewilderment. "What development?"

"My daughter," Narkis said, taking Prima's hand, "believes she is with child."

Prima looked at me, a small smile on her lips.

Marcus cleared his throat. "I am sorry to hear that. I presume you will want to arrange a marriage. If the child's father is unwilling to marry her, I am certain we can find a suitable husband."

"The child's father should be willing." Narkis gave my husband a bright-eyed glance and extended his hand. "The father was wearing *this* the night the child was conceived."

Narkis opened his palm, revealing Memmius's signet ring.

I stared in a paralysis of astonishment. I recognized the ring at once because we had just received a duplicate from the goldsmith.

My husband's eyes appeared in danger of dropping out of their sockets. "Where did you find it?"

Prima met his gaze without flinching. "In the stable, where you dropped it. Do you not remember?"

Marcus's smile broadened. "I am grateful you found it." Then, as he looked from Prima to Narkis, the color drained from his face. "Wait. Do you think . . . ?" He stiffened, adopting the posture of a Roman legionary. "On my honor, sir, I did not touch your daughter."

"You did," Prima insisted, and in her voice I heard the steely ring of truth. "Do you deny that you kissed me? Do you deny that we—?"

"Enough!" I closed my eyes and turned away, unable to look at them.

"Mariana," Marcus said, a note of pleading in his voice, "before all the gods, I swear I did not lie with your sister."

I stood and caught the edge of a tray to steady my quivering knees. "If you will excuse me, I think I should go upstairs and rest."

No one protested, not even Marcus.

Our visitors continued talking as I took an uncertain step, then another and another.

"We will have a midwife confirm Prima's condition," Narkis continued, his voice a flat drone in my ears, "but my advice is to divorce Mariana immediately and marry Prima on the first auspicious day. You want a son, do you not? The gods may have answered your prayers in a most unexpected way."

I staggered up the staircase, leaning against the cold marble balustrade as I made my way to the bedchamber that might be mine for only a few days more.

———————◆———————

Salama must have heard the story from other slaves because she entered my chamber quietly and tiptoed to her cot in perfect silence. I lay without moving throughout the afternoon, then the numbness evaporated, only to be replaced by soul-searing agony.

My marriage would soon be finished. I had doubted in the beginning, but Marcus had proved himself gentle and kind, honest and loving. We had shared dreams, laughter, and grief. I had confessed my fear of the unknown, and he had confessed his fear of not meeting his father's high expectations. We had been vulnerable with each other. Naked, physically and emotionally.

And now . . . Prima had thrust herself between us.

Had our marriage been doomed from the beginning?

I curled around a pillow and sobbed, then felt Salama's comforting arms around my shoulders. As she held me, I wept over the loss of my marriage, my husband, and my faith in a man who did not believe in my God. Paulos had taught that we should not be unequally yoked, and I had been proud, even foolish enough to believe I could prevail against an attitude fashioned by the world and its false gods.

"Shh," Salama said, pushing my damp hair away from my face. "Everything will seem better tomorrow."

How could it?

I loved Marcus and wanted to believe in his innocence, but how could I ignore the evidence? Prima had produced the ring he lost the night of our argument. They *had* both been drinking, he *had* gone outside, and Prima must have followed him. Had they arranged to meet? Had he been attracted to her all along? Or had he already begun to consider Narkis's suggestion to divorce me and marry my stepsister?

After we lost the baby, Marcus might have transferred his loyalty to Prima without even realizing it. I failed to deliver his son, so he considered another woman . . . and now he had a valid reason to marry her.

Did love count for nothing?

"Domina?"

Somehow I found my voice. "Yes?"

"Would you like some water?"

"Please."

Salama released me and went to fetch a pitcher. Grateful for a moment of solitude, I rolled onto my back and stared at the ceiling as if I could find answers in the elaborately painted clouds overhead.

How would Paulos advise me? *"If the unbeliever does not want to stay married, let him go."* So I would have to let Marcus go . . . if he asked to be set free.

Salama had just handed me a cup of honey water when Marcus entered our chamber. "More light," he called, and Salama hurried to light additional lamps. When she had finished, Marcus gestured toward the door.

She left us alone.

Looking ten years older than he had that morning, Marcus sat on the edge of the bed and held me in his gaze.

"Prima's story is not true," he said, his voice heavy. "Yes, she found me in the barn. And yes, I was drunk, and she kissed me. But I thrust her away because I would not—I *could* not—be disloyal to my wife. I would not be unfaithful to you."

"She is with child," I said, my voice breaking. "She is giving you what I could not. She is giving you what your father wanted. And she had his signet ring."

"She found the ring after I left. And we do not know if she truly is with child."

"I know Prima. When she wants something, she pursues it until she wins it. If she wanted your child, she would persist."

"If she persisted, she persisted with someone else. Because I did not touch her."

"Who else?" I shook my head. "I cannot imagine Prima pursuing another man. She is the daughter of a high official, a man of power. She is not common, and she has set her mind on having *you*."

Marcus could not answer, and I could not imagine Prima with anyone else.

"I want to believe you," I finally told him, "but you were drunk, and drunk men do things they cannot recall afterward."

"I was not that drunk," he insisted. "And I would never do what Prima has suggested."

"If Prima is carrying a child, when her belly can no longer be hidden Narkis will tell everyone you are the father. If you do not marry her, the entire province will speak against you. Your father will be shamed, and I know what that will do to you. So do what you must, Marcus, and I will not blame you. Marry her. I will go quietly . . . and I will forgive you."

Uttering those words took every ounce of courage I had because leaving him would tear out my heart. But if he did not want me, if he wanted Prima and his father's approval more, I would go . . . because I loved him.

"There is nothing to forgive—why can you not believe me?" Marcus stared at the floor, then lifted his gaze to meet mine. "You love a God you have never seen because you say He loves you. Would your loving God do this to us? To you?"

The question hung in the silence between us. I had no answer. All I had was . . . faith.

"Adonai has forgiven me for many sins and failures." I swiped at my cheeks. "He has loved me faithfully, as I have loved you. If you want me to remain as your wife, I will remain. If you want me to go, I will go."

"I want you," he responded, his burning eyes locked on mine, "to want me. I want you to stay because you *want* to be my wife."

I trembled as fresh tears filled my eyes. How could he not understand? I loved him more than my life, but in that moment, I wanted to leave. I could not imagine a future in which I saw him every day, a constant reminder of love and betrayal. How could I live with a man who left his lonely, grieving wife to sleep with her stepsister? Life would be unbearable.

But Paulos, my teacher, said Adonai would not want me to go . . . as long as Marcus wanted me to stay.

"I will stay if you wish it," I repeated, "because that is what Adonai commands."

Marcus looked at me, his face taut with exasperation. "I do not want my wife to remain only because her God demands it."

"I wish I could tell you what you want to hear," I whispered. "But in this moment, I have no other words."

Thirty-Four

PRIMA

The morning after our meeting with Marcus, I met the household in the lararium and prayed with renewed fervency. Father glanced at me, doubtless noticing the intensity of my devotion, but should I not be grateful? The goddess had blessed my efforts, and her high priestess had given me priceless instruction—far more valuable than any I had ever received from my stepmother.

When we finished our prayers, Father took his leave of us, but Hester caught my arm before I could slip away. "Are you well?" she asked, her tone light. "I could not help noticing the cut on your palm. My handmaid said you have been feeling ill for the past few days."

Father had not told her about the reason for our visit to Marcus. Perhaps he did not want Hester to warn Mariana, or perhaps he did not want to hear her protests. Whatever his reasons, he was now acting solely on my behalf.

I gave my stepmother a polite smile. "A mere cut." I held up my hand so she could see that the wound had closed. "I have always been clumsy with a blade."

"I saw blood on the altar yesterday," she said, cutting a quick glance to the stone where Father usually offered meat, wine, or fruit. "So I have to ask—have you offered blood to Aphrodite?"

"What if I have? Should I not give the goddess my full devotion?"

Hester's eyes, usually so guarded, widened with alarm. "I understand . . . but I want to share my experience with the goddess."

"*You* worshiped Aphrodite?"

"Who has not?" she countered. "But though nearly every Roman performs ritual worship of the major gods, I developed an especially deep relationship with the daughter of Jupiter. Like you, I visited her temple regularly, I sacrificed to her, I prayed for fertility and love . . . everything Aphrodite promises to those who adore her."

I blinked. Though I did not know my father's wife well, I would never have thought her a fervent follower of the goddess of pleasure.

"I understand what you are trying to do," she said, interrupting my thoughts. "I may not know every detail, but I know you want Marcus, and I know you believe Aphrodite can make that possible."

This show of concern, this deluge of motherly wisdom, undoubtedly came from Hester's desire to save Mariana's marriage. She did not care about me. She cared only about her precious daughter.

"You worship your God," I said, lifting my chin. "I will worship mine."

"But the goddess is deceitful." Her mouth tightened. "Aphrodite is a destroyer, and her promises are false. Lust is not love, Prima. Promiscuity does not bring happiness. And though pleasure is enjoyable, that feeling is fleeting and leaves you with nothing."

Weary of her admonishment, I released an exasperated sigh. "Aphrodite pleases me very well. The high priestess has taught me how to be a woman and how to wield my power."

"Your power?" The corner of her mouth quirked. "No, the high priestess has bargained for your soul. I fear for you because I *care* for you. Stop listening to the falsehoods and come with me to the ecclesia. Hear the truth about how and why Adonai created you. About how His Son Yeshua died to save you."

I tilted my head, surprised to see what looked like sincere compassion in her eyes. "Thank you for your concern," I said, lightly tapping her arm, "but I do not know Adonai, and I will not abandon Aphrodite. She has given me all I need. I pray, and she acts. She speaks, and I listen."

Hester drew a breath as if she would say something else, but I turned and walked away. Though she had made a brave attempt, I could not believe her story.

If she cared so much for me, why did she not tell me about Adonai before Aphrodite and I threatened her daughter's marriage?

Thirty-Five

MARIANA

Losing my baby was tragic, but waiting to hear if I would lose my husband was torturous. Despite constant pressure from my stepfather, Marcus refused to make a decision without discussing the matter with his father. But we did not know how long Memmius would remain in Rome.

At least the governor would not have to hear about the missing signet ring. The copy had been melted down, and the ring resided again on my husband's finger.

In late Februarius, a letter arrived from the governor. As Marcus skimmed it during dinner, I searched his face and wondered how many more meals we would share.

"Father writes that he will return in late Aprilis," Marcus said. "He also writes of Lucius Pedanius's slaves."

"The man who was murdered?"

"Pedanius was not a mere man; he was a senator. The Senate voted that all four hundred of his slaves should be dispatched to the arena because some of them must have participated in the plot to kill their master."

My stomach clenched, so I lowered the piece of chicken

I'd been eating. "That is horrible. Surely most of them were innocent."

"Perhaps." Marcus kept reading. "My father writes that Gaius Cassius Longinus effectively argued that because we have so many slaves with different customs and foreign religions in our homes, we can control such a motley rabble only through terror. Though some innocent lives were condemned, the injustice was outweighed by the advantage to the community."

I thought of Salama, who had been a friend to me ever since our first meeting. "What of slaves who are born into a household? Surely some of them have loyalty and natural affection for their masters. I cannot see how they could be described as a *motley rabble*."

Marcus lowered the letter. "Who can know what thoughts occupy the mind of a slave? In Rome, nothing is more likely to strike fear into the hearts of nobles than the threat of an uprising."

"Still," I said, dipping my fingers into a bowl of water, "many masters grant freedom to their slaves after years of faithful service. And is it not better to be a slave than to be poor and starving?"

Marcus lifted his goblet and smiled. "Perhaps you should go into politics."

I felt a blush burn my cheeks. "I would prefer to remain in the shadows."

I would prefer to remain your wife.

Thirty-Six

PRIMA

I should have had more faith in the goddess—after all, she had already accomplished far more than I expected—but with every passing day, my nerves frayed and my belly tightened. I had been fairly confident of my condition when Father and I went to confront Marcus, but within a few weeks I was certain of it.

To verify the pregnancy, Father sent for a midwife, who listened to my story and told me to urinate on a sheet sprinkled with wheat and barley seeds. After I did so, Gilda checked the seeds for several days, then reported that the barley seeds had sprouted. "You will have a son," she said, a sarcastic edge in her voice. "Congratulations."

Because we had heard nothing from Marcus, Father summoned the midwife again in early Aprilis. Under Gilda's watchful eye, the woman bade me lie on my back and then palpated my swollen belly. She asked about my monthly courses, and when I assured her that I had not bled in three months, she nodded.

"You are in the second stage of pregnancy," she said. "You can expect to give birth sometime during the eighth month. You may experience stomach discomfort and cravings, desiring to eat such things as earth, charcoal, tendrils of the vine, and unripe fruit. Oil rubdowns will help. Drink cold water with your meals. And if you cannot retain the food you eat, fast for one day."

Gilda nodded and left to share this confirmation with my father. He would send word of the midwife's verification to Marcus. This, I told myself, would surely compel Marcus to act.

I embraced the good news, cherished it, and held it close. I was carrying a child. Marcus might doubt me, but Mariana would not. I had shown her the signet ring, and soon I would show her my belly.

Father became overly solicitous, inquiring about my health every morning. Hester looked at me with a question in her eyes, but until Father chose to reveal our secret, I would not. Why would I inform my opposition? I knew Mariana's desire to avoid distressing her mother would keep my secret safe from Hester.

As the weeks passed, I rejoiced in the way my body changed. Certain smells nauseated me, and I craved strange foods, often sending Gilda on desperate searches for pomegranates and figs.

I visited the temple of Aphrodite and took my place in a seat of honor as Cassia and other priestesses brought flowers for my hair, oils for my skin, and foods to tempt my tongue. They whispered that I was the embodiment of Aphrodite, a fecund vessel that had surrendered to the goddess's will.

At home, Father sat next to me at dinner, tempting me with the best cuts of meat and the most delicious wines. Hester had to wonder why he had suddenly renewed his interest in me, but I drank in his attention, grateful to know that I was once again prized and precious.

❖

As our garden exploded with the golden greens of spring-time, Father often seemed preoccupied, but I could not tell if he was pondering my situation or preparing for Memmius's return. I knew he was upset about Marcus's refusal to divorce Mariana, but provincial political matters also weighed on his mind.

At dinner one night he opened a sealed papyri and announced that the governor would arrive in Corinth at the end of the month. The news startled me. I had hoped to be Marcus's wife by the time Memmius returned. The governor could not object if the marriage ceremony had already been conducted, and any disappointment he might feel would be overshadowed by his pleasure in knowing he would soon welcome a grandchild.

I was imagining myself on the steps of the palace, bowing to my new father-in-law, when Father's words brought me back to the present. "Memmius has written," he said, picking up the letter, "of a new sect that has arisen throughout the empire. Belief in a Jewish rabbi has spread from Jerusalem to the provincial seat at Caesarea, then south to Alexandria. Groups of the rabbi's followers, known as Christians, have been reported at Cyrene and the port of Carthage. The sect is growing with alarming speed, having reached Byzantium in the east and as far west as Odessa and Gaul."

I glanced at Hester, who had paled at his words. In that instant I realized that Father did not know he lived with a woman who followed the new sect. I had overheard enough conversations and prayers to know that both Hester and Mariana considered themselves Christians. But Father had been content to believe his wife had simply added Adonai to the pantheon of gods.

"The emperor has been most alarmed to discover that the movement has even infiltrated the imperial army," he continued, reading from Memmius's letter. "One man tells another about this Christ, then the second man tells his family and neighbors. The movement is spreading like a plague, and Nero considers it highly suspicious. Not because its adherents do wrong, but because they have an ulterior motive. These Christians appear to be good. They pay their taxes, often more cheerfully than Roman citizens do. They support their communities and aid the poor. They are sober, hardworking, and diligent. Slaves who follow the Christ serve their masters well.

"But our emperor has uncovered the root of their deception. They refuse to acknowledge his deity, and they claim citizenship not in Rome, but in an invisible kingdom. When the Senate learned about this group, debate raged for hours until one esteemed member put forth this question: hitherto the law had prohibited illegal *actions*; no law had ever prohibited illegal *beliefs*. Other senators were quick to propose laws to remedy the situation, but the difficulty lies in *proving* such beliefs. I am happy to report that the problem has been addressed by an ingenious plan.

"Since these Christians claim to worship a God more powerful than Caesar, and because they say they owe allegiance to Him above all other rulers, all a questioner must do is ask a suspect to break one of their Christian laws. If suspects cannot honor the emperor by offering even a pinch of incense in his name, they deny Nero's divinity and can be resolutely condemned. The means of execution varies. According to the law, the guilty may be put to death by the sword or by fire; they can be sent to the arena or crucified in the same manner as their Christ—with all their possessions subject to confiscation, of course."

Father lowered the letter. "Memmius says he will speak more of this when he returns and reports to the council."

Surely the goddess had never given me a better opportunity.

"Hester?" I lifted my cup and smiled at her over the rim. "You call yourself a Christian, do you not?"

Father gaped at her like a man who had just been knocked over by a charging sheep. "I thought you worshiped all the gods, including the God of the Jews." His brows rushed together. "When did the Jews become Christian?"

"They have not," Hester answered, a tremor in her voice. "The Jews worship Adonai, as do I. So do many Greeks and Romans."

Father frowned. "Then who is this Christ?"

"A Jewish prophet." Hester gave him a smile as thin as barley water. "He claimed to be the Son of Adonai."

Father shrugged. "Why does this trouble the emperor? Apollo is the son of Zeus, and no one causes trouble in his name."

"As you said, those who follow Yeshua do not cause

trouble," Hester said. "They desire to live in peace with all men."

Father might have been content with Hester's answer, but I would not be satisfied with half-truths. "I know little about the religion of the Jews," I said, "but I understand Mariana and her handmaid also worship this Christ."

Father lifted his cup. "If they do not cause problems, I say we should let them be. Rome has always been tolerant of other religions. But apparently Nero would like to expel them from the imperial city." His gaze returned to Memmius's letter. "The governor says they are not to be trusted."

"What laws are they breaking?" Hester asked.

"None as yet," Father said, studying the papyri. "But any group who will not sacrifice to Caesar cannot be loyal to the empire."

❖

After Father sent verification of my pregnancy to the governor's palace, I waited a full week. I spent most of my time pacing in the garden or praying at the temple of Aphrodite, but despite my frantic prayers we received no word from Marcus.

One afternoon I went to the temple and found Cassia sitting cross-legged on the elaborate mosaic tiles. I knelt before her and pressed my hands together. "Why is Marcus so reluctant to make a decision?"

The priestess arched a brow, then lifted her gaze to the ceiling. A trembling seized her frame, her eyes rolled back into her head, and an ancient voice roared from her slender throat: "You must act, daughter of Aphrodite. You must demonstrate your worthiness by acting against our enemies. You must create your destiny."

I watched, terrified, as the goddess spoke through the priestess. I had heard Aphrodite's whisper in the silence of the temple, I had felt her nudge my spirit, but never had I seen her inhabit another living being.

I took a deep quivering breath to calm the leaping pulse beneath my ribs. "I will do as you say."

That night I went to my father's office and confronted the question that had been haunting me for days. "Father, I must know—has Marcus decided to send Mariana away?"

Father regarded me with a slightly perplexed expression, as if he had an answer, but lacked the courage to share it. "I have heard nothing from the governor's palace," he finally said. "And due to Marcus's authority, I cannot press him."

"Until now, you have never been intimidated by a younger man."

Father lifted one eyebrow, silently suggesting that I had overstepped. "He is waiting to discuss the matter with his father. I will not intrude in that relationship."

Buoyed by my experience with the goddess, I dropped into a chair and frowned. "He could write Memmius with the news. Marcus and I could marry before the governor's return."

Father's gaze drifted toward my belly. "The man keeps insisting he is not the father of your child, and I keep asking myself why he would be so insistent. If, as you say, he lay with you, why is he not eager to claim the fruit of his loins?" He looked up from beneath craggy brows. "Tell me, Prima, could your child have been fathered by someone else? Perhaps someone at Aphrodite's temple?"

I stared at him, my heart pounding against my ribs. Had he heard a rumor? Had someone spotted me at the ludus?

"Father!" I cloaked genuine shock in indignation. "Have I ever lied to you?"

His forehead wrinkled as an indecipherable emotion moved in his eyes. "I do not know," he said simply. "I knew the girl who was my daughter quite well . . . but I do not know the woman at all."

"You *do* know me," I insisted. "I want what you want. I want to elevate our family and influence those who hold power. You have worked hard to grow close to the governor, and I will work with you by growing close to Marcus. Mariana had an opportunity to serve our family and she failed. Now it is my turn."

His gaze rested on me, alight with speculation, then he nodded.

I studied him, hoping to spot a flicker of affection, but his face remained inscrutable. What was he thinking? Had he considered what he would do if Marcus refused to divorce Mariana? Rather than endure the shame of an unmarried daughter, he could command me to marry someone else—probably the first wealthy merchant or council member who expressed an interest. If no one wanted me, Father would have the right to cast me off.

I would have to beg Aphrodite to fan the flames of his affection until it overpowered his anger and shame.

He had not been angry when he first heard my news, but if this baby did not result in a stronger connection to Memmius, Father would have no use for me or my child.

❖

The next morning, after prayers, Father stopped and looked directly at my belly, now clearly visible beneath my tunic. "The child has made his presence known," he said. "You and I must pay another visit to young Marcus. If he does not acknowledge his role in this disgrace, I will be forced to find an alternate solution to your problem."

A premonition snaked up the rail of my spine, and for the rest of the morning I could neither pray nor rest. I returned to my chamber, curled around the burgeoning burden at my waist, and wept, desperate for an answer.

Then, like a gift from Aphrodite's hand, I closed my weary eyes and found inspiration. Though Marcus knew he did not plant this child within me, I was certain he also knew Mariana and Hester were Christians. Though Memmius had not expressed concerns about Christians in this province, he might be persuaded to act against them. All I had to do was influence my father, who would present the governor with a strong case for exposing the Christians among us by means of the emperor's loyalty test.

If Marcus truly loved his wife, he would submit to my demand rather than endanger Mariana.

❖

The next morning, litter bearers carried us to the governor's palace, then Father went to the council chamber while I waited in the atrium and pretended to study the elaborately painted wall mural. Marcus, who was always the last to arrive at such meetings, would soon come downstairs, cross the atrium, and join the council members.

The slap of leather sandals alerted me to his approach. I moved toward the staircase, spotted Marcus between two guards, and smiled.

"Marcus," I called, "I must have a word."

I climbed a step, but his guards stopped me from proceeding. Marcus gave me a speculative look, then glanced at his men. "All is well. Proceed to the council chamber and tell them I will arrive shortly."

The guards strode away as Marcus continued down the stairs, condescension radiating from his countenance. "Prima. What more could you possibly have to say to me?"

"Only this," I said, smiling. Aware that a dozen slaves could overhear our conversation, I chose my words carefully. "Father told me about the latest reports from Rome, specifically mentioning the loyalty tests devised by our emperor. Though Memmius has not yet implemented them in Achaia, I think the councilors could easily be persuaded to implement such tests in Corinth. After all, if these Christians offend by refusing to worship our deities, the gods will not send rain, the crops will not grow, and the poor will starve. The meat merchants are already complaining that they have had to reduce their prices because Christians will not buy the meat that has been sacrificed to idols."

Marcus's eyes narrowed. "What is this nonsense you speak of?"

I stepped closer and looked him in the eye. "With very little effort I could convince my father to initiate a loyalty test in Corinth, perhaps even throughout the province. How would your wife fare in such a test?" I lowered my voice. "If you love Mariana, you must divorce her. My baby needs a father, and you need a wife who worships the gods of Rome. If you want to succeed in this city, you must find a wife with the courage to admit that Caesar is divine."

"You said you wanted a *word*." Marcus's eyes snapped. "You have overtaxed my patience."

"Perhaps." I stepped back and gave him a humorless smile. "I *do* have a word for you, Marcus, and the word is *divorce*. See to it now or I will convince my father that the Christians must be winnowed out."

Thirty-Seven

MARIANA

Salama paused at the threshold of my chamber. "Domina?"
I looked up, puzzled by her reticence. "What is it?"
"Someone here would like to speak to you . . . privately."
I looked past Salama and saw Gilda waiting in the hallway,
so I dismissed my other attendants and motioned for Gilda
to come forward. I could not imagine why Prima's handmaid
wanted to see me, but I would listen to her.

Gilda came forward, wearing the impenetrable mask
most slaves adopted when in the presence of their masters.
I searched her face for some clue about her motivation but
found nothing.

"Gilda." I forced a smile. "It is good to see you."
The woman's chin trembled, shattering the look of indifference. "It is good to see you, Domina, but this is not a
social visit."

"No?" I peered into the hallway. "Where is your mistress?"
"At the public baths." Gilda glanced over her shoulder.
"She thinks I am guarding her belongings. I must hurry back,
but first I need to tell you something."

"You may speak freely."

Gilda stepped closer and lowered her head. "I have news about the child my mistress carries."

Like a wisp of smoke, a sense of uneasiness crept into my mood. "I have no interest in discussing Prima's pregnancy."

"Please." Tears glimmered in the woman's eyes. "You need to know that the child is not your husband's. For months, my domina visited a gladiator at the ludus. She gave him silver, and he gave her the attention she craved. The child is his."

Shock caused words to wedge in my throat.

Gilda turned, ready to hurry away, but Salama caught her arm. "Do you swear this is the truth? Prima has not forced you to bring that story to us?"

"Why would she do that when the governor's son is all she ever wanted?" Gilda's flush deepened to crimson. "She has never liked you, mistress, but since the day of your marriage she has despised you. Her story is nothing but a plan to destroy your happiness. And if she learns that I have come here, I am dead."

Overcome with relief, I stood and took her hand. "You need not worry about discovery, Gilda. Now, hurry back to the baths." I embraced her and kissed her cheek.

As Salama escorted Gilda to the servants' entrance, I sank onto my couch, relief flowing through me. Marcus had spoken the truth—he *had* been faithful. This news might not completely bridge the rift between us, but it would be a start.

I closed my eyes and sighed in gratitude. *Thank you, Lord*.

Salama came back into the chamber and quietly closed the door. "There is more to the story," she said. "Gilda was afraid to share it with you."

I tensed. "More?"

Salama sank onto a nearby stool. "Gilda said her mistress has been absolutely devoted to Aphrodite for months. She has put herself at the mercy of the high priestess and done things no respectable woman would do. Gilda said Narkis would kill Prima if he knew she had behaved like a temple prostitute."

I sat back, stung. "Does my mother know about this?"

"I do not think so or Gilda would have mentioned it."

I pressed my hand over my heart, grateful that thus far Mother had been spared the knowledge of Prima's accusation and her pregnancy. But my stepsister would not be able to hide her condition much longer.

I blew out a breath. "We knew Prima wanted Marcus, but now we know the baby is not his."

Salama nodded. "Gilda thinks Prima wants her father's attention more than anything. She said he used to spoil her, but after your marriage, he talked of nothing but you and Marcus, or Marcus and the governor. When Prima realized she was no longer the apple of his eye, she sought attention elsewhere."

Gilda was probably right. Though I had no power to influence Narkis or Prima, learning the truth about my husband was a priceless gift. And if Marcus and Prima had to present their cases before the governor, I was certain Memmius would believe his son. Prima might lodge a false claim, but Memmius would believe that Marcus had simply dropped the signet ring and remained faithful to his wife.

Perhaps we would soon be on our way to recovering the joy of our marriage.

❖

Later that afternoon, I went in search of my husband. I had things to say, an apology to make, and a promise to keep.

I spotted Marcus sitting in the palace garden, squinting into space as if he pondered deep thoughts. I crept up behind him and placed my hands on his shoulders. "I must apologize to you," I whispered, lowering my lips to his ear. "This morning I learned the truth—the child Prima carries was sired by a gladiator."

He caught my right hand and turned toward me, his eyes wide. "Surely you jest."

"I do not. Someone—I cannot say who—risked a great deal to share the truth of the matter. She should not have spoken to me, but her conscience would not allow her to tolerate Prima's falsehoods."

Marcus pulled me onto the bench. "So you believe this woman?"

"I do."

"And now you believe *me*, even though Prima had my father's ring."

I could not ignore the subtle accusation in his words. "Forgive me for not believing you." I bowed my head. "I was wrong. I do not have much experience with love, and I have even less with being a wife. But where you are Gaius, I am Gaia."

He took my face in his hands and gently kissed me, then wrapped his arm around my shoulders. "I should never have allowed myself to be in such a vulnerable position with Prima," he said, his gaze on the horizon. "I should not have argued with you that night; I should have stayed with you instead of walking away." He smiled down at me. "My father never taught me to be a husband. I have watched him for years, but when I see how distant he and my mother are, I wonder if he has been the husband he should have been."

"What is past is past." I pressed my fingertips to his lips. "And now that we have forgiven each other, I promise I will never doubt you again."

"I will never give you reason to do so."

My head fell against his chest as I drew a deep breath of contentment. "I am glad we can forget this and focus on building our family. I will be grateful when your father returns. It will be good to have you to myself again. You have been far too distracted by the business of government."

"For a while I will be all yours. But this is my life, Mariana. This is the life of a Roman senator's son. And one day, gods be willing, I will be a senator myself. The halls of power are filled with ambitious and malicious men, and they are often married to women of the same mind. I thank my gods I am not."

I had thought my news would relieve him of a crushing burden, but he seemed nearly as pensive as ever. Was he worried about his father's return to Corinth? Or was something else bothering him . . . something he did not want to share?

Thirty-Eight

PRIMA

I paced in the garden, my fury growing as steadily as my belly. I could no more think of it as a child than I could think of Atrox as a man. He had been a creature of sweat and desire and violence, and if I had not been set on disobeying my father, I would never have gone to the ludus.

By the names of all the gods, what was Marcus *thinking*? A full day had passed since I gave him my ultimatum, but I had received no message from the palace. Yet my belly continued to grow, as did the disdain in Father's eyes when he looked at me.

What lunacy possessed Marcus? Despite the evidence of his father's ring, the baby in my belly, and my threat against his Christian wife, Marcus had not acknowledged my victory. Worst of all, Father had to be considering his options in case my plan failed. If Marcus did not soon divorce Mariana, I would find myself back in the tavern, but not as a customer. I would be working there, living lower than a slave, doing whatever was necessary to afford food and drink.

Cassia had told me to determine my desires, and I had,

but what else did the goddess expect of me? I had done exactly what the high priestess advised, and I had nothing to show for it. I had spent a hundred sestertii on sacrifices at Aphrodite's temple. I had prayed until I had calluses on my knees. I had offered my own blood on the altar. I had taken action and debased myself by sleeping with a slave.

So why was the goddess taking so long to turn my dreams into reality?

I sank onto a stone bench and propped my chin in my hand. If only Atrox still lived! He would have been a terrible husband, but if he knew I carried his child, he might be putty in my hands. I could buy his freedom and send him to kill Mariana, Marcus, or both. Then I could go to Memmius and declare that I carried Marcus's son, and who would know otherwise? Memmius would adopt me, call me *daughter*, and my child would be provided with everything he needed or wanted. My father would be pleased by my cleverness and courage, and would finally give me the respect I deserved.

Groaning, I stared into the reflecting pool and studied my wavering image. Apparently, I would have to visit Marcus again, but since he might have told the guards to prohibit me from visiting alone, I would have to convince Father that we needed to visit the governor's house as soon as possible. In a week or two, my palla would not be enough to disguise the bulge at my belly, and strangers' tongues would begin to wag.

If I were not betrothed by that time, Father would not want to be seen with me in public.

❖

While I waited in the hallway for a moment alone with Father, Gilda suggested that I leave the house and take a walk. "Your mood is sour because you have spent too much time in your chamber," she said, smiling as though she had not noticed the oversized lump beneath my girdle. "Why do you not go to the market? I will go with you, and we can see what new wares have come from Rome. I hear a silk merchant from the East has recently set up shop. He travels with a woman who sells exquisite perfumed oils."

I smoothed my tunic and felt the rise of the belligerent bump. "I do not feel like going out."

"Please, Domina." Gilda smiled again, and the look on her face almost convinced me that she genuinely cared about my well-being. "You have spent too much time alone. You are not suited for solitude; you need people to brighten your spirits. Here." She pulled a new palla from my trunk, a cloth woven in the bright colors of spring. "I found this in Mariana's former chamber and thought you might like it. It is long enough to hide . . . the fact that you have been eating like a horse."

Grumbling, I took the palla, looped it around my neck, and let the ends dangle over my chest. The slave was right—the palla's bright colors did distract from the obvious.

"This might do," I said, studying the effect in the looking brass. "If there is a breeze, however, it might blow and reveal what should remain hidden."

"The wind has retreated," Gilda said, picking up my sandals. "Which means our walk might be warm, but at least the wind will not muss your hair."

Reluctantly, I agreed with her. I did feel better after being with people, and the marketplace never failed to lift my spirits.

Within the hour, Gilda and I set out. I wanted to take a

litter, but Gilda insisted that I needed to stretch my legs. "A brisk walk puts color in one's cheeks," she said, trailing behind me as a servant should. "You will look and feel better by the time we return to the house."

"If I do not," I answered, glancing around the street and seeing nothing of interest, "I will have you beaten."

Gilda did not respond, probably because she had ceased to believe my threats. Such familiarity, Father once told me, always led to trouble with slaves. If you allowed a slave to become too close, he or she would assume you would not beat them, yet discipline had to be enforced. "That is why it is always good," he added, "to beat slaves occasionally to remind them of their proper place."

We smelled the market before we entered it. The aroma of sizzling meat greeted us from a block away, and the sound of enthusiastic bargaining made my heart beat faster. We turned a corner and entered the crowded thoroughfare, where we strolled beneath awnings of vibrant colors that were repeated in the exotic garments of foreign merchants.

Despite my inclination to remain depressed, the sight of so much activity awakened my interest. We walked past baskets of glazed breads, a pen of bleating goats, and a counter loaded with pungent spices from far-flung provinces. In one booth, a man sat on a stool and sang of love rejected while passersby ridiculed his voice, his song, and his rustic harp.

I spotted bright fabrics in a distant booth and promptly lengthened my stride. Wearing a new garment was always pleasurable, and if I were going to win Marcus's attention, a new tunic might help—

I halted when I recognized the couple occupying the booth. Marcus and Mariana stood with the man, accompanied by Salama. Mariana was fingering a silk fabric of ocean blue. "It is too costly," she protested, her voice rising above the noise of the crowd. "Please, I do not need another tunic."

"You are my wife, and you shall have it." Marcus nodded to the merchant. "My wife will wear this at the banquet to welcome our governor home."

How close was Memmius's return? Was Marcus so focused on preparing for his father's arrival that he had given no thought to my demand? How could he ignore me when his wife's life hung in the balance?

Behind me, Gilda tugged on my arm. "Come," she whispered. "Let us find another silk merchant."

I remained rooted to the spot, my eyes focused on my nemesis, my heart constricting to a lump of hate. What did it matter if they turned and saw me? Clearly, Marcus had disregarded every word I uttered when we last spoke. There he stood, smiling with his wife, making plans for his father's return.

He was not going to divorce Mariana. I saw the truth as clearly as I saw my stepsister. I was about to lose everything. Where was Aphrodite when I needed her?

Determine your desires . . .

I charged forward, pushing a pair of women out of the way as I entered the merchant's booth. "Marcus!"

He turned, his shoulders broadening when he saw me. "Prima? What—?"

"Have you forgotten our last conversation? About the latest reports from Rome?" I narrowed my eyes. "I do not think you want to ignore the emperor's wishes."

"I have nothing to fear from the emperor." Marcus spoke

in a soft voice, but I heard venom in it. "And neither does my father."

"What about your wife?" I snapped.

Mariana looked at Marcus, her eyes going wide. "What is this?"

"You must do what is expected of you," I said, reminding him of my power. "My father is always eager to please Nero."

"Marcus?" Mariana reached for his arm. "What must you do?"

"Nothing." Marcus gave me a sharp look, then smiled down at his wife. "Your sister cannot command me."

I stared, rage boiling beneath my skin, then fled the marketplace with Gilda hurrying after me.

Thirty-Nine

MARIANA

Though I pressed Marcus for an answer, he would not say why Prima had accused him of ignoring the emperor's wishes. "Prima imagines herself far more important than she is," he said, tucking my hand into the crook of his arm as we walked home. "You need not worry about anything."

"But a wife should be concerned about her husband," I countered. "If you carry a burden, I should help bear the load."

He smiled. "As I have said before, I have never met anyone like you. Have you always been so kind?"

I smothered a laugh. "Kindness was not part of my nature until I met Yeshua. Before that, I was set on having my own way and intent on my own interests. My mother was the same until she began to visit the synagogue. When she heard what Yeshua did for the world, she changed. So did I."

Marcus lifted his chin, a frown puckering the skin between his dark eyes. "What did this Yeshua do? Win a war? Heal diseases?"

I studied Marcus's face and noted the earnestness in his gaze. After the storm that had briefly torn us apart, my husband was *with* me again . . . and asking about my God. "Yeshua did those things, and much more."

Marcus lifted one shoulder in a shrug. "The Roman gods worked wonders, too. They also had sons and daughters."

"Yeshua and His Father are not like the Roman gods. Those gods covet and kill and become jealous—their emotions are like ours."

"But you say your God loves. Does He also hate?"

I bit my lip and yearned for Paulos. He would know how to answer Marcus's questions. But what had Yeshua promised? He said the *Ruach HaKodesh*, or Holy Spirit, would tell us what to say.

I prayed for wisdom, then drew a deep breath. "Yeshua, His Father, and His Spirit *do* love and hate, but they are holy and pure. They are not torn by selfish emotion the way people are, but are steadfast and unchanging. They always love what they love, and they always hate what they hate."

A faint light twinkled in the depths of his eyes. "What do they hate?"

"Sin. Disobedience to God's Law. The Jews have copied God's Law, and they study to keep it."

"They must spend hours studying."

I chuckled. "Yes, they do."

"And what does your God love?"

"You."

The word came out as a whisper and clearly caught Marcus by surprise. "Your God does not even know me."

"Yes, He does. He is the Creator of all mankind, and He knows us all by name. He knows what is good and evil in our hearts. And because He is perfect and holy, only those who are perfectly holy can approach Him."

"Well, then." Marcus shrugged as we approached our litter bearers. He pulled aside the curtain and waited for me to slide in.

I thought he had lost interest in our conversation, but as the litter bearers began our journey back to the palace, he turned. "If only those who are holy can approach your God, then how could someone like Prima approach Him? You say He loves everyone, but how could He love Prima?"

I bit my lip. How indeed? My stepsister's behavior had been deplorable, but Gilda said her actions rose from her desire to gain her father's attention—to be loved. And what girl did not yearn for her father's love?

"If Prima would listen," I said, "if she knew how much Adonai loved her, she would change. I know she would."

Marcus snorted softly.

"Everyone has done things to displease God," I continued. "Prima and I are alike because we are both sinners. But I have given my life to Yeshua because He sacrificed himself to pay the penalty for my sins. In the eyes of God, His holiness obliterates the evil I have done, so that I can approach Adonai through the authority of His Son."

"And Prima?"

I nodded. "If Prima surrendered her life to Yeshua, it would be the same for her."

And you.

Not wanting to fracture the peace Marcus and I had reestablished, I did not speak the thought aloud.

But the words hung in the air like a loving, persistent prayer.

Forty

PRIMA

Anger fueled my brisk walk home, but when we reached the house, fear snatched my breath away. The wall on the opposite side of the street was always scrawled with lewd pictures, most of which I ignored. Yet I could not ignore the stick figure with the oval belly and the words beneath it: *Here lives Atrox's harlot.*

While he lived, Atrox's name had often been scrawled on city walls, usually in taunts or ribald jokes. But *this*? Implying that I was the lowest, crudest kind of prostitute . . .

I stood motionless and shaken. What would people think when they saw this? What would Father—?

A scream rose in my throat, and I choked it off. Father would not believe this. And whoever wrote this could not know the truth . . . unless someone I trusted had spilled my secrets.

I whirled around to face Gilda, who had been following with her head lowered. She looked up, startled, when I cursed her.

"Domina?" A flood of fear washed through her eyes, and I

knew she saw the same treacherous currents in mine. "What have I done?"

With a trembling hand, I pointed to the writing on the wall. "What can you say about that?"

She stared at the pregnant stick figure, then shook her head. "I-I cannot read."

I slapped her so hard she nearly lost her footing. When she had righted herself, I walked to the front door, opened it, and addressed the doorkeeper. "See that slave?" I pointed to Gilda. "Take her to the stable yard and have her beaten. Then send someone to scrub the wall in front of the house."

The doorkeeper stared in disbelief. "How many lashes, Domina?"

"As many as it takes," I said, pushing past him, "until she can no longer stand. Then put her in a cart and take her to the slave market."

The doorkeeper blinked. "If she is injured, you will not receive much for her. Perhaps it would be better to take her straightway."

"Do as I command." I glared at him. "Or you can remain at the slave market with her."

Forty-One

MARIANA

I rose early, knowing I had to make preparations for the governor's banquet. A messenger had arrived the day before, telling us to expect Memmius within two days. Furthermore, the governor planned to celebrate with a banquet the night of his arrival.

I smiled, remembering all the fuss and bother we had endured when Narkis planned his welcoming banquet for Memmius. That dinner would pale in comparison to tonight's event.

I sent Salama to inquire if the cooks had procured everything they needed from the marketplace, then settled into a hot bath. I had just stepped into a warm towel when Salama burst into the bath, her face swollen from weeping.

The sight of her anguish made my forearms pebble with gooseflesh. "What has happened?"

Salama gulped a breath. "Gilda."

"What about her?"

"Prima had her beaten and taken to the slave market."

I sank to the floor as my knees folded beneath me. Surely,

Gilda did not think we told Prima about her visit to us. Neither Marcus nor I would say anything, and none of my slaves would dare betray another.

One of the bath attendants helped me to a bench, and I motioned for Salama to continue. "Have you any details? How could this have happened?"

Salama wiped fresh tears from her eyes. "Apparently one of the guards at the ludus went through the city drawing pictures of a big-bellied woman. On the wall facing Narkis's house, the fool drew the picture and wrote, 'Here lives Atrox's harlot.'"

I groaned. Though prostitution was not part of believers' lives, the practice was freely accepted among both Greeks and Romans. A man could visit such a woman without sullying his reputation, and even boast of keeping a *meretrix*—an educated, well-spoken woman—for his pleasure. Poor, uneducated women, however, often sold themselves out of necessity, and the drawing had implied Prima was the latter sort.

She must have been out of her mind with fury. Not only had the offender revealed her secret but he had also humiliated her by using the most vulgar method of communication.

"I am so sorry," I said, my gaze clouding with tears. "Poor Gilda." I reached out and squeezed Salama's arm. "When you are able, make discreet inquiries at the slave market and see if Gilda is available for outright purchase. She should not have to endure an auction."

"Thank you, Domina." Salama grasped my hand and nodded. "I will go now and see what I can learn."

Forty-Two

PRIMA

After weeks of anticipation, the governor and his retinue finally returned to Corinth. My father left the house before sunrise, eager to be among the citizens who greeted Memmius from the officials' platform.

Hester and I dressed in our finest tunics and went out to watch the spectacle. I had chosen my most voluminous garment and my largest palla, which I draped like a toga, so my belly was fully covered. To add another distraction, I picked flowers from the garden and carried an armful, planning to throw a few before the governor's approaching carriage.

The word of Memmius's homecoming had spread, and the streets of Corinth overflowed with citizens who wished to welcome their governor. After two hours in the bright morning sun, we heard trumpets in the distance. A few moments later the advance guard appeared, clearing the street of overeager citizens and merchants' donkey carts. Finally, amid the blare of trumpets and joyous shouts, Servius Memmius Lupus arrived.

I must admit that our governor cut an imposing figure as

he climbed out of his conveyance, his toga gleaming in the sunlight. Like so many others, I lifted my hand and waved, but his gaze passed over me without even a spark of recognition.

Hester and I walked toward the platform, where Memmius climbed the steps and turned to face the crowd.

"Citizens of Achaia and Corinth!" he called, his baritone ringing over the hushed assembly, "I bring you greetings from the Roman Senate and from Nero Claudius Caesar Augustus Germanicus, our divine emperor. He sends his love and is pleased to commend your efforts to preserve the *Pax Romana*, under which all imperial citizens live in peace. He would remind you to respect the gods, honor our ancestors, and maintain the virtues of fidelity, modesty, and piety that have made the empire great. Always remember—duty to the state is greater than anything, even love to one's family. To act and suffer bravely—that is the duty of every Roman citizen."

I glanced at my father, who stood on the front row of the assembled councilors, his eyes firmly fastened to Memmius's broad back. Marcus stood next to him but watched his father with a speculative look. What was he thinking?

"As a senator of Rome and a servant of our divine emperor," the governor continued, "I hereby proclaim that tonight all Roman citizens, aediles, patricians, and council members are invited to a banquet at our provincial palace. Furthermore, tomorrow shall be a feast day with gladiatorial games and other spectacles in the arena. We will gather to celebrate the glory of Rome as well as the greatness of our province and capital city!"

With theatrical grace, he turned and held out his arms to his son. Marcus stepped into his embrace, warmly welcoming his father home. Then, with an equally bold gesture, Marcus removed the signet ring from his finger and placed it on his father's hand, returning authority to his father.

My mouth twisted in a wry smile. Would the governor ever know I had worn that ring for days?

"How did my son manage in my stead?" Memmius asked the crowd, his arm around his son's shoulders. "Did he do a commendable job?"

The crowd roared its approval, and I smiled when I realized that Mariana was not on the platform. She had nothing to do with the government, but Marcus might have asked her to remain out of sight because he planned to proceed with the divorce. Perhaps he would speak to his father today . . . and announce our betrothal at tonight's banquet.

I closed my eyes and saw myself standing beside Marcus, my hand on his arm, as a roomful of leading citizens cheered the news of our marriage.

Aphrodite, goddess of love and fertility, make it so!

❖

I stopped Father in the garden that afternoon. "I must speak to you about tonight's banquet. I trust you have been privy to the details?"

He lifted his head like a dog scenting the breeze. "What do you want, Prima? A new tunic?"

"I would not ask you for anything, Father. I simply want to know what Mariana has planned for the evening."

He smiled as he took my arm and led me to his office. "It will be exactly what you might expect—a grand dinner with all the usual extravagance. A group of musicians singing praise to Jupiter. A trio of Nubian dancers."

"Is that all?"

He shrugged. "Is that not enough? After the entertainment, Memmius will address the people. Members of the council will be seated near him, of course, so they will be able to hear. Harpists will play in the garden to placate those who are too far away."

I smiled. "Will Memmius address the matter of the Christians?"

Father dropped my arm. "It is not for me to tell the governor what to do at his banquet. He will deal with the Christians when and if he feels inclined to do so."

"Does he know a Christian lives beneath his own roof?"

A muscle quivered at my father's jaw. "Tread carefully, daughter."

"And there are probably others. Who knows how many have been infected by Mariana's belief in this heresy?"

Father stepped behind his desk and dropped into his chair. "Memmius is paterfamilias of his own household. If I tell him his daughter-in-law is a Christian, he might think I am implying that he was not vigilant when he arranged the marriage. Or he may think I am questioning Marcus's wisdom . . . and a wise man does not criticize a father's beloved son."

"But Marcus has been blinded, and what father could think ill of a blind son? Marcus can be excused, but a senator cannot condone a religion that forbids worship of the emperor. Is our emperor not tolerant? He is so long as conquered nations and people offer sacrifices to him. But these Christians refuse to do that. They alone do not acknowledge his divinity."

"Prima, consider what you are saying!" A red tide crept up Father's throat. "The Christians are good citizens. They

314

pay their taxes, and they keep quiet. Look at Hester—she is a wonderful wife and has been kind to you and supportive of me. I will hear no more of this until Memmius launches his own investigation."

He picked up a papyrus, his way of dismissing me, but I was not ready to go. Memmius might have all the time in the world, but I did not.

A pitcher of water stood on Father's desk, along with several lemons and a blade. I seized a lemon and held it aloft. "Father, what do I have in my hand?"

He looked up, irritation in his eyes. "I have no time for games."

"This is not a game. Tell me—what am I holding?"

He sighed. "A lemon."

"And what do you get when you squeeze a lemon?"

"Lemon juice." He narrowed his gaze. "Now be on your way."

I shook my head. "No, Father. When you squeeze a lemon, you get whatever is inside."

I picked up the blade, cut the lemon in half, and squeezed, sending a trickle of lemon juice into the pitcher. "When you squeeze people," I said, dropping the spent fruit onto the desk, "their private thoughts and beliefs are revealed. The emperor wants to squeeze these Christians so that their true intentions are revealed. They worship a foreign god and no one else, so they are not loyal to Rome. If they are squeezed, they will betray the empire."

Father crossed his arms. "My wife is loyal."

"Is she?" I lifted a brow. "Does she love you more than her invisible God? If she does, you need not worry. If she does not, she does not deserve to be your wife."

315

A frown settled onto Father's brow, but he did not interrupt as I continued. "These Christians want to deny the old gods, burn their images, and destroy the death masks of our ancestors. They do not believe in any god other than the one they serve. And since every disaster known to man is wrought by angry gods, we are risking plague, famine, fire, and flood if we do not rid ourselves of this hateful Christian intolerance."

"Yet they are good," Father murmured. "Hester is a modest woman. She is kind." His gaze sharpened. "And say what you will about Mariana, you would never find her seeking the attention of a gladiator."

I snapped my mouth shut. He knew. He had heard the rumor or seen the wall. He knew, and yet he had remained silent until now. Why?

Because he wanted my plan to succeed.

I pressed on. "Mariana is not your daughter, but I am. I am not lifeless and boring. I am Roman, I have steel in my blood, and I will fight for what I deserve."

He tilted his head. "Some would say Mariana is as Roman as you are."

"But Christian worship has rusted the steel in her soul. Put her in the arena with other Christians, and you will see how alike—how weak and timid—they are."

Father stared at the wall, thought working in his eyes. He admired Hester and Mariana, but I was his daughter. Despite my wanton ways, which had certainly vexed him, he adored my spirit because it was like his own.

"I will speak to the governor," he finally said. "But the decision of whether or not to arrange a loyalty test will be his, not mine."

I leaned forward and lowered my voice. "If you want me to be the governor's daughter-in-law, we must move quickly."

"He has only just returned—"

"And what better time to act than when all the city leadership is in one place? You know the emperor is concerned— you must make Memmius *act* on that concern. Action taken tonight will be more than enough to stamp out this dangerous movement, especially if it reveals a Christian among the governor's own family."

Father propped his hand on his desk, covered his mouth, and stared at me. A melancholy frown flitted across his features when he finally nodded.

"I will convince Memmius," he finally said. "But I will not give him specific names. If Mariana or Hester is to be condemned, it will not be my doing. And if you are to wed Marcus, I will not have it said that I arranged the marriage."

I rested my hand on the jutting ledge of my belly, relieved that he had come to his senses. "The banquet will open with prayer and a sacrifice, so why not end the evening in the same manner?" I asked, unable to resist the suggestion. "Those who are not traitors will not mind the inconvenience, and the governor will see their willingness to participate as an affirmation of their loyalty to him."

Father nodded. "Memmius will be able to report that he wasted no time in following the emperor's wishes."

I stepped back, content. "There have been times," I said, softening my voice, "when I yearned for you to be bolder, but I am wise enough to see that your success can be attributed to your caution when dealing with powerful people. In the end, you have always done what is best for our family."

"And the empire," he said, his voice gruff. "After all, duty to the empire is greater than anything . . . or so the governor says."

"Of course." I leaned over the desk and kissed his cheek. "May all the gods bless our endeavor tonight."

He grumbled something beneath his breath, but affection shone in his eyes when he looked at me. "You should have been born male," he said, sighing. "You would have made an excellent chief magistrate."

I snorted softly. "Forgive me, Father, but you underestimate me. I would have made an excellent emperor."

Forty-Three

MARIANA

Despite an afternoon fraught with calamity—a kitchen fire, an amphora of wine spilled, and a slave who broke his arm—an unusual peace enveloped me as Salama helped me dress for the governor's banquet. The sorrows that shadowed me for months had disappeared, and my heart sang with joy. No matter what happened tonight, I would be content because my husband loved me. Marcus and I would remain together, and we would have a family.

The life I had feared losing now seemed within reach, and I could see nothing but joy in our future. Best of all, Marcus had begun to ask honest questions about Adonai and His Son. I was still reading at night, and though he pretended to sleep, I had seen him smile as I read aloud certain portions of Mark's Gospel. What was it Yeshua said? "No one can come to Me unless My Father who sent Me draws him . . ."

God had opened the doorway to my husband's heart. If only He would open the door to Prima's.

Salama had just finished arranging my hair when Marcus

entered our chamber, resplendent in a white tunic and a toga that fell to the floor in graceful lines. "That toga is extraordinary," I said, smiling in approval. "Can we afford such luxuries?"

"A gift from my father." He extended his arm to display the intricate folds. "And yes, it is probably the finest garment I have ever owned. I must be careful not to show off, or I may be the object of jealousy tonight."

I stood and moved into his arms. "All because of your new toga?"

"Because of my beautiful wife." He kissed me, then stepped back to look me over. "You and Salama have outdone yourselves. But before we go downstairs, I want to ask you something. You know Prima so much better than I do."

"I would have to agree."

He smiled, but anxiety flickered in his eyes. "How likely is she to carry out a threat?"

I winced. "Who has she threatened now?"

"That is not important, but I need to know if she will follow through."

I glanced at Salama, who was undoubtedly listening as she cleared my dressing table. "I have heard her threaten slaves more than a dozen times. Often she did not act on her threats, but when she does—"

"Prima's threats have teeth," Salama interrupted, "if her desires are thwarted. Would you not agree, Domina?"

Thinking of Gilda, I met Marcus's gaze. "I would agree. She recently had her handmaid beaten and sold."

His mouth twisted. "But what if she threatened a Roman? Would she be so bold as to act against a person of considerable status?"

I frowned, unable to imagine how Prima could harm a citizen. She had no real power, and even her father's authority was limited.

"I do not know," I finally answered. "She would have to convince someone else to act for her."

Marcus sat on the stool at my dressing table and clasped his hands. "I wish I had the authority to send her away. She unsettles me."

"Do not worry, my love." I pressed my hand to his cheek and lifted his gaze to meet mine. "Tonight we will celebrate your father's return, and tomorrow we will begin a new chapter. Should we go away? Perhaps your father would allow us to spend some time at his country villa."

He squeezed my hand and smiled, yet apprehension lingered in his eyes. But what could Prima do to spoil our happiness?

❖

Every available space in the governor's public chambers had been filled with benches and dining couches. Gauzy curtains fluttered in the breezy garden, and torches sputtered against the gathering darkness. Aromatic incense perfumed the air, mingling with the scents of roasted meat and baked sweet breads.

My husband and I strolled through the garden and welcomed the governor's guests. Marcus greeted each of the local officials warmly, thanking them for making his time of leadership free from worry. They praised his abilities, complimented me, and promised to be available if he needed their help in the future.

I smiled, having acquired a small understanding of provincial politics. One was always polite and friendly in public, even to those who openly opposed you. Diplomacy was the key to survival when playing a political game.

We wandered through the gathering, sampling dishes and sipping wine until our throats grew raspy from greeting so many enthusiastic well-wishers. In the garden, a group of musicians played the harp, the panpipe, and a tambourine, while a trio of veiled Nubian slaves danced in honor of Aphrodite. Another slave, dressed only in a toga, sat on a flower-bedecked throne holding Jupiter's thunderbolt in one hand and a wooden eagle in the other. He was supposed to sit and stare straight ahead, but occasionally he nodded encouragement at the dancers, as if the father of the gods had descended to enjoy the governor's party.

"I am surprised you invited Jupiter." Marcus nodded toward the costumed slave. "Considering that you do not worship him."

"Your father does," I answered. "And he would not consider this a proper gathering without Jupiter present."

"What about your Adonai?" Grinning, Marcus glanced around as if searching. "Have you hidden Him somewhere?"

I nodded. "He has been here all along."

The banquet had begun quietly with the requisite sacrifice and prayers offered by Memmius in the lararium. An hour later, I could tell that the free-flowing wine had begun to affect our guests. Voices were louder, the laughter more raucous, and more than one man left his wife's side to seek another woman in the garden.

I spotted a group of matrons who were friends with my mother but could not find her among them. The large crowd was constantly moving, however, so I presumed she had found a friend elsewhere.

I remained by my husband's side, secure in the assurance of his love. At one point I spotted Narkis conversing with the governor in a quiet corner of the garden, but I was not surprised that he had pulled Memmius aside. Narkis would always focus on the most powerful man in the room.

I was completely content until I saw Prima detach herself from a group of male admirers and stroll in our direction. She wore a short tunic, the mark of a maiden, but her palla had been elaborately draped to disguise the thickness at her belly. How many, I wondered, had realized the truth beneath the concealing cloth?

"Good evening," she said, goblet in hand as she sashayed toward us. "I trust I am not disturbing you?"

I answered before Marcus could draw breath. "You are not," I said, taking my husband's arm. "We are well . . . and hope you are also."

She stepped closer and peered intently at my husband. "I trust you have accepted my offer," she said, her tone as smooth as silk. "Have you told Mariana that you must divorce her? I was hoping you would announce our betrothal tonight."

I stared, her words ringing in my ears. Their *betrothal*? How drunk *was* she?

"You see," she continued, not giving either of us an opportunity to answer, "you may have heard that Nero has become concerned about the Christians infiltrating the empire. Memmius has not yet decided how to handle these traitors, but Father has persuaded him to conduct a loyalty test. If Marcus agrees to divorce you, you can slip away so you will not be caught when tonight's guests are commanded to offer incense to Jupiter." She moved close enough for me to smell the wine on her breath. "You would also be spared the humiliation of being present when our betrothal is announced."

She stepped back and smiled again, her dark eyes gleaming in the torchlight.

Was she drunk . . . or did she truly believe she had won?

I gripped Marcus's arm and forced him to look at me. "Does she speak the truth?"

His face had gone blank. "I had hoped she was only posturing."

I turned to Prima, who smiled at me with remarkable malignity. "Aphrodite," she said, swaying toward me again, "has declared victory over the Christians. Tonight you and your Yeshua will be banished from Corinth."

I gripped Marcus's shoulders. "Listen," I told him. "No matter what happens here, trust in Adonai. And never submit to Prima's demands. People who find joy in destroying others are never satisfied."

Marcus's throat bobbed as he swallowed, and in that instant I realized he had been *expecting* Prima's attack. His eyes filled with pleading. "I do not want to lose you," he said, his voice breaking, "but my father cannot risk offending Nero. If the emperor hears that Narkis proposed this test and my father refused to conduct it . . ."

My eyes welled with tears. "No matter what, we should not submit."

"Mariana." His face twisted. "Prima is giving you a chance to escape. Please, I beg you—take your handmaid and leave the palace."

"I will not abandon—"

"You said you would leave me if I asked you to go. So I

am asking—find Salama and leave at once. It is the only way I can be sure you are safe."

I blinked, wavering in a paralysis of astonishment, until Prima moved into the space I had vacated. Marcus did not object as she slipped her arm through his, but stood like a statue, his eyes wet with frustrated tears. A breeze stirred the veil over Prima's hair, ruffled her palla, and revealed the bulge of her unborn child, which everyone would assume belonged to my faithful husband.

Unable to bear another moment, I turned and ran from the garden.

❖

I flew up the stairs, nearly tripping over my stola, and ran into my bedchamber, where Salama had been resting. At the sound of my breathless entrance, she sat up and stared. "Domina?"

Shaking my head, I lifted the lid of my trunk. "Prima has been working against me for months, and tonight she declared victory. Marcus himself told me to leave."

"He would not! You have misunderstood."

I swiped tears from my face. "Do I *look* like a woman who has misunderstood? He told me to go, Salama. Prima and Narkis have convinced the governor to conduct a loyalty test tonight. Anyone who is not willing to sacrifice to Jupiter will be arrested. Since Marcus knows I cannot do such a thing, he sent me away."

Salama rolled off her cot. "He must be planning to join you later. Let me help you pack. We will find him after he has left the palace."

Her comment halted me. Did Marcus intend to escape? He had no reason to run. He would have no problem offering a pinch of incense, but he ought to have a problem marrying Prima . . .

I sank onto the bed, a flash of wild grief ripping through me. I should not have left him downstairs. I should have waited to see if Prima's plan would unfold as she expected. She was probably clinging to Marcus even now, behaving like a wife, perhaps even telling Memmius . . . what? That her child was sired by my husband?

Fear struck like a blow to my stomach. Where was Adonai in all this? Had I somehow displeased Him? Had I loved Marcus more than I loved Yeshua? Adonai was a jealous God who would not share His glory with another.

If I had erred, I deserved to be arrested. I deserved to lose my husband. Like the man whose eye caused him to stumble, I should pluck it out—leave my husband and enter heaven unmarried.

Where is your faith?

The question, coming from outside my panicked mind, stilled my frantic thoughts.

I am here—have you not said so?

"Yes," I whispered, remembering that I had assured Marcus of Adonai's presence only a few moments before. "You are with me."

Then, on a surge of memory, I recalled Paulos reading the words of Adonai from the holy writings:

> "But now, thus says Adonai—
> the One who created you, O Jacob,
> the One who formed you, O Israel:
> Fear not, for I have redeemed you,
> I have called you by name, you are Mine.

When you pass through the waters,
I will be with you,
or through the rivers,
they will not overflow you.
When you walk through the fire,
you will not be burned,
nor will the flame burn you.
For I am Adonai your God,
the Holy One of Israel, your Savior."

Adonai was with me. He would give me courage and strength and whatever I needed to survive this. And He was stronger than Aphrodite, far stronger than the Roman pantheon.

"Stop." I stood and looked at Salama, who had begun to throw garments into a basket. "You may do whatever you wish, but I am not running away."

She gave me a look of horrified disapproval. "Your husband told you to go. He is worried about your safety."

"Marcus does not want me to be arrested, but he is my husband, not my owner. Adonai owns my life, and no one else."

Salama's chin trembled. "Whatever you do, I will go with you. But if we do not flee, will you not be afraid?"

I nodded slowly. "I will be terrified. But as you have said, Adonai is the only God who asks His followers to do what they cannot do without His help. And we will have Him with us."

A palla fell from Salama's hand, but she made no effort to pick it up. "What is your plan? Do we hide ourselves until the test is finished?"

I smiled with a confidence I did not fully understand. "We are going down to the banquet."

Forty-Four

PRIMA

"Now," I said, firmly gripping Marcus's arm, "was it so difficult to let her go? We would not have to do this if you had chosen me all those months ago."

"I chose the wife I wanted," Marcus replied, his lips curling as if he needed to spit. "And I would choose her again."

"If you value her life, you will ask your father to announce your divorce." I smiled as one of the council members passed us with a nod and an uplifted brow. "After we speak to your father, we should find a dining couch and sit together. No one will be surprised to hear we will soon be wed."

"The guests have already seen me with Mariana," Marcus said, refusing to meet my gaze. "What are they to think when they see you?"

"People have short memories." I nodded and smiled at a council member's wife. "What matters is that we are finally united."

We found Memmius reclining on a couch next to my father, who held a goblet in one hand and a meaty bone in the other. Father lifted both brows when he saw me with

Marcus. He said nothing but gestured to the empty couch next to him. I reclined on it, but Marcus stood between our two couches, staring dismally into space.

I turned to Father, who looked at me with a question in his eyes. If he did not know what to say, I did.

I glanced at Memmius, who appeared confused. "Honored Governor," I said, bowing my head in respect. "Your son has agreed to divorce Mariana in order to marry me."

A flicker of shock widened the governor's eyes, then the corners of his mouth tightened. "My son," he said, his eyes boring into me, "does not appear to be overcome with joy."

I smiled and accepted a cup of wine from a passing slave. "Perhaps he needs time."

Memmius rose onto one elbow. "Marcus, is this true? Would you divorce Mariana?"

"If I must," Marcus replied, his voice thick. "But I will do whatever you think best, Father."

Memmius lowered his goblet, lines of concentration deepening between his brows. "Perhaps you should explain the reason behind this unexpected state of affairs."

Knowing Marcus could not give a truthful answer without imperiling his wife, I stood, pulled my palla away from my waist, and turned so Memmius could see the burden I carried. Then I slid my arm through Marcus's.

I sighed. "As you can see, Governor, I am with child. Marcus has been aware of the pregnancy for several weeks but wished to speak to you before setting Mariana aside."

The governor's gaze darted from me to Marcus, then he turned to my father. "Did you know of this?"

Father dipped his chin in a slow nod.

"I was not expecting this." Memmius paused to drink

deeply from his wine cup, then smacked his thick lips. "If a child is coming, I suppose congratulations are due."

Marcus remained silent, but I smiled my thanks. "Would you like to announce the betrothal tonight?"

Memmius shook his head. "We cannot announce a betrothal until the first marriage has been dissolved. I will not dissolve that union until I have spoken to Mariana."

Though my stomach sank with disappointment, I kept a smile on my face.

Why would the governor insist on speaking to Mariana? She and her slave were probably preparing to leave the city.

The thought of Mariana brought another in its wake—Hester. I glanced around but did not see her. I had not seen her all night.

The corner of my mouth quirked. My father was no fool. He must have commanded her to remain at home.

Father raised his goblet to the governor. "Prima will be a fine wife for your son, Memmius. She is like me, steady and determined."

Memmius met Father's gaze. "I hope you are right. But now I think it is time for this evening to end." He drained his cup, then stood, cleared his throat, and lifted his hand high. Like ripples from a stone thrown into a lake, waves of silence spread from him as he looked out at the assembled guests. "Citizens and leaders of Corinth, before I send you back to your homes, I want to share important news from Rome. Our beloved Nero has recently become concerned about a growing sect within the empire, people who do not believe in our Roman gods. Though they may seem like obedient citizens, they are rebels who dare to risk the gods' displeasure—and the stability of the empire—by not sacrificing to the divine beings who have kept us safe for generations."

A wave of reproachful murmurs passed through the crowd.

"Therefore," Memmius continued, "I have decided to safeguard Corinth and the province of Achaia by ensuring that the leaders of this city are loyal to the gods of our forefathers. You are the council members, officials, and magistrates. As you depart this evening, I am asking you to approach the lararium and sprinkle a pinch of incense on the brazier as a sacrifice to Jupiter. By this simple deed we will know you are loyal to Rome's gods and her divine emperor."

As the listeners burst into enthusiastic applause, I studied my father's face. A formal smile had occupied his lips during the speech, but it vanished when the people began to clap. Father leaned forward, his sharp gaze roving over the assembly. Did he suspect members of the council of being Christians? Or did he hope to find other traitors among the civic leadership?

When the applause began to die down, the governor gestured toward the atrium. "My guards will see to it that every man and woman in the palace, whether free or slave, merchant or patrician, soldier or plebeian, shall walk by the altar and offer a small sacrifice of incense. Anyone unwilling to do so will be held for judgment."

My father stood and pointed to a group of guards, who moved to guard the exits. The guests, who had not been expecting this development, whispered and exchanged puzzled looks. Then an older man stood—I recognized him as an elected aedile—and bowed before the governor. "It is my pleasure to affirm my loyalty to you, the emperor, and the gods," he said, gesturing with the practiced movements of an orator. Then, with his wife trailing behind him, the man walked through the atrium and stood before the lararium.

Every person in the triclinium leaned forward to peer into the space beyond.

"Hail, divine Jupiter!" As we watched, the aedile took a bit of incense from a mound on a golden tray and dropped it onto the coals in the brazier. His wife, a willowy young girl, followed her husband's example, her hand appearing to tremble as she flicked the powdery residue from her fingertips.

I watched as a parade of merchants, magistrates, and other city officials made their way to the lararium to perform the act of worship, along with their wives and attendant slaves. The musicians in the garden began to play, and smiles wreathed the guests' faces as they formed a snaking line and made casual conversation while they waited. Each guest took their place before the altar, and many of them seemed determined to outperform their predecessors' booming voices and flamboyant gestures.

Memmius watched from his couch and nodded, his shoulders relaxing as the leaders of Corinth demonstrated obedience and fidelity. I, too, felt confident that Aphrodite had answered my prayers. Mariana was gone. Marcus and I would soon be married, and my child would be born at the palace. Hester would remain part of the family, but Father would never allow her to become a problem.

As if my thoughts had summoned her, Hester appeared at the entrance to the triclinium. Her face was as pale as her tunic, her eyes wide.

Father, who had returned his attention to eating, did not see her.

I leaned toward him. "I thought you told Hester to remain at home."

"I did."

"Then why is she here?"

He lifted his head, his eyes bulging when he spotted her. "In the name of all the gods, what is she thinking?"

I had no answer, but I could not tear my gaze from her delicate form. She had never been overly enthusiastic about accompanying Father to various functions, so she should not have minded his command to stay home. She might have overheard whispered conversations about the governor's test, but if she knew what lay in store for Christians who attended the banquet, she should have known to stay home.

I glanced at Father. He watched her as one transfixed, a spark of some indefinable emotion in his eyes as she threaded her way through busy slaves and waiting guests. Reflected torchlight shone from her face in radiant beams. Never had she looked more beautiful.

Father swallowed hard, an audible gulp. "By the putrid wax in Jupiter's navel," he said, his voice ragged, "why did she not remain at the house?"

Could this be Aphrodite's doing? I suppressed a smile and relished the possibility. When we were ready to depart, I would insist that Marcus and I stand before the lararium like the others. My father would gladly follow my example, and Hester would be compelled to join him. If she could not bring herself to offer incense . . .

The sound of confrontation interrupted my thoughts. A disturbance came from the atrium, so I turned in that direction. Two guards entered the triclinium with a young man clothed in the short tunic of a slave. The youth walked confidently forward, his chin lifted in defiance.

"Whose is he?" Father murmured.

"One of mine," Memmius answered, his voice clipped. "I bought him in Rome. Apparently, the capital is more infested than Nero realizes." He raised his voice to the guards. "Restrain him and any others in the atrium. I will deal with them later."

As the guards escorted the slave to the atrium, I turned to Father, who would probably earn a badge of honor for his role in ferreting out these Christians. Memmius would trust him with greater responsibility, and when I gave birth to his grandson, Memmius would take more delight in me than he had in Mariana.

And though Marcus resented me at the moment, he could not be completely displeased with my plan. After all, I had given Mariana time to escape. By this time tomorrow night, Memmius would deduce that she had fled because she was a Christian. That should be enough for him to decree a divorce so that Marcus and I could be wed.

I blinked as Hester approached the dais where we sat. I gave her a tentative smile, then reached for a platter of honeyed figs on a nearby stand. I was about to offer one to Marcus when I heard more shouts from the atrium. A moment later, I saw two women, both veiled, being herded into the line of guests waiting for their turn at the altar.

When Hester was within speaking distance, I stood. "Surely we are no exception," I said, glancing at Memmius. "Should we not visit the lararium and set an example for all Corinthians?"

I looked at Father. He scowled at me, but could I help it if his wife had chosen to appear as the guests were being tested?

Memmius rose at once. "Let us go." He nodded at Marcus. "Since we are enacting this test in Caesar's name, we are not exempt."

Father stood as well, and I waited as Memmius walked by us on his way to the lararium. Several guests who had already offered incense were talking in the vestibule, but they fell silent as we passed. Those still waiting to make their sacrifice respectfully stepped back, allowing us to approach the altar.

"Hail, Jupiter." Without fanfare, Memmius grabbed a handful of incense and flung it onto the brazier. A nearby slave pumped a bellows to enliven the smoldering coals, and a fragrant cloud poured from the lararium.

I waited until the cloud had passed, then approached the altar. "Hail, divine Jupiter." With two fingers I pinched a portion from the mound of pulverized frankincense and myrrh. "And all praise be to you, Aphrodite." I flicked the fine particles into the flames and stepped away.

Father followed me without speaking, his large fingers trailing powder as he flung the incense onto the brazier.

As one, Father and I turned to Hester. She approached the lararium, and I alone stood close enough to hear Father's gruff words: "You were supposed to remain at home."

"How could I?" she whispered, giving him only a brief glance. "With my daughter's life in the balance?"

I watched, fascinated, as Hester stepped toward the altar. She hesitated, her hand trembling as she lifted it . . .

"Mother, no!"

I turned, my pulse quickening, at the sound of a woman's voice. One of the women near the vestibule stepped forward and lifted her veil, tears spilling from her eyes.

Mariana.

"Mother," she cried, her face contorted by anguish. "Do not do this. Think of all Yeshua suffered for us."

The sound of whispered conversations ceased entirely when Hester crumpled to the floor as if every bone in her body had melted. "I came," she wailed, her voice echoing against the chamber's domed ceiling, "to beg the governor to show mercy to those who worship Adonai and His Son."

Memmius shot my father a look of reluctant tolerance. "Narkis, see to your wife. Either she sacrifices or she does not, but she cannot stop the test."

Father stepped toward Hester, his arms extended, but she pulled away from him and turned toward those still waiting. "You do not know," she shouted, her voice ragged, "what they plan for those who cannot sacrifice to Jupiter."

"Hester!" Father's voice interrupted. "You are not well; you should have remained at home."

"I do this for Mariana," Hester said, reaching for the golden tray. "Noble Memmius, consider this an assurance of my daughter's loyalty. Let her live and take me in her place."

Then, as I watched in disbelief, Hester threw a handful of incense onto the smoking coals.

Forty-Five

MARIANA

When had such a simple gesture ever caused such commotion? As my heart refused to believe what my eyes beheld, a cloud of smoke rose from the brazier, Memmius bellowed an objection, and Narkis cried out in confusion. Prima screamed, likely out of sheer frustration. Two guards hurried forward, lifted Mother off the floor, and held her upright as she wiped her fingers on her tunic and faced the governor.

Once order had been reestablished, we stood in a quiet so thick that the only sound was the slight whistle of Memmius's strained breathing.

"That is not permitted," the governor announced. "You cannot take such an action for your daughter."

Mother clamped her jaw tight and clasped her hands.

"Have you nothing to say?" When Mother remained silent, Memmius looked at Narkis. "She is your wife—can you not control her?"

Narkis moistened his lips. "I ordered her to remain at home."

"And she disobeyed?"

"She did."

Memmius's frown deepened. "Next time you wish her to remain at home, I would urge you to restrain her more forcibly." He crossed his arms and stared at Narkis. "Do you, Chief Magistrate, wish to keep your wife?"

Narkis nodded. "I do. She has offered incense on the altar, so she has passed your test."

Memmius nodded. "Very well. Let us move on."

"No!" Mother cried. "I recant! Ask me to sacrifice again, and I will not!"

Has a heart ever been so torn? I wanted my mother to live, but I could not believe her action should count as a betrayal to Yeshua. I pressed my hand to my chest, my soul aching, as Narkis put his arm around Mother's shoulders, and she dissolved into weeping.

Memmius turned toward the place where Salama and I had been joined by guards. He motioned the guards forward.

My battered heart raced. Surely, Adonai had prepared me for this moment. For years I had feared the unknown, but in this case I knew exactly what would happen. He would ask me to offer incense and I would refuse. After that he would have me executed, along with Salama if she followed my example.

And my mother's sacrifice would count for nothing.

The guards prodded us forward until we reached Memmius. He bent toward me, his eyes filling with confusion and concern. "Mariana, will you offer incense to Jupiter of your own free will?"

I glanced at my mother and read the anguish on her face. "No, Governor." I turned to face him. "I cannot."

"Neither can I," Salama said, courageously linking her fate with mine. "Like my mistress, I worship Adonai and His Son, Yeshua."

"So do my wife and I," added a male voice.

Behind us, a couple stepped out of the line, and my heart squeezed when I recognized Titius Justus and his wife, Aurora, friends of Paulos, Priscilla, and Aquilla.

A muscle flicked at Narkis's jaw. Titius was a highly regarded and influential member of the city council.

"Are there any others who wish to declare that they are Christians?" Memmius called, his eyes raking over the remaining guests. "Any other traitors in my house?"

I held my breath as silence, as thick as wool, filled the chamber.

"I have not yet made my sacrifice."

The voice, completely unexpected, elicited a ripple of recognition among the men and lifted the hair on my arms. Memmius turned, a smile overspreading his face, as Marcus stepped forward.

"Please, son." The governor backed away from the altar, allowing my husband to pass. "Be our example and make your declaration for the gods of Rome."

I wanted to call out to him, but my heart was so tightly constricted I could not draw breath to speak. I bowed my head and closed my eyes, not wanting to watch.

The empty space between us vibrated, the silence filling with dread. I braced myself for the inevitable—my loss, Prima's victory, and Marcus's declaration of loyalty to a false god.

Forgive me, Adonai. My shoulders slumped as I felt my heart break. *I married him because I wanted to win him to you, but I have completely failed! I was too focused on my own needs, my own grief, and so wrapped up in thoughts of his betrayal that I forgot to trust him . . .*

I heard his steps, followed by the soft rustle of his toga as he approached the altar. Against my will, I opened my eyes enough to see him reach forward, pinch a portion of the incense, and turn, dropping it onto the floor.

Dusting his hands, he addressed his father. "I can no longer sacrifice to Jupiter or Caesar," he said, facing me. "Through my wife, Mariana, I have heard about the almighty God who sent His Son, not to negotiate with men but to redeem them from certain destruction. I have seen His attributes—truth and goodness, justice and strength, all the virtues Rome honors—in my wife, who worships Adonai and His Son, Yeshua, alone. If Mariana is willing to proclaim her loyalty to the kingdom of Yeshua, then I am as well."

Memmius snorted and waved Marcus's declaration away. "Do not be a lovestruck fool. Mariana is only a woman, and there are others you could wed, including her sister. You do not want to be joined to a woman who will pay for this folly with her life."

Marcus looked away, and in that instant I feared he would change his mind. Instead, he walked over to me and took my hand, holding it firmly in his own. "Throughout my life, Father," he said, speaking to his father, "I have been terrified of not meeting your expectations. I have loved you, admired you, and obeyed you without question. I followed in your footsteps . . . until I realized that

342

I have another Father, one who knew me even before He created me. He has promised to give eternal life to those who believe, and I do believe in Him. I am no longer afraid to disappoint you. I will always love and admire you. I will pray for you, but as for me, I can no longer worship any God but Adonai."

An icy silence enveloped us as Memmius's face emptied of expression. "Are you certain?" he said. "This is a life-altering choice."

Marcus drew a breath to speak, but my stepfather moved toward us, his hands clenched at his sides. "You do not want to do this, Marcus. Another woman waits for you, and here stands your loving father, who represents a heritage that goes back generations—"

"The woman I love is here." Marcus lifted my hand. "And before all the leaders in Corinth, I have already declared my surrender to Adonai and His Son. I cannot undo what I have done."

Prima strode toward Marcus, shaking her head as she shrieked protestations. "He is bewitched! Summon the priestess of Aphrodite or a priest of Jupiter! The Christians have bewitched him, so his word cannot stand."

Marcus smiled at his father. "I am neither bewitched nor unduly influenced," he said, his voice resolute. "But I am in love with my wife and with Adonai, who will not fail us."

A scowl twisted Memmius's mouth. "Adonai failed both of you tonight." He motioned to the guards. "Take these *Christians* to the prison. I will decide their fate tomorrow."

My mother sobbed as I gripped Marcus's hand and we left the atrium. Within minutes we found ourselves in a narrow passageway that led to the prison beneath the palace.

Our group was not large—only six—but we were bound by conviction, courage, and curiosity about what Adonai planned to do with our lives.

"Marcus," Titius said, his voice as cool as spring water, "what do you think your father will do with us?"

A half smile lifted the corner of my husband's mouth. "I have no idea. He might have us flogged and released, or he might sell us into slavery."

Aurora swallowed hard. "Oh! And where would we serve as slaves?"

Marcus shrugged. "Only Adonai knows."

"We will be seeds," Salama said, smiling at the young slave who had been the first to refuse the loyalty test. "We will spread the Good News wherever we find ourselves."

Her words reminded me of something I'd read. "Did Yeshua not say that a grain of wheat must die before it produces anything?"

Aurora pulled her palla closer to her neck. "I have not given much thought to dying."

"Everyone dies," Marcus said. "But I do not think my father will be eager to flood Corinth with the blood of valued citizens."

Salama nodded. "As I have said"—she caught my eye and smiled—"Adonai is the only God who asks His followers to do what they cannot do without His help."

I tilted my head. Was she thinking that Memmius would execute us? I could not face death without fear . . . if not for my faith. But with Yeshua's promise of eternal life, death was no longer an unknown.

A small smile brightened my handmaid's face. "Adonai will give us the courage to endure whatever He wills."

"I am certain you are right," I said, peering into the dark stone chamber at the bottom of the steps. A rat scurried away from the light of the guard's torch and water trickled down the rough stone walls. "For now, I pray He will give us the strength to survive in this place."

Forty-Six

PRIMA

I watched as guards led the Christians out of the palace. The taste of bitterness lay heavy on my tongue, and the sound of Hester's sobbing grated on my nerves.

Where was Aphrodite when I needed her? Had she been asleep during the last hour? Everything had been going so well, and then . . .

I could not marry Marcus now, and Father's friendship with the governor had been ruined. Hester would remain with us, but she would be miserable. My child would have no father. Memmius, who had just lost his son, would never trust my father again. And my father would have no use for me.

"Father?" I tugged at his toga to snap him out of his stupor. "Should we withdraw?"

He looked at me, his eyes abstracted, but they cleared when he saw the urgency in mine. "Yes, we should depart."

He took Hester's arm and followed me out of the atrium, through the vestibule, and down the palace steps, not waiting for our litter bearers.

We would walk home. If not for the dozens of eyes watching our retreat, we might have run.

❖

I rose before sunrise, woke a slave to accompany me, and climbed the steep Acrocorinth with only the torchbearer for company. I moved with stiff, brittle dignity, silently placing one foot in front of another, again and again, willing my body to keep moving.

I had lost everything. What little power I had was gone, vanquished by my stepsister's devotion to an invisible God who would not be able to protect her against the might of Rome.

So why did I feel that she had won?

The last of the stars glimmered in the night sky, providing no light and growing fainter with every step. Gloom pressed against the stones at my right hand, pools of shadow that threatened to engulf me. Perhaps, if Aphrodite could not provide an answer for the debacle of my life, I could step into the shadows at my left, letting myself fall off the mountain into darkness.

After an hour of walking, the blue air began to congeal with mist. Behind me, the sky had begun to brighten, so the priestesses would be rising, lighting the coals in the braziers, feeding the images of the goddess.

Dawn moved slowly across the landscape, chasing the shadows of the night. The sun had fully risen when I finally reached the steps of the temple, so I told the slave to sit and wait. Then I studied the marble edifice rising above me.

My eyes felt sandy, and my bones hurt. My back ached between my shoulder blades, and the weight of the unborn child threatened to drag me into the earth.

I gulped a breath and climbed the steps, then entered the temple. Without pausing to admire the paintings or the statuary, I went to the chamber where the priestess prepared for the day. There I found Cassia, sitting cross-legged, her eyes closed and her hands resting on her knees.

"Leave us," I commanded, and the slaves scattered.

Though she did not open her eyes, her lips curved in a smile. "So," she said, speaking in the ragged voice that was not hers, "you have come for answers."

"Yes." I dropped onto the floor and sat in front of her. "I have done everything you told me to do. I have given you sacrifices; I have determined my desires. In your name I have done things that shamed my father and would have sent my mother to an early grave."

The priestess's brow lifted. "And?"

"What have I to show for all my efforts? The man I wanted is gone. My father hates me, and the governor will despise the sight of me. My reputation is ruined, and no man will want me."

The lips curved in a smile, then split into strident laughter. "And you complain? You gave me your soul, and I did what you asked. You wanted your sister gone—a woman who petitioned the almighty God on your behalf. You wanted your father's attention. You wanted pleasure, and you wanted a man. I gave you all those things."

"But now I have nothing!"

"While I have everything. Including you."

Overcome by an urge to flee, I pushed myself off the floor and ran out of the chamber, stopping in the vestibule, where I braced myself against a table. My heart pounded in my chest, and I could barely draw breath. Was disaster my reward for faithfully serving Aphrodite?

I raised my eyes to a looking brass above the table . . . and the image reflected there was not my face, but a demon's. Our gazes met, then the monster tipped his head back and laughed, a raucous laughter that filled my ears and head and heart and sent me running down the steps toward the rocky ledges of the Acrocorinth.

Forty-Seven

MARIANA

Though we tried to rest, only Salama and the male slave Brutus managed to sleep in the dank prison. In the darkness of that stone cell, we were not slave, domina, council member, or governor's son; we were *believers*, united in faith and hope, who had dared to oppose the prevailing culture.

Then we were summoned by the governor.

We made ourselves as presentable as we could, though it was impossible to rid our white tunics of the stains from the muddy prison floor. Marcus had given me his cloak for a pillow, so it was also muddy, rumpled, and smelled of rat and urine. When the guards summoned us, we followed them up the stairs and steeled ourselves to face jeering and mocking as we stood on the platform in front of the palace.

News of our arrest had spread. The palace courtyard was packed—not only with city leaders but also with common citizens.

Dozens of men and women stood in front of the palace as we climbed onto the platform, all of us moving slowly as a result of an uncomfortable night on the floor. Some of the women gasped when they saw our disheveled condition, and several people recoiled when Marcus appeared, as if he represented their worst nightmare. Roman sons did not disobey or disappoint their fathers. Marcus had done an exemplary job of ruling in his father's absence, so what had happened?

Yet not everyone looked at us with fear and distrust. I spotted friends in the crowd, fellow believers from the ecclesia and others from the synagogue. They nodded when they caught my eye, and a few lifted a finger toward heaven, a wordless reminder of the prayers they were offering on our behalf.

Then I saw my mother. She stood by Narkis and huddled in her cloak, her gaze fastened to my face. I caught her eye and smiled, silently assuring her that I was well.

I do not think she believed me.

We halted before Memmius, who sat in a gilded chair on the dais. He stared at us for what seemed like an eternity, then he gestured to a brazier on a table before him. "I have given this matter careful consideration," he said, looking directly at his son. "And I believe your actions last night may have been the result of wine and the high spirits that often accompany such a feast. The consequences of your betrayal are dire, so I offer each of you this single opportunity to amend your action. Will you offer a sacrifice of incense to Jupiter, chief of the gods? If so, you may do it now and be restored to your former position."

I felt the muscles in Marcus's arm stiffen, but he did not speak, nor did he look at me. I remained as I was, as did Salama, Titius Justus, and Aurora.

But the governor's slave fell to the wooden floor, prostrating himself before Memmius. "I will! Pardon me, Dominus, and forgive me, honorable master! I will offer the sacrifice now."

Memmius watched, his face impassive, as Brutus scrambled up and ran to the altar, where he snatched a handful of incense and dropped it onto the coals of the brazier. A cloud of scented smoke rose into the air, filling our nostrils with the aromas of frankincense and myrrh.

"Will any of you do the same?" Memmius asked, his gaze drifting over us. "Given the great affection I have toward all of you, will you reconsider? If you do not, you will stand trial for *Lex maiestatis*, and treason is a serious offense."

The wind whispered, ruffling my hair, but not a sound disturbed the thick silence around the platform.

"Actions are a reflection of the heart and mind," Marcus finally said, speaking for all of us. "That is what you have taught me, Father. And my heart and mind are not set on the gods of Greece or Rome, but on the God who rules heaven and earth. The One who sent me a wife who showed me a different way, a life lived through the forgiveness won by Yeshua's sacrifice."

Memmius looked at his son, the hard veneer of the governor fading to reveal the father's heart beneath. "Then it grieves me to sentence you to death," Memmius said, his voice breaking. "Though as Roman citizens, you have the right to appeal to Rome . . ."

He paused, and in that silence I heard his unspoken invitation. *Save your lives and make the appeal.*

Marcus heard it, too. "We appeal to Rome," he said, squeezing my hand.

Memmius looked at us with mingled relief and sorrow in his eyes. "So be it. I will send all of you to Rome on the first available transport. Until you depart, you will be confined in a nearby house."

I slumped in relief, then turned and hugged Salama. As she wept tears of relief, I turned to Marcus. "Paulos and Luke are in Rome," I reminded him. "And Priscilla and Aquilla. We have many friends in the city."

Marcus gripped my hand more tightly. "We will need them and their prayers."

"I am not afraid," I said as I slipped my arms around my husband. "I cannot believe I am not concerned about the future. But it is enough to have you with me and to know Adonai holds our lives in His hands."

And then, before Memmius, Narkis, and all of Corinth, my husband pulled me closer and kissed me with the ardor of a man who had finally surrendered to the love of his wife . . . and to his God.

Epilogue

The young orphan climbed the steep path to the Acrocorinth, his eyes intent on the ground. Occasionally, wor-
shipers lost a coin or two while making the climb, and even
an *as*, the lowliest coin in Rome, would buy a loaf of old
bread.

He paused, lifting his head as the scent of cooking reached
his nostrils. One of the merchants' women must be cooking
a good meal. His starved senses, made overly sensitive by
desperation, detected the mouthwatering aroma of meat.
The boy inhaled a deep breath, hoping the smell of the
stew would give him strength enough to reach the top of
the mountain. There, if the priestesses were feeling generous,
a starving boy could beg for a bowl of gruel or a lamb bone.
He had once gnawed a lamb bone for two days, eventually
licking the marrow from the shards.

He walked farther, bending to pick up a bit of metal that
glinted in the sand. He studied the metal, scratched it with
the stub of a fingernail, and tossed it aside. He shook his

head when he encountered a new odor—the heady aroma of incense from one of the small shrines.

He lifted his head. There it was, a shrine to Asclepius, god of healing. An auspicious location because anyone could fall and injure themself on this perilous path. The route was steep, the ground uneven, and the precipice dangerous. He peered over the cliff at his left hand. The city of Corinth lay far below, nestled beneath rising plumes of smoke from family kitchens. A veritable cloud rose from the palace, where the governor was probably feeding over three hundred slaves and a handful of family members.

His stomach clenched, protesting its emptiness. He moved away from the drop-off and continued to climb.

There had been a ruckus near the palace that morning. The governor had issued a judgment against a group of rebels, and they were to be taken to Rome. Lots of people had jeered and cheered and scurried back to their homes, indifferent to the orphan who sat in a corner with his hands outstretched.

He wouldn't mind going to Rome if the ship fed the passengers a decent meal every day. He had done a fair bit of begging at the port. Fishermen were always happy to toss the heads and entrails to anyone who needed to fill his stomach. Of course, a boy had to be careful not to mind the stench. The smell of offal was often enough to tighten his stomach, but combined with the smell of rats, the stink was enough to make him lose whatever he had found to eat.

He glanced at the sea beyond the escarpment on his left. A pair of white sails danced above the blue waters, and for a moment he closed his eyes and imagined himself swaying on a wooden deck. The seamen said it took time to get used to the rocking, but captains were always looking for skilled hands and steady stomachs.

He blinked when another sail caught his eye—a white sail fluttering not on the sea, but on the rocks across from him. Wait. That wasn't a sail; it was a garment . . . still attached to a person.

His pulse quickened. Unfortunate soul, whoever that was. Someone must have been walking in the dark, most likely drunk, and slipped. The drop was not as steep in that area, but large boulders littered the escarpment, ancient rocks that had withstood wind and weather and the efforts of quarry workers. One of those rocks had stopped the body from falling all the way to Corinth, but the body might lie there until the ravens picked the bones clean.

Unless . . .

The boy moved closer to observe the body's location. From the top of the Acrocorinth, the victim's downward fall would have been steep and swift, but from where he stood, the journey was a sideways scramble over the stones. Whoever the unfortunate one was, he or she might have a purse, and that purse might well be the means by which the gods would save the boy's life.

He inched closer to the edge and looked down. The view was enough to pebble his skin. But if he looked straight ahead, the distance between him and the body was not insurmountable. He could make his way across by holding on to the weedy grasses and scampering like a mountain goat over the boulders. Best of all—he glanced around—thus far he seemed to be the only person who had noticed the victim lying on the rocks.

He sat, placed his feet on the steep slope, and turned so he would not have to look down. Moving slowly and carefully, he scrambled spider-like over the scarp, testing his weight on protruding rocks, holding on to stubborn saplings that grew from small cracks between the stones. While he worked, he imagined the foods he would eat once he had recovered the victim's purse. A silver denarius would feed him for a month, an aureus for an entire year. If he found a denarius, perhaps he could buy a decent tunic and persuade a silversmith to teach him the trade.

The thought of having food, clothing, and a roof over his head spurred him to move faster. In his eagerness he misjudged a step and slipped. Only his grip on a ledge kept him from meeting the fate of the body on the rocks.

Finally, he could see the victim clearly. What he had imagined to be a sail was a woman's tunic, caught and tossed by the wind. She lay upside down, her head slanted toward the city, her legs toward the temple of Aphrodite. Her palla obscured her midsection, and when he finally reached her, he saw that it was stained with blood.

He lifted the fabric, hoping to find a purse tied within the folds of the woman's voluminous tunic, and at last found the item he sought. He opened the leather pouch and counted a dozen sestertii inside it.

Not the silver of his dreams, but still, he would eat well tonight. He tied the pouch of coins to his tattered garment, then looked for the best way to return to safety.

When a groan shattered the silence, the boy flinched, terrified that the woman's spirit had returned to chide him. When he turned to look again, her eyelids fluttered.

What could he do? He could not carry a grown woman, and why would he? Unless . . .

He studied her face, noting the cosmetics and the pearls at

her ears. This woman was important. Perhaps there would be a reward.

He stood as straight as he could without losing his balance. He looked up and spotted signs of movement by the entrance to the goddess's temple.

"Oy!" he cried, waving his arm. "This woman is alive!"

Author's Note

Readers often want to know why I made certain choices in my historical novels, so I've tried to address some likely questions below.

Q. Venus was the Roman name for the Greek goddess Aphrodite, so why does Prima, a Roman citizen, call her Aphrodite?

A. Because Corinth was a Greek city, and its citizens had worshiped Aphrodite long before the arrival of the Romans. Important provincial officials and their families were often granted Roman citizenship—Paul of Tarsus was one example. Paul's father was a friend of the Roman governor, so Paul's family had Roman citizenship, though they lived miles from Rome.

Q. Mariana mentions that when the Romans worship their gods, they are actually worshiping demons. Where did she get this idea?

A. In the story, Paul explains this to Mariana through a passage from Deuteronomy 32:16–18.

> They made Him jealous with strangers,
> with abominations they angered Him.
> They sacrificed to demons, a non-god,
> gods they had not known—
> to new ones who came in lately,
> ones your fathers had not dreaded.
> The Rock who birthed you, you ignored.
> You forgot God who brought you forth.

Q. **The midwife verified Prima's pregnancy by having her urinate on seeds. Does that method actually work?**

A. The ancient Egyptians had written that if a woman urinated on wheat and barley seeds, she could determine the sex of her unborn child. If the wheat seeds sprouted, a female child could be expected; if the barley germinated, the woman would bear a son. No germination of either seed meant no child was on the way.

Did the method work? Yes, but only to a point. Researchers in the 1960s tested this hypothesis and found that higher-than-usual levels of estrogen in a pregnant woman's urine might have stimulated the germination of seeds, but had nothing to do with predicting the child's sex.

I wonder what they would have thought if *both* groups of seeds sprouted.

Q. In your earlier novels, your Jewish characters refer to God as HaShem, but you didn't use that term in this novel. Why not?

A. Because I learned something new. HaShem, which literally means *the Name* in Hebrew, is a euphemism modern Jews use to avoid speaking the holy name of God. While modern Jewish readers may appreciate my use of HaShem, the term was actually not used in the first century. Jews and Gentile believers of that era would have referred to God as *Adonai* or LORD. As a writer, I had to choose—historical accuracy or modern sensibilities? I decided to go with historical accuracy.

Q. You have the Greek Gentiles in Corinth calling Jesus "Yeshua," but wouldn't they have called him *Jesus*? After all, that's how we know Him in the New Testament, which was translated from the Greek.

A. Actually, Jesus wasn't called *Jesus* until the sixteenth century with the publication of the Geneva Bible. I had the Gentiles in this novel call Him *Yeshua* because that's what Paul would have most likely called the Messiah.

The Corinthians did speak Greek and Latin, as did Paul, who also spoke Hebrew. But Greek has no "sh" sound, so the Greeks would have had a problem saying *Yeshua*. Early Greek documents refer to the Son of God as *Iesous*.

For generations, the Son of God was known as

Iesous. But when Catholic Queen Mary I (who would have used a Latin Bible) ascended to the throne of England in 1553, Protestant scholars fled to Switzerland, where they produced an English Bible. In Swiss German, the letter *j* is pronounced more like the English *y*, thus Iesous became *Jesus*.

"In short," explains writer Gina Dimuro, "the name [Jesus] used by English speakers today is an English adaptation of a German transliteration of a Latin transliteration of a Greek transliteration of an originally Hebrew name."[1]

In this novel I thought it best to call Him *Yeshua*.

Q. You used some foreign words in this novel. Why didn't you include a glossary?

A. I like to use foreign words in my novels because they impart a genuine historical flavor to the story. When I use one of those words—*triclinium*, for instance—I always try to make the meaning clear in the context of the story. Since people are always eating in the triclinium, you can safely assume it is the Roman version of a dining room.

Q. When Mariana considers how Salama's life has improved since joining Narkis's household as a slave, it almost sounds as if you are making a case for slavery.

1. Gina Dimuro, "What Was Jesus' Real Name? 'Yeshua' and the Story behind It," All That's Interesting, accessed November 8, 2022, https://allthatsinteresting .com/yeshua-jesus-real-name.

A. I'm not. I have received letters from readers who took me to task for my *characters'* opinions and attitudes, but please remember that this is a novel. My job as a historical novelist is to portray ancient people as they thought and felt. I will admit that modern sensibilities do guide me—for instance, if I *honestly* portrayed everything that went on in a temple fertility ritual or how sternly a paterfamilias could rule his household, modern readers would be aghast. So I try my best to paint an accurate historical picture without offending my readers' sensibilities.

Q. **Is this the end of the story? I need to know what happens to the main characters.**

A. This is not the end. Book three in the series will be set in Rome. I fully intend to have characters from books one and two appear in book three. After all, *All roads lead to Rome.*

Reading Group Discussion Guide

1. *The Sisters of Corinth* begins a bit like the story of Cinderella. The prince is giving a ball, and a conniving stepsister is determined to snag him. But the prince—in this case, the governor's son—is charmed by the sister, who prefers to be true to herself. In the beginning, were you rooting for Prima or Mariana?

2. Mariana has grave concerns about whether she could marry Marcus. After all, he isn't a believer in Adonai, and she knows she should marry a Christian. If you were her mother, how would you advise her?

3. Roman families were under complete control of the father—the *paterfamilias*. If the wife, a child, or a slave dared to disobey the head of the household, they could be severely punished or even killed. Mariana, Prima, and Hester had to obey Narkis or risk the consequences. If you were Hester, how would you have handled the betrothal situation?

4. Hester and Mariana, both of whom believe in Jesus, attend the morning prayers but pray silently to Adonai, not the Roman gods. Was this wrong of them? Were they being hypocritical or simply trying to keep peace in the household? What would you have done?

5. The early Christians didn't have a printed New Testament. They had the Jewish Scriptures if they were fortunate enough to have access to a copy of the Septuagint (our Old Testament written in Greek), and some of them had access to letters from Paul, Peter, and other apostles. How did they learn how to live a godly life with such few resources available?

6. Why did Prima dive so deeply into a sordid lifestyle after Mariana's marriage? Why did she visit a gladiator? What drove her to the temple of Aphrodite? Was she driven by lust or a desire for love?

7. History tells us that many slaves came to faith in Christ. He appealed to the poor, the helpless, and those without free agency. Why do you think Hester and Mariana found it easy to trust Christ, while Prima and Narkis could not?

8. When the banquet guests had to offer incense to Jupiter, what did you think of Hester's decision?

9. Do you think Marcus will ever be a Roman senator? What do you think the future holds for him and Mariana?

10. What new information about Rome and the Romans did you learn by reading this book? What surprised you?

11. When comparing/contrasting Roman society to our modern culture, what are the similarities? What are the differences?

12. In the epigraph, the author tells us about ancient relay races where runners passed a torch to the next runner in line. In what way did Hester and Mariana "pass on the light" of the Gospel? How are you passing that light to those around you?

Coming Soon

Look for characters old and new
in the third and final book of

THE EMISSARIES series
by Angela Hunt

In Emperor Nero's Rome, Calandra helps her father, a renowned sculptor, complete the most significant commission of his career. But when an unforeseen tragedy shakes the great city to its core, Calandra finds herself dependent upon people unlike any she has met. Who are these Christians, and how can they worship the Son of an invisible God?

Her mistrust of the outsiders gives way to appreciation when they help her and her father return to life as they once knew it. In time, her Christian acquaintances become dear friends, though she cannot forsake the gods of Rome.

When the emperor begins building his golden house, the people of Rome become resentful, suspecting that Nero set a devastating fire to create space for his gigantic palace. Needing a scapegoat, Nero points at those who follow the Jewish Messiah, forcing Calandra to make an impossible choice between right and wrong, friends and family, love and death.

Available in the spring of 2025

Angela Hunt has published more than 165 books, with sales exceeding five million copies worldwide. She's the *New York Times* bestselling author of *The Tale of Three Trees*, *The Note*, and *The Nativity Story*. Angela's novels have won or been nominated for several prestigious industry awards, such as the RITA Award, the Christy Award, the ECPA Christian Book Award, and the HOLT Medallion Award. Romantic Times Book Club presented her with a Lifetime Achievement Award in 2006. She holds ThDs in Biblical Studies and in Theology. Angela and her husband live in Florida, along with their mastiffs and chickens. For a complete list of the author's books, visit AngelaHuntBooks.com.

References

"Ancient Roman Weddings." Accessed November 7, 2022. https://mari amilani.com/ancient_rome/ancient-roman-weddings.htm.

Nero: A Life from Beginning to End. Hourly History, 2018.

Achtemeier, Paul J. *Harper's Bible Dictionary.* New York: Harper & Row and Society of Biblical Literature, 1985.

Beal, Matthew S. *Lexham Bible Dictionary.* "Corinth." Ed. John D. Barry et al. Bellingham, WA: Lexham Press, 2016.

Byfield, Ted, Ed. *The Christians: Their First Two Thousand Years.* "A Pinch of Incense, AD 70 to 250." Canada: Christian History Project, 2002.

Cahn, Jonathan. *The Return of the Gods.* Lake Mary, FL: Frontline/ Charisma Media, 2022.

Campbell, Colin J. "Ancient Rome: An Unknown History of Alcohol (7 Facts)." Accessed November 8, 2022. https://www.thecollector .com/history-of-alcohol-ancient-rome/.

Davids, Peter H. *Baker Encyclopedia of the Bible.* "First Letter to the Corinthians." Grand Rapids, MI: Baker Book House, 1988.

Dimuro, Gina. "What Was Jesus' Real Name? 'Yeshua' and the Story behind It." Accessed April 14, 2023. https://allthatsinteresting.com /yeshua-jesus-real-name.

Hughes, Robert B., and J. Carl Laney. *Tyndale Concise Bible Commentary.* Wheaton, IL: Tyndale House Publishers, 2001.

Sanna, Stefania. "Perfume in Ancient Rome." Accessed November 10, 2022. www.officinadelleessenze.com/en/perfume-in-ancient-rome/.

Smith, William. *Smith's Bible Dictionary*. Peabody, MA: Hendrickson Publishers, 1986.

Tan, Paul Lee. *Encyclopedia of 7,700 Illustrations: Signs of the Times*. Garland, TX: Bible Communications, Inc., 1996.

Vos, Howard Frederic. *Nelson's New Illustrated Bible Manners & Customs: How the People of the Bible Really Lived*. Nashville, TN: Thomas Nelson Publishers, 1999.

Sign Up for Angela's Newsletter

Keep up to date with Angela's latest news on book releases and events by signing up for her email list at the link below.

AngelaHuntBooks.com

More from Angela Hunt

Three Philippians whose lives were changed by Paul—a jailer, a formerly demon-possessed enslaved girl, and the woman referred to as Lydia—find their fates intertwined. In the face of great sacrifice, will they find the strength to do all that justice demands of them?

The Woman from Lydia
THE EMISSARIES #1

In her JERUSALEM ROAD series, *New York Times* bestselling author Angela Hunt carries you away to ancient times and into the lives of the friends and family of Jesus during his life on earth. From his first miracle, to his death and resurrection, this series presents a poignant portrayal of Christ's ministry and the profound impact it had on those He served, offering you a fresh perspective on these transformative events.

JERUSALEM ROAD:
Daughter of Cana, The Shepherd's Wife, A Woman of Words, The Apostle's Sister

♦ BETHANYHOUSE

 Bethany House Fiction

 @BethanyHouseFiction

 @Bethany_House

 @BethanyHouseFiction

 Free exclusive resources for your book group at BethanyHouseOpenBook.com

 Sign up for our fiction newsletter today at BethanyHouse.com